To Those Who Survive

A Monksblood Bible novel

Isabella Anton

To Those Who Survive © Isabella Anton

ISBN 978-1-9999415-2-9

eISBN 978-1-9999415-3-6

BIC/BISAC: FM – Fantasy | FA – Modern & Contemporary Fiction / FIC009000 – Fantasy | FIC009010 – Contemporary Fantasy

First published in Great Britain in September 2019

ibellaanton.com

FIRST EDITION

Text and Ebook Design © Isabella Anton, ibellaanton.com
Cover Art & Design © Anita B. Carroll, Race-Point.com

The moral rights of the author and illustrator have been asserted.

All rights reserved. No part of this publication may be reproduced or transmitted by any means, electronic, mechanical, photocopying or otherwise, without the prior permission of the publisher.

This is a work of fiction. Names, characters, places, and incidents are used fictitiously and are not to be construed as real. Any resemblance to actual events, locales, organizations, or persons, living or dead, is entirely coincidental.

Printed and bound in Great Britain by TJ INK, Padstow, PL28 8RW

To Beth.

To those who survive, do not pity those who have died but those who live, for they feel death over and over throughout their lives and fight against it each day. The dead, on the other hand, look on from another plane to their loved ones suffering, unable to do anything. So live a life that is full of happiness and not one soaked in despair, for all you are doing is creating a cycle that cannot be easily broken.

- The Thoughts of Henry Fitzalan-Howard, 15th Duke of Norfolk

NI EDRYCH ANGAU PWY DECAF EI DALCEN.

DEATH CONSIDERS NOT THE FAIREST FOREHEAD.

I

My breath caught in my lungs as I walked to where Jackie was standing, a confused and worried look on her face. Both my parents and Bowen were positioned behind me in my small dorm room, and when I looked back at them, his face was ashen.

Something's wrong...

I peeked around the corner from my door, the dark varnish worn from its many previous occupants opening and closing it, and when I did, I almost tore it off its hinges.

It was Finch.

He looked the same. The same short brown hair with the same hazel and caramel eyes, but this time they were calm, not manic as they had been in the past. Instead of the Brotherhood's black robes that had seemed to permanently shroud his figure, he wore a tailored three-piece suit, which was as dark as slate.

"Hi, Jade," he said, waving slightly, innocence playing on his lips.

I lost it. I moved on instinct—on fear—as I tackled him to the ground, my magic on full display for everyone behind me to see. Red sparks spluttered from my fingertips, higher than

I had anticipated, their power strong as they licked their way toward him—to burn him.

"Jade!" Bowen's voice boomed behind me, its Welsh-ness cracking against the walls of the narrow hallway. "Don't."

He came to stand next to me, a challenge in itself as the corridor could only fit two side-by-side in its limited space. He also wore a tailored suit, its deep gray offering a sharp juxtaposition to the angles of his face that were hidden by the scruff of his beard—though it did little to hide the fact he was the gorgeous man that I had completely fallen in love with. His brown hair was tousled back in luxuriant waves. If I were to run my hands through it they would have interrupted the hair product that was holding everything in place. His eyes were the color of brown tree bark with strips of morning sun running through them, their intensity holding my stare for only a second before I glanced back down at his pitiful excuse of a brother.

"Why are you here?" I snarled at him, my other hand gripping his previously pristine tie. He didn't look afraid or nervous, just calm, which made my blood boil.

"I'll tell you, but only if you'll let me up."

"How about you tell me or I kill you?" I could hear Mom's intake of breath behind me as she heard my words. *I would do it.* She didn't know, but after everything Finch had put me *and* Bowen through, I would kill him right then and there.

Bowen rested a hand on mine, the red sparks instinctively dulling their voltage at his touch. "*Cariad*, please…"

The word was unfamiliar to me, as he had never called me it before, but I knew the translation instantly: *my love*.

"But after all he's done…" My voice broke. I couldn't leave

it. Finch had been part of the Black Plague Brotherhood and their villainous plot to rid the world of magic had succeeded—and they had used *me* to do it.

"And everything he has done after... You don't know." Bowen looked to his brother, cautioning him against making any sudden movements. "Let's sit down and we can discuss everything." He waited for me to make a decision, his hand hesitant as he stroked the back of my hand with his thumb, the movement meditative.

My thoughts protested at the insanity of the notion, my mind whirring with conflict at the prospect, but finally I extinguished my magic and got up from the floor. My parents' and Jackie's faces were frozen in shock, not just at my aggressive behavior but at my magic as well.

What must they think of me?

"Not here," I said, knowing well that my dorm room was nowhere big enough to contain the tense emotions that were to come.

"We'll all go back to my place." Bowen reached out his hand and helped his brother to his feet, Jackie glaring at both of them as she went off to get her coat and purse.

"We'll meet you back there, sweetheart." Mom came over and gave me a hesitant kiss on the cheek. I hadn't seen her for six months. Her eyes were still the same pale blue but now they held more worry in them, just as there were lines on her face that hadn't been there before, etched in deeply. The only thing that hadn't changed was her hairstyle, the blonde curls falling just short of her shoulder. "Go straight there. We'll be timing you." Her voice sounded strained.

Dad, on the other hand, was the opposite, and in a chance

to lighten the mood, he mouthed, *No we won't*. He pushed up his glasses as he said it, their wired frames slipping from the heat of the situation. His black hair was peppered with white and cropped short at the back, while his dark, green eyes sparkled with mischief.

I had forgotten how goofy they were together.

And how much I had missed them.

Finch stood up, not making a sound as I went back to my room to grab my stuff, Bowen following me in. His muscular figure leaned against my desk as I wound my way around him, tight-lipped as I gathered my things.

"He's different here," Bowen began, his voice taut.

My body went tense as I held my hand up in protest from whatever defense Bowen wanted to continue with. That man had stripped me of my will in the rite of passage and forced me to become the slave of that *vile* creature—the Black Prince of Wales. "There is *nothing* you can say right now that can convince me that that piece of *shit* is reformed."

Despite the month being May, the Welsh weather was still chilly. I wrapped a scarf around my neck, the wool slightly dusty and damp from not being used for months, and stomped out of the room. Slinging my bag over my shoulder, I shoved past Finch, joining Jackie at the bottom of the stairs.

The quad in Old Building was quiet except for the bubbling of the fountain at its center. I had apparently come back to Lampeter during finals week, the other students either busy with their studies or out drinking to celebrate the academic year's end. The tranquility was like a foreign world to me.

The four of us walked down to the library car park and piled into Bowen's Mercedes. If I hadn't been so irritated I would have marveled at the interior, its cream leather soft against my body as I sat next to Jackie in the back.

She still wore her thick white-framed glasses that highlighted her midnight-black skin. Her tight curls were pulled up into a ponytail—like they had been when I had first met her at London's Heathrow Airport—though now their length was shorter by a finger.

Driving through the town of Lampeter, it was weird seeing the world so different from what I had just left in 1351. Instead of the bustle of carts and horses or peddlers shouting out their wares, cars and lorries dominated the streets. Rows of houses and stores lined Bridge Street, their facades ranging from off-white to the deepest of pinks.

The car sped up as Bowen headed out of town and into Cwmann, its fields of grass and sheep welcoming us at its border. Dark clouds had transformed the morning sky, raindrops falling unsuspectingly onto pedestrians. The windows of the car soon blurred with the rain, making it feel as if everything I had experienced was nothing but a dream.

The world felt empty of magic. Though there were still trace amounts of it here and there, it was as if they were a distant memory I was trying desperately to hold on to, only for them to slip through my fingers.

"How long have you been living here?" I asked finally, the silence eating away at me. My leg bounced up and down out of habit, my hands sweaty against my thighs.

Bowen's eyes flashed to the rearview mirror, the gold in them glinting in the oncoming headlights. "Since the Renaissance. I didn't want to stray too far. I knew I would be living for a long while before you'd show up. Lampeter seemed out of the way enough for me to lie low and not have any prying eyes into my personal life."

He was right about that. Lampeter was a secluded sleepy town in South Wales—the most popular topic of gossip was who slept with whom—no one would ever suspect a six-hundred-and-ninety-two-year-old to be living amongst them, especially not how Bowen looked.

He pulled up a dirt road, the hedges along its sides acting as a partition along the winding route. My breath came in heavy waves as I scanned across the area, the anxiety of the possibility of a sudden attack creeping its way further into my mind. I grabbed for the door's handle, ready to leap out of the car at a moment's notice.

I was ready to bolt as we rounded the last bend, and before us was Bowen's home.

"Welcome to *Y Goedwig*," he said as light-heartedly as the situation allowed.

The first thing that caught my eye was its size. A pebbled driveway ushered us to a circular parking area in front of cobbled steps that led to a large double door. The walls were beige limestone and its roof was made of tiled gray slate covered here and there with moss. There were two gabled bay windows at the front of the house, their stone awnings as intricate as church glass. To one side of the house was a conservatory filled with a variety of flowers and plants, and further back I could just make out a light-green barn-like structure with black doors and windows.

The car came to a stop and Bowen cut the engine, got out, and held my door open for me. It was a nice gesture, but that didn't mean he was off the hook.

The large front door opened and a man who looked to be nearly seventy-five stood in the doorway. He had an air about him—both of wisdom and of knowledge—and he came over and handed us umbrellas, unperturbed at getting wet himself. He had thin, graying hair and a mustache, his pale face etched by lines and wrinkles.

"Arthur"—Bowen pulled me under his umbrella—"this is Jade."

The man in front of me bowed. "Milady, I've heard so much about you."

I was caught off guard at his use of my own title and fell into my old routine, my legs bending into the curtsy I had perfected months ago. It felt both familiar and odd, my body no longer encumbered with the heavy fabric of skirts and undergarments. No one knew of my upgraded status—magical or otherwise—and that was something I was looking forward to in the coming discussion.

"Are we all to convene in the master's office?" I asked Arthur, Jackie's face full of questions at my old-fashioned sentence. "I mean... should we talk in the office?" As gracefully as I could, I held out my hand to Bowen and waited for him to take it. He hesitated, unsure whether I was giving it to him out of hierarchal respect or because I wanted him near. At that moment, it was the former.

"Actually, I believe the library would be more suitable," Bowen answered, placing his hand under mine while his butler led us in. His fingers felt gentle, the calluses that used to be on his palm almost nonexistent; the modern world no longer required swordsmen.

The decor inside suited the outside architecture. Dark

mahogany flooring ran throughout the foyer, linking with a grand staircase that any princess would have wanted to descend—as if the whole room had been created from the wood of a single tree. The walls were painted in a soft blue that invited our imaginations to run wild as to what the Welsh sky would look like on a sunny summer day. Paintings adorned the walls, their heavy canvases and frames lighting the room. Some were of Bowen wearing a military uniform from one era or another, while others were of people I didn't recognize.

A room opened up to the left, where sofas and love seats were positioned on thick Persian rugs in front of a high-definition television, speakers placed in each corner to give a full surround-sound effect. A black piano sat in front of a bay window, allowing plenty of light for whoever wished to play it.

On the other side of the foyer was a large dining hall comprising a long wooden table on a rug that ran the length of the room—grand enough to host a party of fifty if the occasion called for it. A bay window with French doors and deep-green drapes led out to a small garden, yellow roses and pink peonies already in bloom. What really caught my attention was a canvas framed in ornate gold that was as tall as the height of the dining hall. My heart was beating fast at the sight of it.

It was me.

My hands were held up in a pose, one hand containing luminous green flames, the other red. My raven-colored hair was flowing freely down my back, gently lifted by a phantom breeze, while my sea-green eyes were piercing as they stared back at me. A silver and golden tree twinkled behind me with Saint David's Cathedral in the distance.

"I had Cosimo Tura paint this when the loneliness was too much to bear. I think he captured your likeness exactly, though he thought me insane and I had to pay him extra to add the magic fire details."

His smile made my display of pissed-off-witch quickly fade and I fell back into academic mode, my anthropologist's mind whirring away. "How did you get all this stuff?" I whispered as we moved back into the foyer, unable to contain my curiosity as I glanced at an hourglass where black sand slid through three interconnected tubes. The house was gorgeous, exactly the type of place where I imagined Bowen would have lived. There was a sort of manliness to his home, with hints of femininity only a Renaissance man would have been bold enough to own up to.

"We'll have time enough to recall every item in the house if you wish, but for now, I think we should make our way to the library." A slight grin crept to his mouth. He looked… tired.

I let go of his arm and sped past Arthur, who was directing us through the living room and was just about to open the door to the library. With a wave of my hand, the door banged open, and I cringed inwardly.

Before I could step into the room I felt it, that nagging pull I had become accustomed to since my magic had manifested. The books… their pages whispered. I examined the bookshelves. The newer books seemed to be located near the door, and as we made our way further in I could see as the books grew older, every volume with its spine facing out. I chose a title at random, the smell of myrrh pervading the air around it. In an elegant hand was written: *Time Travel: A Theory on Everything*, and I looked up in disbelief. This was one of the books from The Forest, its magical archives knowing no bounds when it came to information—information that was now lost to the modern world.

"You didn't?"

Bowen's smile widened, further melting a section of my heart. "I did."

"Every volume?" I went up to the second floor, where a platform jutted out into mid-air, letting those standing on it survey the shelves below. There was an oval table there as well, with a bookstand next to it, and scouring the other shelves I found other familiar titles dotted about. I couldn't stay mad at him, not when he had delivered such a present.

"Not every book. Some are at the library on campus, but the most important and rarer editions are here. Including those from Master Lewis's private study."

Tears threatened to appear at my hearing my old magic tutor's name, as Bowen appeared behind me.

"Thank you," I whispered, leaning into him.

"I didn't want them to go to waste." Quickly, he stepped away.

I took the opportunity to wander up and down the aisles, surveying the books I had once held and researched from in 1351. They had yellowed and browned with age, but they were still in reasonable condition.

"Does someone want to fill the rest of us in on what the *fuck* this is all about?" I hadn't noticed Jackie looking mad, beyond mad… She looked like she was about to throttle the life out of me and Bowen. "Why the hell do your hands glow? Why do you know Prince Charming with his huge house and fancy-ass library? Who the *hell* is this guy?" she asked, pointing at Finch, "and where have you been?"

I forgot that some of us weren't as up to date as others, though my parents didn't look as freaked out as I thought they would be.

"Jackie, calm down." Right as I said this, the ambience of the whole room seemed to alter, and Jackie relaxed to the point where she looked as if she had smoked two joints.

Bowen glared at me, a stern look crossing his face.

"I didn't mean to," I apologized, honestly surprised. *Something's definitely wrong with my magic…*

"It's not nice to suppress other people's emotions." His words didn't match the light tone of his voice or the happiness on his face at seeing me use my magic.

"I don't think I can help it right now… Something's off…"

"Jade!" Jackie yelled, breaking the hold on my spell.

There was worry in his eyes, but before Bowen could question me further on what I had meant, my parents went over to the table and sat down.

"Come, everyone," Mom said, ushering us, "let's all sit down and talk about this. Arthur, can you ask Louis for tea please?" Arthur nodded and made his way out of the room. Before I could ask her how she knew all these people, she pushed ahead. "Now, Jackie, I know you have questions, as do we, but we won't get through this conversation with interruptions." Though clearly still annoyed, Jackie nodded in agreement. "Good. Now, Jade, how about you start from the beginning?"

Arthur returned with a tray filled with a teapot, cups, and hefty sandwiches of ham, chicken and beef, with veggies poking out from the sides. It seemed Louis had been prepared for our arrival, and I realized I hadn't eaten since Finch had kidnapped me the previous morning. It made me homesick for Gran's cooking—a woman I had made sure to make a close ally of at Llansteffan.

I gobbled down the first sandwich, washed it down with black tea, and started on the second. "Right," I began, as I finished chewing, "I don't know who knows what, so I'm just going to tell everyone everything."

I began my story, starting from when Jackie had last seen me running out of our flat to the library, but I only made it to when I first met Bowen before my voice trailed off. I didn't want my parents knowing what he had done, the scar on my clavicle burning hot as a reminder. He had been a different man back then, hell-bent on revenge for his murdered wife and children, which was understandable. But it seemed I didn't have to.

"And he tortured you," I heard Mom say point-blankly. I looked up in surprise. "Don't give me that face. Do you think we don't know *anything*? We knew what we were getting into before we adopted you."

"You what?" The table shook as I set down my cup, my meal forgotten.

"Of course we knew," she said defensively.

"I'm sorry. I'm not following what's happening right now… Can we just focus on Jade's story?" Jackie pleaded, pushing her glasses back on her nose.

Mom looked at her apologetically. "Yes, forgive me, Jackie. We'll get to my part later." She gave me a look as if to say I shouldn't push the subject and to continue.

"Fine…" The argument still churned in my stomach as I tried to calm down.

There were times I had to stop or get up and pace, anything

to get through the struggle of remembering all the people I had so recently left behind, who had now been dead for almost seven centuries.

There was silence once I was finished, the only thing breaking it the sound of a far-off cuckoo clock letting us know that night had fallen, until Mom turned to Finch, revulsion curling her lips.

"How *dare* you!" she exclaimed with a cold, dead stare.

Dad's chair fell to the ground as he reached over to Finch. The screwed up thing was, Finch looked like he wasn't going to stop him.

"You… you…" He could barely get the words out, rage pouring off him. "*You* did *that* to my daughter? *You* let such a disgusting human being use her like that?" Dad brought his fist back and connected it with Finch's nose, blood dripping from it and staining his pastel pink shirt. His next words were directed at Bowen, the venom in them potent. "You let us live with this bastard for *months* and never said a word?"

"It was not my tale to tell," he stated defensively.

"Wait, you guys have been *living* here?" I shouted.

"Of course we have," Mom shot back. "Did you think we would have stayed away, not knowing whether… *when you* were coming back?"

"I was a different man back then." Finch cut us off, but the look in his eyes wasn't convincing enough.

"And that means you're different now?" I asked from behind.

Mom put a cautionary hand on Dad, her own shaking with indignation, but as always, appearances were everything.

I would have done more than just hit him…

With all the commotion I had forgotten to check how

Jackie was fairing. It wasn't every day you learned that there had once been magic in the world. "Jackie, you okay?"

"I just…" She looked like she was about to hyperventilate. "Can we open a window or something?"

Before I had the time to wave my hand, all the windows in the room swung open, letting in the cold breeze of the evening. Jackie's eyes opened wider, my use of magic overwhelming her senses, but there were more pressing matters.

I took stock of everything. "Now that we're all on the same page," my voice rang with confidence as I directed my attention to the still bleeding Finch, "*what the fuck is he doing here?*"

II

Arthur brought Finch a hand towel to wipe his nose with, the blood now caked above his lip.

"The short answer," Bowen said as he went to sit down again, "is that I actually don't know what he's doing here."

"Well, that's a load of shit," I stated defiantly. "How do you *not* know?"

He raked his hand through his beard, frustration showing in his words. "Jade, I don't even know why *I'm* here. You vanished before Tristan and I figured out what you'd done. All we knew was that I was alive and you were gone. For a long time we... we thought you'd sacrificed your life to save me." His voice cracked, as if the memories of a lifetime ago were still fresh in his mind. "I had to live with that for decades."

I pulled out the chair next to him and sat down, placing my hands atop of his, trying to somehow take all the pain that he felt away with my touch.

"The next time we went to war I was hit with a spear. Went right through my arm... Hurt like a bitch, but when I pulled it out the wound was gone. Healed itself right up, like magic..." He smiled. "It was then that I started to look through

The Forest again, well, what was left of it at least, looking for anything that could explain what had happened to me. It took me decades more to find it, but I did. I found the spell you used."

"That's impossible," I protested. "I made it up. There's no way you could have found it."

"But I did. It was there… Stuck between two pages of the most obvious book." He looked over by the edge of the table to the bookstand.

I recognized what it held. "The Monksblood Bible?" It looked just as it had last year when Lampeter's resident archivist, Paul, had first handed it to me. Its thick covers were wrapped in taut leather that had now faded and cracked with age. When I picked it up its weight was still off, the size of it tricking its readers into thinking it would be heavier.

"Technically it's Evans' blood," he said with a smirk. "But I thought I'd spread the rumor about it being monk's blood to keep the genealogists entertained."

"Those poor genealogists." I laughed lightheartedly, something I hadn't done in weeks. "That still doesn't explain what Finch is doing here," I continued, getting back to the question at hand.

"Ah, yes, well from what I can tell from the wording of the spell, you probably messed up," he said hesitantly, like he knew I was going to take offense at the accusation.

And I did.

"How can I mess up a spell I created?" I recounted it, the words feeling familiar to me. Everyone else in the room waited on bated breath for something to happen and sighed in relief when nothing did.

"You didn't create the spell, *cariad*." Bowen moved to my side and took the book from me, the tome seeming smaller in his hands than my own. Opening it to the end of the binding, he peeled back the parchment from its heavy wooden board and took out a flashcard-sized piece of parchment, the spell written on it.

"You kept it in there?" I asked as I took the paper from him. The parchment was heavier than the book itself, carrying with it the weight of what I had used it for.

"Never remove an object from its original setting, the consequences can be too great to fathom!" he said, hunching over slightly and imitating Master Lewis's voice.

"He would be cautious, wouldn't he?" I said, smiling, remembering all that I had learned from him.

"Get back to the problem, Bowen," his brother reprimanded. Finch was leaning against one of the bookshelves just behind the table looking anxious.

My face flushed as I snapped at him, my tongue unyielding. "Why don't you just crawl into a hole and die? Or would you rather be set on fire? I recall you like setting fires, don't you?"

He pushed off from the bookshelf, the vein in his forehead popping out as he understood the meaning to my words.

Bowen moved between us before I could take another step, acting as a barrier between me and Finch. "Jade, I'm sorry to say, but you really did make a mistake when performing the spell."

"That's not possible. I literally made the spell up at that moment. The Forest must have made a record of it afterwards."

Finch got in my face so quickly I didn't have time to respond, but my muscles automatically tensed at the threat.

"That's not how these things work, Jade, and you know it." The mood in the room got more tense with each passing tick of the clock above us. "At that moment you had an all-access-pass into The Forest's knowledge. You did it on purpose to torment me all this time!"

After extracting all the magic from the world I'd only had a split second to think as I saw Bowen bleeding to death. At that moment, I hadn't been concerned with anyone else, especially not Finch.

My hand went for the small blade I had become accustomed to wearing, only to grasp at air. "A happy coincidence," I sneered through clenched teeth.

"Enough!" Bowen slammed a hand onto the table, making my parents and Jackie jump. Finch retreated back to the edge of the room. "Read it again," he half snarled.

Feeling annoyed, I looked down at the black script ingrained into the parchment, skimming the letters. "It's the same."

"Jade, come on now. Look."

I looked at the spell, re-reading the words over and over. "I still don't see it."

He pointed to one of the words. "What's its translation from Latin to English?" he asked.

"*He*," I answered confidently, a numbing headache forming at the front of my lobes.

Bowen tutted, prolonging my agony. "You didn't pay enough attention in Master Lewis's class."

"I did so!" I said, feeling hurt at the accusation.

"Then you should know that this word actually means *two*, as in double."

TO THOSE WHO SURVIVE

The realization hit me head on. I gripped the sheet of paper tighter, looking closely at every stroke, every flourish of the calligraphy. "That's just... No..." He was right... so right I was too shocked to grasp the concept.

"And what is the title of the spell?"

My gaze shot to the top of the sheet. "*For the Use of Extending Bloodlines.*" Every ounce of energy drained from me, a headache now pounding throughout my whole body. "I didn't know," I argued numbly, the fragile paper on the verge of ripping from the tremors that shot through my hands.

"How could you not *know*? You performed the bloody thing!" Finch snapped.

My cheeks flushed again. "I had no idea what I was doing then, words just spilled into my mind and I followed their lead."

"Well, maybe you shouldn't have," he cried, his voice strained. "Do you know how many years I've lived?"

"Maybe I wouldn't have had to do it if *someone* hadn't kidnapped me, forcing Bowen to come to my rescue and then be mortally wounded!" I reached again for my blade and this time made contact with it. In a swift movement, I pulled it out of its scabbard, only to discover it wasn't made from metal and pewter as my original one had been, but that it was glowing hot with green flames. It was much larger than my usual one, its shaft thicker and the hilt forming comfortably in my hands. I readied myself, preparing to take him down, the books rumbling in unison with my anger. It was only when one went flying across the room and almost hit Jackie that someone intervened.

"Darling..." Mom came and stood next to me, her brows

pulled together in worry—or horror. "We know it's not your fault, but we need to talk about this rationally. You may have rushed into everything too quickly—"

"What?" I turned on her faster than when I had accidentally enchanted Bowen's legs and stuck him to the ground, the blade burning brighter with each second.

"Jade." My mind reeled as Bowen got too close, my instincts taking over as I pointed the tip at his throat, his features tranquil as the heat lightly singed his collar. "Jade," he said more softly, trying to calm me down.

"I did it for you," I whispered as I lowered the tip ever so slightly before finally letting it drop from my fingers. Instead of the sound of metal hitting the floor, the flames dissipated before they hit the polished wood. I looked straight at him as I came back to my senses. It sounded so pathetic but it was the truth. "I didn't know Finch would be affected. I just didn't want you to die. Is that so bad?"

"No, *cariad*, I am happy you did it. *Dyma'r rheswm yr wyf wedi bod yn aros i chi i gyd y tro hwn*." His answering smile calmed my anger and I went to be encased in his arms, his body stiff.

"*Et factum esset arbitrium eadem iterum, si essent interrogavit*," I countered in Latin.

"English please," Jackie reprimanded curtly. "My Latin is rusty as hell…"

I let go of Bowen as I saw Dad come over, his face grim at the whole situation. "Now that's settled—"

"Nothing is settled!" Finch interjected, but he was ignored.

"—we can move on to what we're going to do now."

It was the farthest thing from my mind. The headache that

had spread through my body had moved back to its former location, piercing the front and back of my brain. I had been so focused on what had happened in the past that I hadn't even thought about what was happening in the twenty-first century.

"I need to go back to university. Finish the year if they'll let me." I had missed so many classes and exams I would probably have to retake the year. That meant another year's worth of loans and debt.

"I think the school board can be persuaded, through a hefty donation, to allow you the credits," Bowen said slyly, as if he had already lined up the money. "You did technically fulfill the ethnographic experience, and I believe that counts for something."

"And what will knowing how to shatter a man's ribcage and being able to make mead get me in this century? Will it help me get a job?" The real world was catching up with me. I had no idea what I was going to do with an anthropology degree, though seeing as I had lived in a different period of history, I could always make the switch and become a medievalist.

"You will have more than enough time to make those decisions. You are only twenty-one, Jade." He had meant it as a compliment, as he looked deep into my eyes, but I didn't take it as one.

There were so many things those eyes had seen that I would never be able to understand, and the thought haunted me. To a six-hundred-and-ninety-two-year-old, twenty-one years was practically nothing, but in human years… I was almost a quarter of a century through my own life.

III

I didn't want to have to think about my existence, how fleeting it was compared to Bowen's. What I needed to know was what was happening *now*. Other than the obvious, who knew what my actions in the past had changed in the present.

Bowen led me back to my chair, and I was happy to have the cushiony fabric to rest my head against. The day felt as if it would never end.

"Right now we're having some political issues that are… moving in quite a tumultuous direction."

My eyes glassed over for a second, bored of the topic already.

Bowen seemed to see it as well, quickly moving onto more exciting things. "But I think we should start with what happened after you left." I slightly perked up at that. "After you disappeared, the Black Plague Brotherhood was happy with the outcome: Magic was no longer prominent in the world." I looked over to Finch, still not trusting him being here. Bowen continued. "You not only sucked the magic out but also the history. Every book was altered so there was no mention of the craft, except for the few stories here and there that are considered fairy tales and folklore. The Forest started to die. The magic that once protected its many books and artifacts was no longer there."

Guilt ate away at me. "What about the Tree of Life? I know it's not dead." Though most of the world's magic was gone, not all of it was eliminated. The Tree of Life, the origin of all magic, was somewhere. I could still feel its faint heartbeat periodically thrum through the earth, though the beat was too weak to pinpoint exactly from where.

"I can't say. You were the only one who ever encountered it. Not even the Roderic Bowen Library and Archive has any information."

My heart ached at hearing what my actions had done to the world. *There's no more Forest?* I could barely even fathom the idea…

I glanced up in surprise at hearing Bowen's full name. "What did you say?"

"The library on campus is named after its founder," he said with a roguish playfulness, "and I am he."

Mom chimed in with: "And he's also your generous benefactor. The reason you persuaded us that you should come to Wales."

It was like being slapped in the face twice over. The only reason my parents had agreed to me studying abroad was that my education and living expenses would be paid in full by an anonymous benefactor. Knowing now that it was because of Bowen, all the pieces fell into place.

"Whoa. Hold on. You're saying that you *own* the archives and library?"

"Not own per se, but I've donated a substantial collection

of books over the centuries that would have otherwise not put the library on the academic map. Though it doesn't have the same prestige or size as the Bodleian in Oxford, we do hold our own on how unique our materials can be. I started it so Wales could have their own national library, but that honor ended up going to Aberystwyth."

"Why? Why set it up?"

"For this exact reason. For you to find the Monksblood Bible and set things in motion."

If Bowen hadn't paid for me to come here then I would never have gone to the archives—excuse me, the Roderic Bowen Library and Archives—and been sent back to the Dark Ages. "You wanted me to rid the world of magic?" I asked in disgust.

"Jade, if you haven't noticed, which I very much doubt, magic still exists. Maybe not what you or I would consider it to be, but just think of all the innovations humanity has created? Electricity... Technology... Things no one in the past would have ever thought of if magic were still around. Humankind created them through necessity, if not laziness. Yes, in the beginning, I thought a grave mistake had been made, but centuries later, I started to see the bigger picture."

"Only because I was there to help," Finch said, sneaking in. He really did need to get his mouth sewn shut.

I had never thought the twenty-first century to be a place of magic. Magic was being able to create spells and summon rain on a whisper of words, not turning on a light switch, but after hearing Bowen's way of thinking... it was kind of hard not to. "And the part about you paying for my education?"

"Well, that's still on the table if you want it. I am quite

wealthy. Over the years I made the right investments, some more fruitful than others. You told Master Lewis you were from the twenty-first century, didn't you?"

I nodded.

"News travels fast in a bustling castle. I knew as well by the end of that day, and when I had searched in your bag—"

"You went through my bag? I don't remember that!"

"You were unconscious… Sorry…" He skipped over this quickly. "As I was saying, I found some interesting things. At the time I didn't think anything of them: some papers, a wallet, and what I now know to be a mobile phone. They were hints enough to know where I should place my money and where not," he finished triumphantly.

"I don't know how I feel about you paying for my education. I'm more than capable of paying my way through school. Dad's job keeps us pretty happy in that department and I get a loan from the government every year." When I had first heard my time would be fully financed while I was in Lampeter I was ecstatic, but knowing now that Bowen was the benefactor changed things. I didn't want to mooch off him. "Plus, I don't know if I want to continue with anthropology anyway."

My parents' heads shot up faster than a jack-in-the-box.

"Jade…" Dad said in a cautionary tone.

Mom seemed to have a bit more to say. "You *will* finish school, whether this year or the next, or in three years' time. You *will* have a diploma. One way or another." The teacher in her was leeching out, making sure my education came first. She hadn't stepped into a classroom for years, now only a substitute when needed and a freelancer at other times, but that never stopped her from lecturing.

"Calm down. I didn't mean *not* finish school, just that I don't think I want to be an anthropologist anymore." My headache had turned into a full-blown migraine that was getting worse and worse by the second. If this conversation didn't end soon, I knew I was going to take my frustrations out on *someone*.

My parents relaxed after hearing that, my future looking bright in their eyes once again.

"Oh, I haven't told you the best part," Bowen said, smiling.

"What?" I snapped at him, my anger lashing out.

"I am a wealthy man, yes, but you, Jade Elizabeth *ferch* Morrison *ferch* Gruffydd, are as well."

"What?" Everyone in the room almost simultaneously said the word, leading me to believe that none of them knew about this.

At that moment my attention was distracted by Arthur, who had returned for a second time to turn up the brightness of the chandeliers, their crystals throwing rainbows onto the books. The smokey gray night was now pitched in ebony, surrounding us with shadows. Shadows that reminded me of the cloaks of the members of the Brotherhood. My breath caught in my throat, my words barely getting out. "What do you mean?" I asked, looking nervously around the room, making sure there was no one hiding in the darkness.

"Exactly what I said: You are just as wealthy as I am, perhaps even more so." Bowen laid a reassuring hand on mine. He could see the panic in my eyes, feel my tension as I prepared myself for anything unexpected.

"And how wealthy are you exactly?" A flash in the corner of the room caught my eye and muscle memory took over as I jumped to my feet. Bowen stood with me, deflecting my action so the others wouldn't notice, his hand resting on my lower back. It took everything I had to ignore my instincts.

"About as wealthy as Luxembourg at the moment, and I'm equating this to pounds sterling, not dollars."

I could barely hear what he was saying, the sound muffled as I concentrated on the phantom threat I sensed in the room.

Dad let out a high whistle. "That's close to fifty-four billion pounds. Sixty-seven point seven billion in dollars."

That brought me back. "But that amount is absurd," I countered. "Why would you even do that?"

"I've been investing here and there, wherever I could over the years, not only in my name but in yours as well. Her Ladyship Joan de Somervile knew that you would be returning to your time at some point or another and made me promise to build up your inheritance until we met again. And not all of it is in cash—though with what computers do these days, cash is irrelevant. But you also own property throughout the world."

I really didn't know how to take all this information in. Would you believe it if someone randomly said you had won a million dollars? And, apparently, I had won insanely more.

"I have all your financial records if you want them." He motioned to Arthur, and as his butler left the room, so did Finch.

"Yes…" I said in a daze. "No, we can look at them later tomorrow. I think I just need to process everything." I made to move back to my chair, only to miss a step and catch the table on the way down.

Jackie pulled out her phone. "Whoa, it's almost midnight. We should be getting back." She stood and waited for me.

"Come on, Jade. The girls in the flat are gonna flip when they see you're back."

The thought of leaving Bowen made me nervous, a crusted speck of blood still under my fingernail catching my eye. His blood.

I came so close to losing him...

"I'm staying here," I announced resolutely.

"Jade, you can't," she protested.

I looked up to him for confirmation. It was his decision in the end.

"I see no problem in you staying," he said, and I could see the relief flooding through him. "It's up to you, Jade."

"I'm staying." I didn't need to think about it.

"Dave, perhaps you can drive Jackie back to her dorm? My mechanic, Reo, will still be in the garage if you want to get a lift." Bowen didn't take his eyes off of me.

"Can do." Dad stood up. "C'mon Jackie." He led her out of the library, her face a mask of hurt.

"You need sleep," Mom announced resolutely.

"I agree," Bowen said, hovering around me. "I'll show you to your room."

He guided me out of the library, his arm strong around me. We didn't say much as he led me through the hallways of his home. The emotional toll of today's events finally became too much for me to handle, my legs wobbling enough that he finally scooped me up, my head resting on his shoulder. His scent encompassed my every sense, the mulled spice and forest musk enticing me to bury my face deeper into him.

Even with me in his arms, he managed to open the door to the room, revealing something I never thought possible.

The inside was decorated in the same way as the First Room back at Saint David's. The mustard-yellow walls were the same shade as the wheat that had greeted me in the First Room, while a rich blue rug that mimicked its stream cut the room in half, with the bed on the one side and the en suite on the other. I expected to see a likeness of the Tree, perhaps made out of books, at the end of the room but what instead held my attention was the twelve-foot glass wall that separated us from the garden outside.

Where the Brotherhood could be hiding...

I shook the thought from my head, reminding myself that they had died out long ago.

Wooden spiral stairs led to a loft above, two lounge chairs looking out through the glass wall into the distance.

"It's gorgeous," I whispered in amazement.

"It took a couple of tries, but I thought of you when designing the mansion, this room especially."

"I can see that." He put me down but stayed close as I walked around looking at the paintings on the walls. All of them looked like originals that should have been part of a museum collection, rather than kept in someone's home. "Do you sleep here?" I asked, as I passed by a Rembrandt.

"Every so often, but ultimately this is your room. There is a change of clothes in the dresser..." He hesitated, stepping back a pace. "So it's here that I bid you goodnight."

"Please..." My hand reached out to him, not wanting to let him go. "Please don't leave me again."

He seemed affected by the truth in that sentence. We had both lost each other, me for only seconds, and him for hundreds of years, but there was still a hesitation from him.

Since my return there had been something off about him, how he would position himself around me. Back in 1351 there was no time for love, no time to be caught up in infatuation, but somehow our feelings were linked to each other. Even now, there hadn't been time to acknowledge each other, to tell one another exactly how we felt.

He lifted my hand to his face, gently brushing it against his lips. The warmth of his breath tingled all the way up to my wrist, and he took my face into his hands. I could feel his hot breath on my cheeks, his mellow and musky smell mixing with the lavender that I could smell in the room.

I stood on my tiptoes, close to his lips that parted with every breath I took, matching me.

He bent toward me, his lips eager for my own. "Never."

IV

Blood dripped from my blade as I brought it across the chest of a Brotherhood soldier, the sounds of the battle deafening as I made my way through the throng of black-hooded men and women that surrounded me. I kept thrashing and cutting until bodies were piled high, their limbs limp and their hearts paused forever. Finch, in all his Brotherhood garb, sauntered up to me, his eyes looking wicked.

And then they changed.

No longer were they brown, but startlingly blue, almost silver. His dark hair was pulled back toward the nape of his neck and his mouth curled into a sadistic smile I would never be able to forget.

The Black Prince stared back at me.

I could feel the weight of my sword, what it would feel like to run him through, yet my hand wouldn't move.

"*Jade…*" His voice rang in my head, my body now petrified, frozen to the spot. He came closer and I could feel his hand on my lower back… the way he had placed it before. His lips grazed at my neck. He said, "*Thank you,*" and bit down hard.

****

I jolted awake and felt the weight of an arm around my body. Adrenaline took over all my senses as I instinctively pushed away and fell from the bed onto the polished wooden floorboards. My sweaty hand slipped as I skooched into the corner of the room, bringing my legs up into a protective ball, eyes closed.

"Jade?"

I could hear his voice and the *thump* of feet against wood as they hurried toward me. I tightened my defenses as power shot through me, readying myself for an attack, when I felt a hand on my shoulder. I lashed out with too much force, hitting flesh. The sound of a body slamming hard against the floor forced my eyes open, and I saw Bowen, his lip bleeding.

"I..." Tears sprang to my eyes. *What am I doing?*

He recovered quickly from the attack and came to kneel by my side, his face a mask of emotions. "Jade, it's okay."

The fear in his eyes... the pity...

"I'm sorry! I'm sorry!" I had no idea what was happening to me. The present and past were all jumbled, mixing up not only my magic but my emotions.

He took me into his arms, trying to calm my trembling body. "Shh, it's not your fault..."

Before I had time to answer, there was a knock on the door and Mom unceremoniously came in. She looked for us in bed and, finding it empty, was surprised at the sight of us: me on the floor and Bowen with a welt of blood at the side of his mouth. "What happened?" she asked, rushing over, her hands stroking my face, trying to see if I was hurt.

"Nothing. I had a bad dream..." I got up using the wall and Bowen as support, cautioning him from telling any more.

She wasn't convinced as she checked me over, Bowen standing there as he tightly held my forearm. *How long had I been asleep?* It had felt like seconds, but the clock on the bedside table indicated that a day had already passed since my arrival.

He led me over to the bed and we sat as Mom handed me a bottle of water from the side table. The thought of water sloshing around in my stomach made me nauseous and I tried to push it away, but the look she gave me had me cracking it open and taking a small sip to please her.

"Is there something that you need, Janet?" Bowen asked, deflecting the situation.

"Ah, yes. The reason I was going to wake you is because the police are here."

That got Bowen moving. "When did they arrive?" B-lining for the dresser, he grabbed some clothes for me. It looked like he had been ready for my arrival, most of my stuff already laid out neatly in the drawers.

"About five minutes ago," she said, her voice pitching up higher than usual.

"Whoa, why are the police here?" I went to change in the bathroom so they couldn't see how much my hands still shook, though my voice probably wasn't all that convincing.

"I told you that we had to give them an excuse as to your absence. I believe they've found out you're back and want to follow up," Bowen called out.

"How would they even have known I'd left?" I yelled back, trying to pull on my jeans.

"It's a small town, remember," Mom chimed in.

"Or Finch told them," I said, disgruntled.

"Either way, they're here and waiting for the both of you in the foyer."

I looked in the full-length mirror, my black hair a disheveled mess that even a run through with the comb wouldn't put into submission. In an effort at normality (and to forget last night's nightmare), I washed my face vigorously, hoping the thoughts would go with the water down the drain.

"Why not the sunroom?" I heard Bowen counter.

"Arthur won't let them past the threshold until you're there to supervise," she answered.

Minutes later, all dressed and ready to go, we hurried from the room.

When we got to the foyer, Arthur was still standing there, barring the police from the rest of the house.

"Here they are, Ron," Mom said informally to the policeman.

How many times had they met?

"Cheers, Janet." He moved to take off his hat and grabbed his badge, flashing it toward me. "Chief Inspector Ron Kant. This is my partner Constable Amy Noble. She's in training." The woman behind him was staring at Bowen, and she fumbled for her badge when she realized she had been introduced.

"Hello." I smiled as sweetly and innocently as I could. The man in front of me was ordinary-looking; his receding hairline and pudgy stomach made it look as if the most exciting thing this detective had done in the past year was drink at the pub. "I guess you're wondering where I've been for the past six months?" I started.

"Yes, miss, we need to take your statement for our documents. It's procedure." He had a no-nonsense attitude about the situation and made to move further into the house, only for Bowen to stand firmly in place, not wanting them to intrude.

"It is just as we have explained before, Chief Inspector. Jade was going through a rough time. She was just rebelling and wanted to know who her real parents were." Bowen was telling the story as if explaining to someone how to boil water. "She believed going behind her adoptive parents' backs was the best option as they wouldn't have been able to understand where she was coming from." He ended with a flashing smile.

"Come now, Mr. Evans..." The chief inspector wasn't buying a word he spouted. "Though your position in our community has enhanced us greatly, especially what you've contributed to the Coal Industry Social Welfare Organisation, I think the girl is more than capable of speaking for herself."

Bowen looked as if he was going to argue the point, but I wasn't going to give him the satisfaction.

"It's as Bowen describes," I said, playing along earnestly. Somehow the lie sounded better coming from my mouth. "I wanted to find my biological parents. I even went as far as the Netherlands, but I came up empty."

The chief inspector's skepticism rolled off him. "Am I to believe that a girl of twenty-one did all this?"

That got my blood boiling. "You shouldn't judge a person on their age, Chief Inspector Kant, it is both belittling and insulting." I had been underestimated before by adults, and it always annoyed the hell out of me that they tended to treat younger people as if they still had a pacifier in their mouth.

"No," he said, looking me up and down, "I guess not. But we'll still need you to come down to the station and make an official statement."

"Ron, really…" Mom was using her persuasive-teacher voice, a tone I had been subjected to many times over my younger years. "I've only just gotten my daughter back. Could we please wait with the formalities of the law?"

"I'm sorry, Janet. Jackie filed the missing person's report, and 'said' person is no longer missing."

Jackie filed it?

"Then how about I have her fill something out later and I'll personally come by and drop it off?" Mom was always good with compromises.

He flipped through his notebook, trying to come to a decision that suited both parties involved. "I think that's acceptable." His partner looked like she wanted to protest the arrangement, but one look at Bowen's stone-cold face shut her right up.

"Right. Now that's settled"—Bowen moved to the front entrance, holding the heavy door open—"we don't want to keep you." If there was ever a better line in the British culture, I don't think it would even come close to how well it politely invited people to fuck off.

Chief Inspector Kant shoved his cap back on and left the house, his partner following quietly behind.

We all waited at the door until they had sped off down the driveway, Bowen releasing a sigh of relief as they did. "Who wants breakfast?" he asked lightheartedly.

As if I was going to let him off the hook for giving such a cover story. "Bowen, have you heard the saying 'hell hath no fury like a woman scorned'?"

He moved to my side, trying to play the innocence card. "I believe it was William Congreve who first uttered it. Good man, though that interpretation doesn't do its original justice: *Heaven has no rage like love to hatred turned, Nor hell a fury like a woman scorned.*"

He was right, the latter quote intended a deeper meaning, but that didn't mean what he had done wasn't wrong. Before he could move out of reach I grabbed him by the arm and swept my leg under him, and as he fell, I pinned him to the ground, forcefully pushing out the air in his lungs. "That's for making up such a shitty lie."

Mom stood by with an amused smirk on her face, like she was glad someone had finally had the balls to do it.

I stood up and walked past him further into the house, Arthur waiting on my command. "Arthur, could you show me where the kitchen is?" I asked, as ladylike as possible.

"Yes, madam," he said, trying valiantly not to react at his master's predicament.

"Please, don't call me that. I'm just Jade." The scenario left me with a sense of déjà vu as he walked in front of me, leading me to the French-style doors into the kitchen.

When we entered, it was exactly what I had expected. It was a professional-grade kitchen, with a big chrome gas stove in the middle island. The fridge and dishwasher on the side wall were as large as a household could ever need, and the quartz stone countertops and white cabinets gave it a farm-y feel.

"Hey, pumpkin," Dad said, manning a pan, a spatula in hand. "Want some pancakes?"

"I'd love some." My stomach growled loudly as I sat down at the breakfast bar across from him, content in putting this morning behind me. When Bowen and I had finally fallen asleep, my headache had disappeared only to be replaced with a day's worth of my torturous unconsciousness. Suffice to say, I was starving as I watched him flip pancakes in the air, the sound of their sizzle as they hit the high-heated flattop enticing.

"Dave, could you try not to burn them this time."

I hadn't seen the other man who now returned from inside the pantry, but he was obviously the full-time chef. He wore the typical garb of one—accompanied by an Italian accent. He looked comfortable in the kitchen, not as Gran did when she was busting out dish upon dish—though this guy looked like he would be up for the challenge.

"I would never burn pancakes that were meant for my daughter, Louis," Dad said as he plopped a pancake onto my plate. "Here. Eat up. Louis will make you eggs and bacon if you want."

"*Si*. I will make you something with protein. You will need it when you are to train with the master." He moved a pan onto the high heat and threw some eggs and bacon in. "By the by, where is he?"

"Probably still lying on the floor where I left him," I said, getting astonished stares from both of them. "We just talked with the police. Bowen made up a cover story—a good one—but that didn't mean I liked it."

"No, we didn't either…" Dad scoffed.

"You are the first to best him," Louis sang with confidence. "Maybe the master will rethink his actions."

"I doubt it." The Bowen in this era didn't seem any different to when I had first met him, his stubbornness prominent. But now it was different. Things were slightly calmer, no war was impending, and we could finally start the relationship I had been waiting for.

I heard the door swing open and turned in surprise to see Finch, everyone in the kitchen going rigid at his presence. Dad looked like he was about to throw the spatula right at his face, while Louis paid more attention than necessary to the eggs.

Finch came straight up to me, his eyes lowering to mine, and I couldn't help but wonder if they would turn silver in a split second. "Can we talk?"

I wanted to slap him right there. For him, it had been centuries since we last saw each other, but for me, it had been only forty-eight hours ago that he had strapped me down and used magic on me.

"I don't think that's a good idea," Dad began.

"No, Dad, it's fine. I think we need to get everything out in the open." Hopping down from the breakfast stool, I made my way through the kitchen's back door and out into the garden, Finch following right behind.

The crunch of the tan-colored pebbles beneath our feet only stopped when we were out of earshot from the house, right next to the marble and wrought-iron gazebo I had spied earlier from my bedroom window.

Before he had a chance to utter a word, I whirled around and slapped him so hard across the face *my* fingers went numb.

"That's for everything you did to me." He was bent slightly over in agony and, taking my next chance, I uppercut him in the jaw. "And that's for everything you did to Bowen." He didn't move for a while, trying to handle the pain that I'd inflicted on him, and I had to walk around the gazebo's small perimeter a couple of times before I was able to fully calm down.

"Okay," I said, my nerves now somewhat even-tempered, though still teetering on fury, "what is it you want to talk about?"

He went and sat inside the marble structure. Its wrought-iron roof was covered in a glass dome, protecting its occupants in case of stormy weather. Thankfully today was as sunny as I had ever seen Wales, with white clouds being swept across the sky by the wind.

He pulled out a pouch of tobacco and rolled a cigarette. I didn't even know he smoked, but he lit the end of it and puffed out fumes into the air. "I want to apologize."

I stood by one of the ivy-covered pillars, not wanting to get too close to him, keeping my mouth shut to avoid the colorful assault that wanted to escape from my lips. Was I ready to forgive him? Last night's dream flashed before my eyes again and I could feel the taste of bile rise to my throat. I thought about everything he had done, everything he had put not only me but Bowen through.

I went and stood over him, staring straight into his eyes. I knew that the power of forgiveness was mine to use however I wanted, my emotions torn as to whether to cling to the past or throw it away and move forward. I chose the middle ground. "I'm not going to say what you did was okay, because it never will be, and know that you will never have my full trust." I closed my eyes and screamed every curse word I knew at him, my throat going hoarse at the effort. When finished, I opened my eyes again and stared him down. "For the time being, I will overlook your past regressions."

I think I actually startled him into silence as he gawked at me with his mouth slightly open.

"Jade, you have no idea what that means to me." He leaned forward, elbows resting on his knees, his head in his hands. "For centuries I've been trying to reconcile the guilt I'd accumulated all those years ago. After you disappeared, I managed to slip away and find passage to Germany. I had nothing, no one… You don't know what I went through. The Brotherhood had accomplished their goal and the world spun into despair, if only for two hundred years. By then the last generation of magic users had all but forgotten about the Brotherhood. But I never did." He raised his head. "I knew that if I were to move on with my life, the only person that could grant me this was you." His eyes were teary as he took an unsteady breath. "It was only years after, when I returned to Lampeter with Bowen, that I knew I had to reconcile with him and find closure. It took a couple of centuries, but finally we were brothers again."

"Why are you telling me all this?" I was torn between still hating him with all my might and accepting Bowen's own forgiveness toward his brother.

"Because I want you to understand that no one blames themselves more than me."

"As you should." I wasn't going to hold back. If he was laying out his cards, so was I.

"I was a different person back then. Zanna, my master," he paused, trying to form his words, "…thought we were headed down the right path, but I got consumed by it." His eyes shifted uncomfortably. "Please understand."

"I don't think I'll ever be able to understand your reasoning, Finch. But you also need to remember that these events only happened days ago for me, and you've had centuries to figure out your feelings. Let me have my time, whether it be tomorrow or in thirty years."

He smiled a boyish smile. "I think that's fair."

I had never seen him so gentle. Before, he had been crazed, sadistic in his pursuit of me, and my every instinct still screamed at me to keep my guard up. "Come on. My dad will send out a hunting party soon."

Finch took a last drag of his cigarette. "I think you're right. He does have a mean left hook." He rubbed his jaw emphasizing the fact, but Dad wasn't the only one who could give a good punch.

We walked back to the kitchen, Dad and Bowen looking as if they were seriously about to send out the hounds. Bowen zeroed in on me and came to stand between us.

"What happened?" he growled.

"It's alright. We just talked. We're... okay now."

No one could hide the surprise on their faces. Even Louis just about choked on his bite of bacon, his cheeks going purple trying to cough it out.

"Oh"—Bowen faced me, his features softening—"I'm glad."

Dad went right up to Finch, a threatening spatula in hand. He wasn't going to let him off that easy, and I was thankful for it. "Don't for a second think *I* will. You hurt my daughter."

"I understand, Dave," Finch said, backing away. "I wouldn't expect you to."

With everything uneasily settled, I was able to get back to eating breakfast. Mom had gone out with Arthur for groceries and other necessities, leaving the rest of us to entertain ourselves.

Bowen wrapped his arms around me as I sat at the breakfast

bar chewing away at a pancake. "What do you want to do today? We could go into town, or spar, or relax in bed..." His beard tickled my neck as his lips met my skin.

The prospect of going anywhere today made my insides churn, and while lounging in bed would have been exactly what I needed, the thought of spending another day lying down made me antsy.

"I think sparring is in order." Since our time in the Dark Ages, I had gotten into the rhythm of training every day. I wasn't going to let up now.

"Sure. Go change and meet me in my office." He gave me a kiss before he sauntered out of the room, his back broad and tall as he went.

I wasn't sure how we would be able to maneuver in his office but I followed his instructions and changed into my gym clothes. It was still weird not spending an hour being primped and prepped for the day.

When I got to his office, Bowen was already inside waiting for me. It was what you would expect of a bachelor's cave. There wasn't much in terms of decor, with dark wood everywhere, and the carpet and red drapes made me feel like I was in one of those secret Victorian gentleman's clubs where people whispered about politics rather than in Bowen's home, but it somehow suited him.

"So how are we going to fight here? There's not much space." Though it looked like the room could hold a maximum capacity of twenty people, I doubted it could withstand our blows.

"We're not going to train here." Going over to his desk, he reached for something under its surface.

"We're not?"

"No. I have a better place…"

All of a sudden his desk slid forward, and where it had been positioned there was now a large gaping hole with stairs leading down.

"Whoa!" As a child, I had always wanted to live in a house with secret passageways and trap doors. Now I was.

"You ready, oh great Exalted Witch?" His lip curled upward confidently.

I accepted his challenge, the first smile of the day touching my lips. "Bring it."

V
Finch

Finch hated lying to Jade so outright about following Zanna's orders in the Brotherhood, but it was a lie he felt needed to be told at that moment. She was still too immersed in what had happened in the past that telling her *he* was the one who helped the Black Prince start the whole genocide would have only caused more of a rift. He needed her trust—now more than ever.

He sat on the porch step and rolled himself another cigarette, a filthy habit he had picked up over the years but could never find the will to stop. So many times Bowen had chastised him about it, but really, it wasn't like they were going to kill him. His mind wandered back to the day when the Black Prince first came to him.

Finch had been sitting on a low wooden stool in Zanna's house, the cold Welsh air drifting in through the spaces between the worn floorboards. His hands had been beaten raw from the thrashes he had received for every spell he hadn't perfected that day, his failings costing him dearly.

"Are you paying attention, Finch?" Zanna slapped the

back of his hand again with a thick stick, the crack splitting against his knuckles. He had been training with her for the past, grueling, thirteen years. Compared to his brother, he was the best sorcerer in the family, maybe in their entire village, but that meant little to his master. He could *do* better, he could *be* better, and at the age of twenty-one, he was already a high-class mage.

"Yes, Zanna, please. Let us end the day." He had to get back home to his parents and help them deliver that day's bread, the coming hours the most important for their business.

"You will leave when I tell you to. Now, again. Start the potion again."

Finch went back to training. The sun had already started to set beyond the horizon, the valleys hidden in dusky shadows. The herbs he was working on were tied together, their limp stems wilting in the heat of his hands, and it was only in the early morning hours, when they had finally finished, that he was allowed to trudge his way back home to Tenby.

Their house was not grand. It had four walls and a thatched roof for protection. He opened the rickety door and, stepping through, propped his coat on the small chair that sat next to the entrance, the pegs on the wall already adorned with his parents' own cloaks and aprons. The air was cold, misty from that morning's dew.

"Mam, Dad?" He moved further into the room, dreading the coming day. Sleep was out of the question, his deliveries more important. By now he should have smelt the fresh aroma of yeast rising, dough and flour should have been caked onto the counter, yet he found the place dry, empty of any ingredients. Instead, when he turned the corner into the kitchen he found his parents on the floor, their blood seeping into the packed dirt. His heart broke as he bent down to them, their bodies already cold and heavy as he swept them into his arms.

"Nonononononono." Tears streamed down his face as he rocked back and forth, his hands and legs becoming covered in their blood.

He heard a rattling behind him and felt a shift in the air as a shadow crept up. With every magical muscle in his body he produced a charm strong enough to bring down a platoon of men, yet when his eyes focused on the intruder, he found him still standing.

"I've not come here to harm you," the voice purred, his face hidden in the corner of the room.

"Better men have tried and failed." It was a hazard of living on the edge of town, but they had liked the quiet. The way the sea's waves crashed against the cliff's edge with a meditative hum was what had drawn them to the place.

He tried his spell again, this time putting every ounce of his concentration into the words as they almost silently slipped through his lips and into the air that now crackled with lightning. The intruder deflected the blows with a wave of his hand, no spell needed to bat them away. Finch stumbled back onto his hands, their blood-coated stickiness now caked in dirt, his face flushed as he tried to register what was happening.

"I saw someone leaving this house in a rush," the intruder murmured. "I thought as a concerned third party that it was my duty to make sure whoever lived here was safe. Naturally." The man finally came to stand in what sparse sunlight dawn gave off. "Royalty has no need to kill commoners."

When Finch saw who he was conversing with, he scrambled to his knees, his head bowed in acknowledgment.

"Prince Edward... I had no... Your Highness, what are you doing here?" He cursed himself for thinking that his magic could bring down Edward of Woodstock; his name was renowned as being the best sorcerer of his era. He probably would have been named as an Exalted Witch if Gwenllian, the Lost Princess of Wales, was not still alive and in hiding.

"I was here to invite you to a private dinner. You and your brother, of course." The prince's words rolled elegantly off his tongue.

"I am honored." Finch shook with anger and remorse, his nails biting deep into his palms as he looked over to his dead parents. "As you can see... My family needs me at the moment."

The prince moved to Finch's shoulder. "There are more important things in life than family. Like loyalty. Are you loyal to me, Finch?"

"Yes, Your Highness. As my brother serves as one of your father's captains of the Royal Guard, I too take pride in being one of your subjects." Finch was still on his knees as he waited for permission to stand.

"Good. I have been watching you for a while now, ever since you came to visit your brother after the Battle of Winchelsea. Your fervent defense against Spain's rudimentary magic was riveting... to say the least. It was then I knew you were just the man I had been looking for." Edward placed his hand lightly on top of Finch's head, caressing his hair as if he were a parent consoling a child. "*Vivens lucem videret!*"

Finch could feel the spell work into his mind but wasn't

quick enough to counteract it. It wouldn't have helped either way, as he had never heard it before, but no one could disguise the energy needed to produce such a thing. "Your Highness!" He struggled under the pain of the charm, his legs going limp as he slammed into the stool next to him, trying to steady himself as a rush of dizziness encompassed him. "What… are you doing?"

"Showing you the light, Finch. You need to *see* what will happen to this world. And I want you by my side to help me."

"Help you… what?" Suddenly, Finch could feel sparks in his brain, and his eyes rolled into the back of his head.

"Help me rid the world of magic."

With a last jolt, Finch's body fell to the floor, convulsions racking through him from the effort to process what the premonition was telling him. His mind was no longer in his home but far away, as if he had been swept up in a dream and transported to another time.

It looked nothing like any place he had ever visited, with its fancy carriages that moved without the help of horses and the cluttered sky filled with magic, its waves and currents drifting through a multicolored dimension. He thought it beautiful, but when his gaze came upon the people that walked around, he was taken aback by the comparison to his time.

They were skeletons of themselves. Their skin was stretched over their bones while sunken eyes vacantly stared ahead. Finch could hear the cries of children, the clap of taut skin as they were slapped to stay quiet. Women were half-naked in the streets, a babe latched to a breast while more sophisticated patrons flipped the odd coin at their feet, as if the action made up for their division in class.

Finch walked along a cobbled road, where lanterns were positioned on every corner. A small lad was going around extinguishing them with the flick of his wrist. Just like the others he saw, the boy was wearing trousers, his under-robes poking out from a tight vest. Another boy shouted from down the street: "Come one, come all! Now is the time to get your fix! We have fresh bottles of Magi for all who want it!" The peddler roared over a crowd of people, everyone jostling to get closer. The boy threw bottles at them and the crowd surged like hungry animals going in for the kill.

A bottle of the bright pink liquid landed at his feet. Before he could pick it up, a woman scratched his hand away and made to take the vial, only for a younger lad to punch her in the face and take it for himself, scuttling away before anyone else could steal it from him.

Finch looked at his hand, the pain already subsiding. He couldn't believe what he was seeing. His lip curled up in disgust, the people around him clawing away at each other.

This is not right...

He peered deeper into the eyes of those around him, their minds looking as if poppy-dragon had taken away their sanity, the rest being drowned in the necessity of magic—peddled magic that could no longer be classified as what he had learned since he had been a small child.

No. No magic could ever do this.

"Oh, but it will." The prince's voice resounded in his head. "It was not the magic's fault here, but the people. There are those who, in our lifetime, will exploit the powers of magic to create this future."

Finch was suddenly brought back into his own mind, the

prince still standing over him. "Your Highness… what…?" He could feel fresh tears running down his cheeks.

"I showed you the future, in about six hundred years. What will happen to our world if we do not act now."

Finch laughed, the sound raising even the prince's hair. It held no joy in it; it was the manic cackle from a man who had cracked, his psyche now only held together by spider threads.

"Yes! Haha!" Finch grabbed his coat and headed through the door, leaving his parents' bodies forgotten behind him. "We must go, sire. On the hunt!"

"I was going to visit your brother next." The prince had followed him out into the foggy morning mist, the sun now just over the horizon. "Hoping he would join us."

"Bowen? Yes. My brother and his family would side with us!" Finch seemed unhinged, jumping all over the place.

"With *you*. For now, no one must know of my involvement, otherwise that idiot Richard of Bordeaux could become king."

"Yes. Yes, sire. I will not tell a soul until the time comes." Finch's body twitched as he made his way to the back of the house, his horse grazing on a small patch of grass with the prince's horse now right beside his.

"And if he refuses and gets in your way?" Edward asked with interest.

"Then he has to go." Finch filled in the blank as if it was the most obvious solution. "Anyone who gets in my way has to go."

Another sadistic smile passed Edward's lips. "Good. Now, visit Zanna and the other villagers, and spread the word." The prince finally got a hold of Finch's bouncing figure long enough to look him straight in the eyes. "It is all up to you."

Finch nodded in agreement. "And what will you be doing, sire?"

"I will be heading to Calais on an… expedition, so to speak." Edward let go of him and mounted his steed, his form now towering over Finch. "When the time comes, I will send word about our next move."

He kicked off and left Finch there bowing in respect to the man that had corrupted his mind.

VI

The next couple of nights were restless. Bowen pushed my body to the point of utter exhaustion when we trained but my mind still wandered through my memories, revisiting the past and the Black Prince who haunted them. It wasn't until days later, when I could no longer distinguish what was happening around me, my nerves strung to the point of snapping, that I finally shut down long enough to have a different dream altogether.

> "Oh hush thee my dove, oh hush thee my sweet love
> Oh hush thee my lap wing, my dear little bird.
> Oh, fold your wings and seek your nest now
> The berries shine on the old rowan tree
> The bird is home from the hills and valleys..."

"Gwenllian, you need to let her go." Bowen looked down to where she sat in the rocking chair and I... I was the baby sleeping soundly on this woman's chest.

"Is it already that time?"

Her alto voice was rhythmic as the lullaby floated in the air.

"Yes." He delicately took me in his arms, cradling my head

ever so slightly. He was so caring... "I know of a good family that has been destined to have her."

"Who? Are they kind?" Gwenllian asked, the worry in her words not lost on him.

"Dave and Janet Morrison are the best of people."

I startled awake, the scene too real for it to be anything but a viewing of my recent past. When I thought again about the woman that held me in her arms, the lullaby that she sang from her lips, it was with a loving warmth no other woman but a mother could hold.

But that wasn't what captivated my attention. It was the fact that I had seen her before—as clear as day, just weeks ago in The Forest's First Room.

She was the ghost that had led me to the Tree of Life.

But that's impossible! If she was a ghost then... she's dead...

My limbs were stiff as I got out of bed and tried to stay as far away from the glass wall as possible, still unconvinced nothing was hiding out there. The morning sun had just risen, though most people wouldn't have been able to tell with the gray clouds that blanketed the sky.

What was Bowen doing there? He hadn't made any previous mention about knowing my biological mother. Should I even trust what I'm seeing in a dream?

I didn't care about getting dressed. I had slept in my training clothes last night, too tired to even move let alone change into anything decent. I thought about taking a sweater with me, an old habit that wouldn't die until warmer weather emerged, and went in search of Bowen.

I searched every room, my mind tired and foggy, until I finally found him with the rest of the household in the dining room, the morning paper open in his hands. I walked in and didn't even notice as the others greeted me, just waited until Bowen looked up from his paper, the question now stuck in my mind.

"How did you know Gwenllian?"

Everyone in the room stopped what they were doing. Dad poured coffee that was now spilling onto the table, Mom had a piece of toast still stuck in her mouth, and Bowen's newspaper slid from his hands. It was like some horrible scene from a sitcom, but I wasn't laughing. The only one who answered me, I knew, wouldn't have the answers I needed.

"What are you talking about?" Finch took a sip of his Scotch, unperturbed by the tension around him.

"Where did you hear that name?" Bowen stood and came next to me, concern in his eyes, the newspaper forgotten.

"In a dream I just had. You were there." I was trying to be understanding, but I needed to know what was happening.

He knew my dreams weren't getting better. For the past couple of nights I had been waking up in cold sweats on the ground or with the bedsheets singed. Something was definitely wrong with my magic, which made sleeping even worse, wondering if I was going to wake up with vines wrapped around me or the house on fire. Thankfully, only Bowen was a witness to my nightmares.

"Are you okay?" he asked.

"Who is she?" I asked.

"Your biological mother."

"Bowen." Mom's voice held a warning to it.

"No, Janet, I'm sorry, but she deserves to know." He took me by the hand and led me to the dining table, seating me in the chair next to him. He started again. "Gwenllian is your biological mother."

"Is she dead?"

His eyebrows shot up in surprise. "She's still very much alive, and living just outside Cardiff."

"So she's not dead?" My mind was still catching up, the fog taking its time to clear away. I had always thought that my mother wouldn't have given me up for any other reason. "Because that's what I assumed when I saw her ghost in The Forest that day."

"*She* was the ghost woman?" Bowen sounded absolutely astonished.

Well, it would have helped me a whole lot more if you'd just talk to me. It felt like he was keeping so much from me, trying to protect me, but I needed to know. I could feel my cheeks flush, my vision going blurry with both tears of joy and anguish.

"Did you always know where she was?"

"Yes, *cariad*, but things were tricky… I only met her when she found me one day, showing up on my doorstep, pregnant," he said with a smile. "When she said that you were to be born in a couple of days, I almost passed out in excitement."

I couldn't picture Bowen passing out from anything, let alone my birth. I wiped my tears away with my sleeve, and Arthur offered me his handkerchief. I thanked him, took it, and patted my eyes. "Why did she give me up?"

"She never said…"

"You never asked?" I whispered accusingly.

"What position was I in to deny her actions? I was just happy that you were being born and that I knew the perfect family to take you." He looked over to my parents, who sat listening to the tale.

Dad came over to console me, as always, trying to add a bit of humor to the somber moment. "We thought it was odd when we got Bowen's call. We'd only just made the decision to adopt that day and then out of the blue he tells us you're waiting."

I mustered a smile, my head swimming with questions they couldn't answer. "I'm going to go back to my room. I think I need some time alone."

Everyone stood up as I made my way to the door, Mom stopping me before I went. "Alright, sweetie. We'll be right here when you need us." Pushing my hair back, she kissed my forehead, her hands hesitant on my arm.

"Thanks, Mom."

Back in my room, I flopped onto the bed trying to sort through my thoughts. Before, I would have gone to Tristan and he'd have made some stupid joke about it all, but that wasn't going to happen again, and that hit me harder than I wanted to admit.

Bright sun shone through the window, the light piercing through to warm the room as the scent of fresh cotton wafted about the place. I tore my eyes away from the ceiling, its fine details and whorls holding nothing there but wasted time, and took out my phone.

Midday... Would Jackie even be awake?

I dialed her number and waited as it continued to ring.

"Hello?" She still sounded half asleep.

"Sorry, Jackie... did I wake you?"

Her voice no longer had the tiredness of the morning, the realization of who was on the other end jolting it from her. "No, no! I just got up. What's up?"

"I just got some shocking news."

"How shocking can it be? You were in freaking 1351, remember?" The sound of her laughter lightened my mood, infecting me with its positive energy.

The corners of my mouth pinched tightly as I took a big breath to calm myself. The line went silent, ready for the reveal. "I found out who my biological mother is."

"Holy shit." I heard the ruffle of her bedsheets as she tried to disentangle herself from them.

"Ya..."

"Did you *find her*, find her?" she asked, the phone rattling as she held it against her shoulder to steady it, her earrings hitting the receiver.

"No, I just saw her in a dream, and when I confronted Bowen and my parents, they didn't deny her."

"Of course you saw her in a dream," she said sarcastically. "Wait, so Bowen knew this whole time?"

"Yup."

"That asshole!"

"That's what I thought at first, but with so many things happening... He just thought he was protecting me, Jackie," I half-heartedly protested.

"I don't care! He had no right to keep that from you." The line went silent again. She was right of course, but I didn't want to tell her that.

"So are you going to try and find her?" she asked finally.

"I don't know. That's what I've been struggling with all morning. I don't know *what* I should do."

"Do you want me to come over?" Her tentativeness left me longing to see her—how she would be able to take away all my worries with a simple wave of her hand. I could hear as she opened her closet, the squeak of the old hinges.

"Can you? I think everyone in the house is a bit on edge, except for Finch of course."

"And I can't picture you wanting to spill your guts to *him*." Her laughter was infectious and so carefree. A hint of a memory, long forgotten, lingered in my mind as she and I took hours trying on second-hand dresses at one of the charity shops, preparing for that night's club night. I couldn't recall what I wore in the end, the evening like a wisp of haze in my mind.

"Hell no," I replied, joining in with her. "So you want me to get you?"

"If you think Bowen would even let you out of his sight."

It's not that Jackie seemed to hate him… it was just that she *hated* him but I didn't care, I just wanted someone—some normalcy in my life at that moment. "He doesn't really have a choice," I replied rebelliously.

"Good. Then I'll see you in twenty minutes." She hung up the phone. I changed into more decent clothes, leaving the comfort of my pajamas for more robust fabric. Grabbing my brush, I raked it through my mess of hair. It had gotten longer, the length now almost all the way down my back. I tried to tie it up as Elian always did, but the twists and pulls were hard to maneuver without her nimble fingers pulling them this way and that. Giving up, I braided it into a simple plat and made my way to the foyer and out to the garage, where Reo was already working under an old Beetle.

His workspace was littered with work-tools, the smell of grease and oil pervading the warm air. It was a different sort of trade compare to what Master Lewis and I knew, the tools clunky, yet as his hand reached out for one, he guided it with such deftness, I wondered which one of us was the real witch.

Before I had a chance to interrupt, he slid out from under it, jumping to his feet as he saw me. His fine black hair was cropped short at the back, while faded bleach-white bangs were plastered onto his forehead from the sweat of his work. Though the weather was nowhere near what it should be for the season, he wore a tank top, much of his arms and body covered in intricate Japanese tattoos, their paths interrupted by a scar here and an old bullet wound there. But it was the bright smile on his face that got my attention.

"Ah, *Anesan*—Jade. What do you need?" He set aside his tools and grabbed an already dirty cloth, wiping away the grease from his fingers.

"I was wondering if you could drive me into town? I want to pick up Jackie." I had my license in the States—had been driving for almost eight years—but I wasn't going to chance that when driving on the wrong side of the road.

His almond eyes glanced away as the muscles in his neck tensed.

"Sorry, *Oyabun*—Bowen—expressly said I shouldn't..." His Japanese accent was soft, making his tentativeness even more pronounced.

"Oh, did he now...?" He really was being too overprotective. "Well, how about I just fly there then?"—not that I had any experience with the spell—"And you can explain to Bowen why he's seeing 'Lampeter's Flying Woman' on the news."

Reo squared his shoulders, my playful threat mimicked back in his eyes, wickedness dancing around them. It seemed the idea of rebellion was catching.

"Okay, okay," he relented, with feigned defeat, "I'll do it. Don't want to start an uproar in the town." He was already putting his tools back in their box. "I'll bring a car around in a minute. Which one do you want?"

"I don't know. How many does he have?"

"Over fifty."

"*Fifty*? Okay… well… just get me a black one. Don't want to stand out too much."

Reo's smile broadened, mischief playing on his lips. "I know exactly which one will do."

When he came back five minutes later, my jaw almost dropped to the floor. He had gotten a black car alright, but even I knew what a Rolls Royce looked like when I saw one.

"I can't go in that!"

He rolled down the driver's side window, bouncy and ready to go. "Oh, come on. It'll be fun. Jackie will love it."

It was a case of six of one or half a dozen of the other. "Fine. Let's go before Bowen notices." I jumped into the back, having trouble with the door handle on the way.

"Oh, he'll notice us, no doubt," he emphasized, revving the engine.

"Great," I said sarcastically. "Then drive fast."

"Will do!" He hit the acceleration and we were barreling down the graveled road.

We got a couple of stares while passing through town, but

nothing out of the ordinary, the tinted black windows letting no one know who was behind them.

When we finally arrived at the dorms, Jackie was waiting outside for us, her jaw dropping as much as mine had when she saw her carriage waiting.

I rolled down the window.

"No!" I heard her squeal. "You can't be serious!"

"Get in, bitch!" I exclaimed at her lightheartedly and opened the passenger door.

"This is some *Princess Diaries* shit." She slid in next to me, gawking at the interior. Plush gray leather seats and a television positioned in the back of Reo's headrest had us feeling like we were flying first class.

"Well, I am filthy rich you know," I said with a mockingly posh British accent, and flipped my hair over my shoulder. We laughed our heads off as Reo sped back to *Y Goedwig*, the more normal atmosphere a reprieve from the last couple of days.

As we made our way back up the driveway, we saw that Bowen was already standing outside, his arms crossed with a displeased look on his face.

"Oh, here we go," Jackie said, ready for the attack.

Bowen came and opened my door as the car stopped. He jumped the gun before I could even get a word in.

"You know you shouldn't do that," he said, a playful look on his face as he pulled me into his body and I could feel his warmth.

At least he trusted me.

"Just keeping you on your toes." My mouth found his, the kiss lasting seconds before my hunger set in. "Come on, Jackie. Louis makes a mean burger."

"Yes! I'm starving." She followed me in, Bowen hanging behind to give us space.

Our bellies were full from the copious amount of food as we all sat on the porch balcony, glasses of homemade beer and lemonade on the metal table. The day had brought with it an unseasonal humidity together with the damp smell of impending rain.

Despite the gayety of the moment, my parents were still tiptoeing around me. It was understandable, it's not every day you find out who your birth mother is, but now that I knew, there was a hollow part inside of me that I had never noticed, never made mention of, that seemed to be filling by the second.

"Now that everyone's here, we need to talk about Gwenllian." I wasn't about to openly call her my mother. It wouldn't have been fair to the woman who had raised me for the past twenty-one years.

"What is it you want to know, pumpkin?" Dad sat across from me, his eyes ringed with sleep. Obviously the pressures of trying to work and deal with my magical problems were taking their toll.

"Well, it seems from our earlier talk that there isn't much you *do* know," I countered. Dad resigned to the statement, as did everyone else, and I switched my attention. "Bowen, you say she's still alive."

"As far as I know. I haven't had much contact with her since your adoption." Bowen sat there looking as if he wanted to say more, but he kept his mouth shut while Jackie got up and moved to the other side of the balcony, her eyes squinting out across the valley.

"But she's still in Cardiff?" I affirmed.

"Yes. She said she wouldn't be moving. Last I saw her, she was living as simple a life as possible to keep herself under the radar," he answered.

"But why? What's the threat?"

"The Order."

We all looked over at Finch in surprise.

"What Order?" I asked.

"The Order of the Garter," Bowen spat. "The Black Plague Brotherhood was a branch of the Order, though no one knows of their affiliations, the Brotherhood still lurking in the Order's shadow."

"Whoa, what? And they're still around today?"

"The Order is one of, if not *the*, most prestigious groups in the EEA," Finch affirmed. "Not that anyone knows of their sordid creation. The rumor was that the Prince of Wales was in Calais when the Countess of Salisbury's garter fell from her leg as she was dancing. There was outrage at the incident, but Edward of Woodstock was one of the few defending her—or so history tells. He was said to have created the chivalric order to protect those who couldn't protect themselves. Meanwhile, the Brotherhood was using the Order to gather information and hide behind. Now it's the most senior honor of knighthood the Queen bestows."

"How do you know all of this?" Mom asked, the ice-cold lemonade in her hand seeming to tremble as she held it.

"Because I was one of its founding members. In all honesty, I had no idea what we were really doing, and looking back on it, I'm sure the prince used the *Persuasio* spell on me, a very powerful one at that, but I bought into the cause. You can find my name in the records—Henry Eam, I went by—but nothing more."

He told his side of the story as if he were recounting the actions of a foolish child, but that wasn't going to make him any less guilty in my eyes.

"And what does Gwenllian have to do with them?" I asked through gritted teeth.

"Nothing, really," he continued, in the same casual tone. "They're threatened by her is all." Finch took out his pouch of tobacco and started to roll another one, Dad eying it as well.

"That's not entirely true, Finch," Bowen remarked.

"Guys…" Jackie was still staring into the sky.

"Well…" Finch said, "there is one reason…"

"*Guys…*" Jackie backed away from the edge.

"That *one* reason is the main reason," Bowen continued.

"GUYS!" Jackie's voice was frantic as she caught all our attention, her hand pointing toward the sky. "What is that?"

We all looked up, each of us trying to make out something barely visible in the distance flying toward us.

"It's just a plane, Jacqueline," Bowen said, waving her away.

"Don't call me that! That's not even what Jackie stands for." It seemed their relationship wasn't ever going to get better. "And I don't think a plane flaps when it flies."

Dad pushed up his glasses. "Must be a Fregatidae."

"Those are seabirds, darling," Mom pointed out gently, as we were far inland.

Finch's face went as pale as death as he looked up. "*Y Ddraig Goch,*" he whispered in terror.

Before I even had a chance to comment, the animal came bearing down on us, its wings knocking the glasses and chairs across the balcony. Large talons reached for me, and in seconds I became weightless. My eyes snapped shut as a piercing screech left my lips. I felt my hair as it whipped around, slapping against my face. As I pulled in gulps of air, a taste of dew lingered on my tongue, but also something else... I opened my eyes to see that I was no longer sitting peacefully in a deckchair, but flying hundreds of feet off the ground.
   Holy shit, holy shit, holy shit!
   My mind reeled as I tried not to look down, which was absolutely impossible, and the trees below looked like the tops of broccoli, their branches bowing against the assault of the wind. I clung to the smooth talon as I strained to see above me and I saw long spikey horns protruding from a scaled head.
   I was being kidnapped by a dragon.

VII
Finch

Finch almost went deaf as Bowen shouted from the balcony, his brother frantic as he tried to see what had happened to Jade.

"Oh my God! She's out there!" Janet covered her mouth in horror.

"*Get up there now!*" Bowen was right in his face. He hadn't looked this mad in decades. Strike that. He hadn't looked like he was about to *kill* something in decades, his eyes pools of onyx against the lush Welsh countryside.

"You know I can't fly anymore, Bowen," Finch lied easily as he pushed him away. It wasn't a total lie—he did still have some magic left in him compared to his brother, who possessed none, but he was saving it for the right moment, and this wasn't it.

Jackie's voice shook with terror, bringing their attention back to the sky. "It's flying away! Where's she going?"

His brother ran back into the house, Finch just managing to catch him as he bolted for the car and got the keys into the ignition. "You won't be able to follow them."

Bowen growled in frustration as he ran his hands from his beard and into his hair, making it stick up in one spot. "What would you have me do?"

He was on the brink of breaking.

The years Jade had lived in California had been hell for Bowen, not being able to see her, to talk to her and tell her of what was to come, and when she had finally come back to Wales... It was like dangling bait from a fishing line. Finch watched as he barely slept, barely ate, so he could keep a watchful eye on her. Now, after all they had been through, everything that happened from this point on was unknown, and that was scaring the fuck out of Bowen.

"There's only one person that would send a dragon to her. Gwenllian."

Bowen got out and paced by the side of the car.

Finch could see exactly what his brother was thinking, his mind ticking away as to why Gwenllian would kidnap her own daughter when it would have been just as easy to show up and ask her to come with her.

"Can you call her?" Finch had only been to Gwenllian's hideout once, but even then he had never stepped foot out of its surrounding tree line, making sure she never laid eyes on him. The Order on the other hand... They had found her and paid a dear price.

Bowen groped for his phone, his fingers fumbling with the screen to dial. It took a couple of rings, but finally, they connected.

"Bowen?" Jade yelled over the thrashing wind.

They could barely hear her. "Jade! Jade, are you alright!?" The line disconnected.

"I meant Gwenllian, you idiot!" Finch exclaimed, for once being the sane mind in the conversation.

"I don't have her number! She changes it so often and I've never needed to be in contact with her until recently that—" His phone rang, the caller ID coming up empty. Finch was shocked as a prayer escaped his brother's lips, an action he hadn't performed in years.

He picked up.

"Bowen, so nice to hear from you after all these years. You still have the same number," she said, tutting. "That's not particularly safe."

Finch could hear the smug tone of her voice even from where he stood—a tone he would never forget as she sicced *Y Ddraig Goch* onto the defenseless Order.

"Gwenllian, you—"

Silence cut the line as she interrupted Bowen, and a second later, he hung up.

"What did she say?" Finch had his hands in his pockets, the stress of the situation egging him to roll another cigarette.

"She says I have to wait until Jade tells me it's alright to come." He shoved the phone roughly into his pocket, agitated but resigned to wait like the pup he was, and started back for the house. "You coming?"

"No." Finch pulled out his pouch, Bowen shrugging his shoulders, the fight in him lost. He waited until his brother was finally inside and then replaced the pouch with his phone, dialing his personal assistant.

"Malcolm, any news?" He paced the pebbled driveway, small puddles of dirty water pooled in places where the ground was too saturated to soak it up.

"I was able to find the documents you asked about." His Irish accent wavered.

Finch rubbed at his brow as he could hear the "but" about to drop. "But?"

"But the curator won't let them out of Edinburgh Castle, insisting that if we want to see them, we have to go there." He paused, and Finch knew exactly what his PA's next words would be. "Don't you think it's time we brought Bowen in on the search?"

"No," he snapped. "Not yet. As I guessed, we'll need Jade to handle everything magical. I need to save my strength, and I'm not about to let their suspicions of me cloud the importance of this mission." In truth, it was a question he had asked himself every day for the past two hundred years—his search for the Tree of Life now a journey to find out about himself—but involving Bowen meant playing by his rules, and that was something Finch was not prepared to do. "For now I'll play the helper, and by the grace of the Gods, even Gwenllian has joined into our fold. I'll tag along when Bowen goes to them, see what she knows about the Order."

It had been a calculated move to reveal he was one of the founders of the Order. He was at a cliff's edge, his toes just over the brink enough that he would be safe, but every move, every word, had to be accounted for so that everything would go to plan.

"And Scotland? Do you want just me to go?"

He thought about it. "We'll all join you up there. Arrange some meetings with the city council so it looks like a legitimate business trip." Finch had been an official for the Welsh government for a little under three years now, but his connections and influence went back longer, allowing him to travel as he liked, which came in handy when searching for the Tree.

"Will do, boss," Malcolm confirmed, hanging up the phone.

This time Finch did pull out his tobacco and roll a cigarette, trying to piece together the leads he had searched his whole life for. If he hadn't played a hand in killing the Tree of Life, then perhaps he wouldn't be struggling so hard to find it, a last-ditch attempt to suss out the origins about his cursed life.

He remembered the exact day he had decided to go in search of the Tree.

11 August 1890—London

Finch glanced at the worn faces that sat at the Round Table in the Order's meeting room at Westminster, the group comprising some of the richest and smartest men in the world, which meant little to him. He took out his pocket watch, the minute hand seeming to move backward rather than forward in its attempt to prolong the godforsaken meeting. They had meant to be out of there hours ago, their stockpile of sherry already down to its last dregs.

"We can't let this keep happening." The Marquess of Salisbury, Robert Gascoyne-Cecil, banged his hand onto the table for emphasis. He dug into his breast pocket and pulled out a blue handkerchief he used to wipe away the sweat accumulating on his brow. His stomach sat over the top of his suit trousers, the buttons on his vest seeming as if they would pop at any moment if he moved incorrectly.

"And what would you have us do, Robert?" The Earl of Leicester, Thomas Coke, stubbed out his pipe, the smolder rising into the heavy velvet curtains that lined the room, keeping others from prying. The sweltering day had caused all their patience to run thin, the air stifling as the earl unbuttoned his cufflinks and rolled up his sleeves. He reached over the table to the tobacco pot to freshen his blowfish pipe, lit it, and brought it back to his white-whiskered lips. "Riots have broken out for centuries. Finch, tell them, you have been a part of this Order the longest."

Everyone there knew of his position as a founding member, one of the best-kept secrets in all of history, besides the Order's creation.

Finch swished the remnants of his port around his glass, sediment collecting at the bottom. "It is as Thomas says. Chaos has always played a role in the world. But I see your point. The Old Price Riots, the Merthyr Rising, Rebecca Riots? And that's just here in the United Kingdom. The Americas have had a riot almost every year—several in some. The world, gentlemen, is at a turning point."

They harrumphed in agreement.

"You know the cause of it."

They all turned to their brother, the tension growing as he bitterly spat the truth.

"Fitz?" Finch asked inquisitively.

Henry Fitzalan-Howard, 15th Duke of Norfolk, was no fool, and Finch had become close friends with the man, divulging even the many attempts at taking his own life and his years spent in Bedlam—better to be locked up and drugged than to keep reliving the horrors of his past. They all knew about his predicament of immortality; some were jealous, others suspicious, but Fitz… It had taken him years, but after meeting him, Finch had managed to find some semblance of balance in his outlook on life.

He was a good-looking fellow with a strong brow that slightly hid his pensive eyes. His brown beard was so long it reached to the bottom of the knot of his tie, his hair parted at the side and the front cowlicked. His cane was positioned beside him, though he had no real need of it except when wanting to push his way through London's pedestrian traffic.

"Especially you, Finch…" Fitz stood and pried open one of the curtains to look out onto the cobbled lane just outside Westminster, the lantern flames already turned up high for the pitch-black night. "The Tree of Life is dying."

Silence filled the room.

Finch had tried to forget that part of his life, the reformation of his psyche dependent on surviving the here and now. His past was a mess and the relationship with his brother was only just starting to form again for that century. He wanted nothing more than to forget about the Tree of Life, to forget the whole sodding affair that started this mess.

Fitz continued. "Our private archives have essentially been butchered by the loss of The Forest, the amount of information that is unknown to us astonishing." Finch looked away, shame eating away at him. "I have pored over every book in there, have even asked you, Finch, about those years of the Dark Ages, yet you always deny me the specifics." He came and sat on the edge of the table, arms across his chest. "From what little information I have gathered, the Tree of Life is connected to everything, all the political, economic, and environmental strife that is afflicting this world. And it is on its last legs, gentlemen."

"The Tree is just a myth," the marquess countered, his hand waving the notion away as much as the smoke from the earl's pipe.

Finch's steely gaze fell onto the man, the venom in his voice striking. "The Tree is as real as I am, Robert, and you should not speak of it as if you yourself are not a beneficiary of its existence."

The marquess shifted uncomfortably. "My apologies." He bowed his head slightly, bringing the argument to a close.

"If it is as powerful as you say, then perhaps we should take action and bring it under our wings, so to speak," Thomas suggested, stroking at his white beard.

"It would take an exorbitant amount of magic, and I imagine it is heavily shrouded." Finch knew it was next to impossible to find the Tree, let alone to try to control it afterward. The last known sighting was when Jade herself encountered it.

What a fool I had been.

"There may be answers it has to your questions, Finch." Fitz placed a reassuring hand onto his shoulder.

He was right. If there was a way to find out how his immortality could be reversed, then finding the Tree of Life would be worth it.

Hope, so long lost in Finch's mind, crept in once more.

VIII

The massive dragon swooped straight down to the ground, and when only a few feet away, his talons opened, dropping me into the meadow. Bile rose to my throat as my eyes fell upon a sea of blood… no… not blood, but a field of blood-red poppies, their stems waning and waxing like an ocean's tide in the wind.

"Are you alright?"

I flinched at the deep voice behind me, its vibration softened by the thick woods that surrounded us. My mind shut down as the wind shifted, the flowers catching my attention once more.

"You need not fear anything here," the dragon said, grinning. "*I'm* the scariest thing you'll find."

In lieu of what should have been terror, curiosity pricked my senses, as I turned and looked at the beast. He was much larger than I'd first thought, his red scales smooth against the bright sun, though I could see a few spots where his skin dipped from scratches and scars.

Tentatively, I rose, wiping at my hands to rid them of petals.

This wasn't the first time I had been kidnapped, the chaos and adrenaline an all-too-familiar sensation.

From my position I took in the surroundings of the meadow. We were enclosed by trees, their thick trunks and branches rich with blossoms, their leaves creating patches of darkness beneath them. The more I stared into their dark depths, the more I thought I could see the shrouded outline of Brotherhood figures waiting to attack. My eyes never left them as I addressed the dragon.

"Who are you?"

He made himself more comfortable, his scales almost merging with the colors of the flowers. "In the Arthurian language, I am known as Myrddin, but you may call me Hawk."

"I'm Jade," I said, introducing myself.

His shoulders seemed to relax. "Yes, I know. We have met before."

That caught me off guard. "We have?"

"It was only for a short while with Gwenllian in the First Room."

The giant dragon that sat before me looked nothing like the toy-like version I had encountered in The Forest's annex, my lips stretching into a smile as he tilted his head in the same way I had seen him do before. "How are you still here?" I asked.

"Gwenllian sent for you," he replied, brushing off my question.

I froze, nerves eating away in my stomach.

It was too soon. I hadn't even thought about what I would say—what I would ask!—if I were to meet her. "And she couldn't have just phoned because…?"

"Because Gwenllian has always been one for… grandiose

gestures." He chuckled, small tendrils of smoke escaping from his nostrils.

That seemed like an understatement.

"Where are we?" I could hear the soft thrum of cars in the distance, but they sounded too far away for me to be able to reach them.

"About three miles outside Cardiff. Gwenllian's home is just ahead." A bright flash erupted and my hands flew up to shield my eyes. When I could see again, Hawk was no longer his large dragon form but the one I remembered first meeting, his little wings beating softly against the air. "Head straight for ten minutes and you'll find her place." He flew in front of me as we walked, guiding me in the right direction.

The forest dwellers seemed to feel Hawk's presence, and they scurried away, leaving the place eerily quiet. I could smell the scents of pine and mud intermixed with a whiff of petrol from the road in the distance. The silence ate at me and I finally caved, striking up a conversation. "Hawk… can you tell me anything about… my mother?" The word still felt foreign in that context.

"Well, you met her before, did you not? What did you think then?" His tiny body floated next to me and the urge to pet him as if he were a dog rather than a dragon was increasing by the second.

"She was someone I could trust. Calm, gentle, but didn't take any shit." In the First Room I was more preoccupied with my surroundings and honing my magic than anything else, but there was enough time to know that if I would have met her out on the street, I would have stared at the sharp lines of her face, the beauty in how she moved, the happiness in her eyes.

Hawk came to perch on my shoulder, his wings drooping as we finally emerged in front of her home. "Her traits have not changed much over the centuries," he replied.

I had imagined she would have been living in some cabin in the woods, with stacked logs and a chimney that spouted aromatic smoke, but what greeted us was the *exact* opposite. The house was modern. It had a boxy shape with black tinted windows and smooth white walls. The roof had graphite slate roof tiles, with a rustic quality to the house that mixed well with its exterior surroundings.

"Are you sure this is the right place?" I looked around the side of the house and then came to stand back at its entrance.

Before I could stop him, Hawk floated from my shoulder and pushed the doorbell, its chimes barely ringing out.

At first nothing happened, the silence of the forest weighing heavily upon me. I could feel invisible eyes at my back, drilling uncomfortable holes that made my anxiety hitch up a notch. I saw my reflection in one of the windows, my hair windswept and a tangled mess. I tried to smooth it down as much as possible. And then I heard it… A distant pecking noise from inside the house, the sound like a hammer tapping against wood. Or maybe it was my own heartbeat thrumming against my temples? As it got closer I registered that it was, in fact, the sound of high heels on a tiled floor.

I held my breath when finally the door opened, with Gwenllian standing in the doorway.

She looked exactly as I had seen her in the First Room, minus the transparent ghost form and medieval gown. She now wore black slacks that fell beyond her ankles and a green button-up blouse, the shade of it enhancing her eyes. I had been correct in thinking the tapping noise was her high heels; the height of them would have even astounded Emma (my former flatmate and party-goer). Her hair was free-flowing, shining brown against the dark color of her shirt. Even with such simple clothes, the first word that came to mind when I saw her was *regal*.

I looked back at her face, a huge smile spread across it. She looked so much like me, or I guess I looked so much like her... The only difference was in our skins, mine slightly tanned from playing in the California sun, and the lines around her mouth and eyes were nearly nonexistent, but I could see them all the same.

"Jade."

There seemed so much love put into my name that I forgot what I was going to say as she beckoned me forward. I hesitated at the threshold of the door, my legs trembling as I stood in front of my mother.

She looked me up and down, appraising the woman I had become without her. "You are beautiful," she whispered, her hands moving to pat a section of my hair down that was still sticking up. "Come."

She took me further inside, and I struggled to think of something to say. All I could think was to ask why she had given me up... Not a proper topic to start with. I tried to focus on other things.

The inside of the house was far more spectacular than its exterior. The open-plan design allowed me a one-eighty view of the ground floor. Just as in Bowen's home, the foyer opened onto stairs, yet compared to his, this house seemed more science fiction than fantasy. The stairs seemed to be made of glass, the steps floating up to the next floor. In the back left corner of the expansive room was a kitchen that, surprisingly, seemed even more professional than Bowen's. The couch, coffee table, rugs, and television offset the straight lines of the living room, giving life to the somewhat sterile area. Though Gwenllian was the only one living there, the rectangular dining table was big enough to hold a party of twelve, its chairs high-backed, as if each was a throne for its occupant.

I followed her into the living room, where she had already prepared a pot of tea and some biscuits.

"Please, sit."

I sat opposite her on a leather couch. Not trusting myself not to spill anything on its pristine surface, I forewent the tea and drank hot water with lemon. My legs bounced of their own accord as they always did when I tried to calm myself, but this time it wasn't working.

"So," Gwenllian started and turned to me. She laid her tea cup down so gently it barely made any noise. "Where to start?"

I set down my own cup—not so gently—ready with an answer. "At the beginning, I guess."

Gwenllian smirked at my boldness and stood up to pace by the fireplace, obviously wrestling with exactly where to start. Finally, she turned toward me, a serious expression on her face. "That is a complicated request in itself."

"Try." Even though I was out of my mind with nerves, that didn't mean my patience would last, since she had technically kidnapped me, but her eyes were soft with understanding.

"My father, Llywelyn the Last, was killed in 1282 by a hired hand of Edward I. The history books say the man didn't know he was battling a prince, but that's just talk. My father was assassinated. My mother, Eleanor de Montfort, went into hiding after that. She was pregnant with me at the time and knew they would be after her next. I was born that year, only for my mother to die in the process."

Her father was a prince? That means...

"It was then that I was taken from my home in Abergwyngregyn to a nunnery leagues away. The English king knew that I was hidden away but took pity on me, thinking that because I was a child, and a girl at that, I posed no threat, and stopped looking. Little did he know..." she said mischievously. "The nuns had their hands full with me. My powers had manifested more quickly than in regular children and the townspeople started to notice. I would flit here and there through time, warning them of bad weather or raids. As compensation they never told the king of my whereabouts, and I was left to live a peaceful life. It was only when I met your father that things got... interesting."

My ears perked up at the mention of my biological father. I knew even less about him.

"He was a cobbler, of all things. But I saw the love that he put into his work and I knew that he would love me in the same way. We eloped (the nuns none too happy about it) and settled in a small house a few towns away. I knew the risk I was putting him in, but he didn't seem to care. I stored my magic away, using as little as possible so as not to stand out. A couple of years later in 1305 I was pregnant with you." Her eyes lit up, taking in my every feature, but they also held a sense of caution. "That's when things went wrong. You had so much power in you, so much raw talent before you were even born that it messed with my own powers. In the end—" She took a breath, readying herself. "In the end I couldn't control them any longer, and Geraint... your father... ended up in the middle of one of my fits and..." She couldn't continue, but she didn't have to.

"And we killed him," I whispered, my use of pronoun not lost on her.

Her voice was fierce as she defended me. "You had no part in your father's death. It was my fault and it's a burden I came to terms with long ago." Her thoughts trailed off, caught up in the horrible memory. "He was trying to help me... but that's when I had the strongest premonition in my entire life." She smiled with pride. "I saw you fighting. You were beautiful, but there was something odd about you, as if you hadn't grown up in the same world as me. Something told me I had to follow my gut... I never thought I would have jumped such a long distance in time, the Tree of Life sending me farther than I ever imagined. I left a part of myself there, knowing that one day you would find it, and me with it. Eventually, I found Bowen, and he told me more about the adventures you were to go through, all be they horrible, but there were some good parts too."

She was right. Through all the awful interactions I had with the Brotherhood, there were powerful memories of the people that had become like family and that would always stay with me as well.

Tears were streaming down my face, and she came to sit next to me, her hand placed atop mine like an anchor. I couldn't leave the question any longer. "Why did you give me up?"

The pain on her face...

"You need to understand, things right now aren't as

hunky-dory as they're made out to be. The Order has been after me since I got here, you too, and I didn't want that kind of life for you. Always moving, always looking over your shoulder..."

"Finch mentioned them before… Said they were threatened by you…"

Gwenllian sneered at the comment. "The only thing they're threatened by is the giant sticks they've got shoved up their asses."

"Then what do they want from us?" I asked, sniveling.

She squeezed my hand. "The only thing that matters, magic."

I stiffened under her grasp, new questions buzzing around my head. *Who wants my magic? For what purpose? Maybe they need it for something good… or something very bad…*

No longer being able to sit still, I stood and surveyed the pictures that were positioned on the walls and mantelpiece. They were all of *me*. There were photos of me from every school year, one where I'd actually dressed up as a princess on Halloween, and another of me at a track meet.

"How'd you get all these?" I said, a bit out of breath, there were so many of them.

"Bowen sent them to me." Gwenllian lounged against the back of the couch, the trials of her past over, though who knew what future ordeals were ahead. "I'm not sure how he got them, but I'm eternally grateful. They were the only times I got to see you."

Frustration ran through me. "You could have called or emailed at least." How many times had I thought about why I had been given up? How many times had I thought of what my biological parents would be like? I didn't know why the Order wanted magic, but was the threat so great that we couldn't even *talk* with each other? That all communications had to be cut off?

Gwenllian came to stand next to me, her arms holding me for a tight hug. She could see all my questions floating in the expression on my face. "I didn't want to risk them finding you." She pulled away, wiping tears from my cheek. "And Bowen thought—"

"Bowen seems to think a lot of things without *actually* thinking them through," I snapped. "And he'll be hearing more than a mouthful from me when I call him here."

What I must have looked like at that moment, her face full of motherly pride. "You're exactly like me…"

My emotions were running amok. I wanted to remind her that she was not the one who had nurtured me for the past twenty-one years, but at the same time, nature also had a strong influence on who I had become today.

"How about I show you your room? It's been a long day and I imagine you want some sleep." She guided me to the bottom of the free-floating stairs, her grip surprisingly tight. With the tinted windows and the lights on throughout the house, I hadn't noticed the sun setting, leaving the world in darkness.

"Wait, I have more questions," I protested. We hadn't even gotten to the part about my powers.

"We will have more than enough time tomorrow, and the day after that, and the day after that to answer everything. I'm not going anywhere now that we've found each other again."

IX

I settled into my new room, the place almost hospital-like in its cleanliness, smelling of cotton, fresh and clean. It wasn't as grand as my room in *Y Goedwig* but looked more pristine. The beige walls were accented with tints of white and sky blue while the king-size bed was low to the ground and covered in bright pillows and a duvet. There was no en suite, but Gwenllian had pointed out the bathroom just two doors down. Narrow windows, small enough that no one could climb through, were positioned near the ceiling, leaving me (for once) feeling secure.

I had nothing but my phone with me, so I pulled it out, forgetting that I had turned it to silent. There were thirty missed calls from Bowen. I pressed his number and held it up to my ear, the tone only lasting a second.

"Where are you?" His voice was strained, no doubt concerned at my impromptu absence.

"I'm fine, just…" I didn't know where to start. "I met Gwenllian."

"Jade, *where are you?*"

Why wasn't he surprised? "Just outside Cardiff…"

"So she's still there?" I could hear what sounded like the ruffle of clothes at the other end. "I'm coming to get you."

"No!" I protested a little too loudly. "I mean... I need to talk with her more, and I don't think I can handle any other distractions." The day had left me drained.

"Am I a distraction?"

I could picture the way his mouth would have curled up seductively at that statement. "Yes," I affirmed. "Yes, you are."

He chuckled. "I get it. How long do you want? A day?"

A day seemed too short, but I knew he wasn't going to agree for longer. To tell the truth, I didn't know if I could either. The nightmares weren't getting any better and I didn't know how I was going to manage a night without him to hold me together. I knew I had to talk with Gwenllian, get answers about my powers and persuade her to pick up where Master Lewis had left off... I couldn't concentrate properly on that while he was here.

"Get here for dinner tomorrow?"

"I won't be a second late."

I woke with sweaty sheets clinging to my body. It was the first night I hadn't had Bowen there, and I was paying for it, my joints stiffer than before and a migraine forming.

I slowly made my way to the kitchen and found Gwenllian already there. Her idea of what breakfast consisted of was a cup of coffee and a sliced apple. She looked perfect, her hair already fluffed out in brown waves and her blouse pressed—purple this morning. The only thing that looked out of place were the white cat slippers on her feet. I eyed them with a grin.

"They were a gift," she explained with embarrassment.

"I like them."

Putting on the kettle, I prepared my cup of tea—sugar and tea bag first, then water, and just a dab of milk—while Gwenllian popped on some toast.

"Butter and jam?"

"Yes, please." The tension in the air felt heavy; I was unsure of how to start. *How much will she be able to answer? Should I wait until we're done eating?*

"You can ask me, you know." Her voice caught me off guard.

"I know..." The toast popped up and I went over to butter it. "Would... would you train me? In magic, I mean... There's still so much I don't understand... can't understand. Since coming back to the twenty-first century my magic has been acting weird. It either takes me forever to get the spell complete, or it blows it out of proportion." Now that there wasn't any magic in the world, she and I were the only ones left.

Then it hit me.

I dropped my knife, the edge of it just missing my foot. How could I have been so blind? That shouldn't have been my first question...

"Are you alright?" Gwenllian came over and picked the knife up from the floor, butter smeared onto the white tiles.

"Do... do you even have any magic?"

She looked shocked by the question, maybe even a little hurt, but it was odd. If she had as much power as everyone thought, why hadn't she taken out the Order already? Why send me away if she could have protected me?

Gwenllian took my hand, her eyes fierce. "No."

We stood there together, our drinks and food forgotten.

"It took all my magic when having that premonition *and* to set things up for you in the Dark Ages *and* bring us here *and* also setting up my life so that we would be both comfortable and hidden." She shook her head in disappointment at herself. "I used it for years without realizing how much of a toll it was taking on my body and on the world."

"So will you be able to train me?"

"The art of magic is still the same. It will just be harder as I won't be able to *show* you anything."

It wasn't a huge loss. Master Lewis never demonstrated anything for me, adamant that I had to figure it out myself and have a feel for the magic. It was a heavy conversation to have at ten in the morning, but if this was what would get things started, I'd take it. "Is that what will happen in the end? The Tree will die and every last ounce of magic with it?"

"It's already happening. I don't know how much you've caught up on current events, but the world is in turmoil right now. Politics and war are one and the same. There's not much time left."

If the Tree of Life were to be truly eradicated from the earth, then what would we be left with? Bowen had already filled me in on the many terror attacks that were racking the world, and the freak weather… There had to be something I could do, and the only thing I could think of was harnessing my magic to its fullest abilities.

"I want to show you something." She motioned me away from the counter and to a white door set into the wall. There were filigreed leaves delicately etched into it, and it had no doorknob.

Gwenllian placed two fingers on its frame and started to

trace its outline, then, with ease, she pushed the door open without needing a handle.

"How'd you know to do that? I thought you said you didn't have any magic!"

Gwenllian's lips turned up with a smile. "It's a touchpad lock I created based off one of the more ridiculous spells parents would teach their children so they could keep their doors and windows locked away from monsters. It was more based on the fact that many children were kidnapped, this being a preventative measure. I designed this house with all the latest technology."

Ridiculous or not, it was a cool spell, er... security system.

We descended the stairs into what turned out to be her office, or what I imagined was her office—it looked more like a hub at NASA than anything else. Monitors were mounted onto the far wall and on her desk were three different keyboards.

"Whoa!" *She wasn't living in the Dark Ages anymore...*

"Computers are a bit of a hobby of mine," she confessed.

"I got that." I went over to her desk and looked at the screens, some displaying a different article or news station, while others were on social media sites, automatically bookmarking tweets and posts deemed important. "What is all this?"

"It's my research into the Tree of Life." She sat in her chair, the wheels of it smoothly rolling against the worn Persian rug underneath.

"Have you found anything?" My eyes lit up. Maybe this was going to be easier than I thought.

"Not even close. There've been rumblings about something in Scotland, but my contact hasn't gotten back to me yet."

Scotland. Just the mention of the place had me reminiscing

of a time when I had promised Jackie we would travel there together.

"Do you think you'll ever find it?" I had to know. What if finding the Tree of Life could restore magic to the world, and if not that, maybe some semblance of balance?

"I didn't before, but now that you're here… well… here's hoping."

X

Bowen and Finch showed up exactly on time for dinner. I don't know how they managed it, but just as I was popping the cork from a bottle of 2006 Malbec, the door opened and in they walked.

"I didn't hear the doorbell," I said.

"I didn't ring it," Bowen countered, shaking his set of keys. "The old ones still work. You really should get them changed, Gwenllian."

She went and took her place at the head of the table. "Why bother? You and I are the only ones who have a set."

I only noticed Finch as he stood by the dining room's entrance watching the scene unfold.

"Finch, you okay?" I asked out of feigned interest.

He ignored me, his eyes never leaving Gwenllian as he walked up to her. Seconds later he was kneeling in front of her, hand over his heart and head bowed.

"Princess."

That one word was enough to stop all conversation.

"Rise," she commanded, seeming to sit taller at the

recognition of her title. She glanced over to me. "You don't seem surprised?"

"I was yesterday when you dropped the hint about your father, but now... I don't know what to think."

Finch had barely moved, Bowen having to go over and drag him up. "Pull yourself together. Her title has little standing nowadays."

"Perhaps to you, but many of us still remember the old ways. No matter what time we are in, she is the Lost Princess of Wales, and that means something."

"It means *nothing*," Gwenllian snapped, glaring daggers at him. "Now, shall we eat?"

We all sat around the dining table, the food getting cold from the delay. I had to say something, anything, to get us past the shaky start.

"Gwenllian, I mentioned earlier that I wanted you to train me..." I shoveled a forkful of peas into my mouth, waiting for her response.

"I think that's a great idea," she answered, smiling, her teeth stained red from the wine.

"Are your powers back to normal?" Bowen asked her, taking a sip from his glass.

So he knows she doesn't have magic anymore.

"No, they're actually almost gone. The Tree dying has left a huge impact on my lifestyle." Her hand shook as she tried to cut her chicken, her knife clattering to the plate. She quickly picked it up again, trying to mask her fumble.

I peered at Finch across from me, accusation in my eyes. He was sweating, his collar almost soaked, even though the room was much cooler than the temperature outside. Something was wrong, but before I could comment on it, Gwenllian stepped in.

"I will still be able to train you, as I promised, Jade. And Bowen is taking care of the physical aspect, I assume?" she asked, trying to move the conversation on.

He choked on his bite of potato, hearing the innuendo in the comment.

"We haven't made much progress, I admit, but we're getting there." I played along, trying to drop Bowen the unsubtle hint. The first night I had come back, the extent of our physicality was our lips, exhaustion encompassing the rest of my actions. Since then, Bowen had trained me harder than ever and we always fell into bed too tired to do anything else but sleep.

"Well, you've only been back for less than a week." She directed her next words to Bowen. "You'll need to get on top of that."

"Oh God, guys. I'm eating!" Finch exclaimed.

Bowen's face was bright red as he took another sip of wine.

With dinner over, Bowen and I retreated to my room. I sat down on the bed, the day's adventures having taken its toll.

"What are you thinking, *cariad*?" Bowen joined me, lying down comfortably at my side.

"Nothing." My head settled onto the pillow next to his as I scanned the ceiling. I couldn't exactly tell him that what Gwenllian said about us bugged me. At the time I made light of it, but ever since my return, we had done nothing more than kiss and fall asleep together. With everything that was happening, it should have been the last thing on my mind, but…

He propped himself up onto his elbow, his eyes searching my face.

"It's not *nothing*. I can see the cogs in your head turning."

With a sideways glimpse, I met his stare, my eyes telling more than my mouth ever could. I tried to switch the conversation.

"Did you know that when I was really little I wanted to be a teacher? It didn't really matter about the subject. I just wanted to teach elementary schoolkids, the smaller ones, not those snotty-nosed fourth or fifth graders." It wasn't what we really needed to talk about. I had always had sexual partners, either whatever boyfriend I had at the time or a one-night stand, but this… What I had with Bowen… It was different, and it scared the shit out of me.

"I didn't know," was all he could answer. "You can still be a teacher, Jade, if that's what you want."

I scoffed, my nose turning up. "Yeah, that'll go so well. *Hello class, today we're going to learn our alphabet, but just be careful, I might incinerate you along the way.*" I smiled sarcastically. It seemed that becoming a medievalist was looking better and better every day… if I also didn't burn down the archives in the process.

"You're underestimating yourself again." He moved in closer and I tried to squirm away, only for Bowen to pull me to him. I wanted him to touch me everywhere. "You'll get there, *cariad*. Dreams take time and effort, and once this is all over, you'll be able to follow the path that will lead you to whatever and whoever you want to be."

"You were never this good with words before," I said, and I finally turned to face him.

"I've had centuries of practice," he said, laughing, the scent of wine still on his breath.

I could only guess at how much he had learned over those centuries.

"Speaking of practice… How much have you had? I mean… How many people have you *been with* since…?" I didn't have to finish the sentence, understanding that even bringing up his dead wife's name might cause him grief. I snuggled deeper into his chest, not wanting to look in his eyes at that moment.

"There've been a few but nothing serious."

"Do you… find me attractive in that way?"

He pushed me away, as if to get a better look at me. "Jade, are you serious?"

I couldn't look at him… Embarrassment didn't even come close to how I was feeling at that moment.

"I've wanted to hold you like this for so long. Ever since I walked you to your room on your birthday."

Since then? It felt like a lifetime ago. "I think that was about the same time for me as well," I confessed. "But you never made a move."

"I never thought you wanted me in that way. I thought you were just playing nice so I'd train you… Putting up with the man that had tortured you…"

I stopped him there. "I didn't want anyone more than you, but it was 1351. Did they have condoms? Did they have birth control? I didn't know and I didn't ask, so it was easier just to abstain."

He laughed—full-on, bear-rumbling laughter that made the whole bed shake. "That's what you were worried about?"

"It's a fair thing!" I protested. "Even if we did *other* stuff,

I don't think I could have controlled myself. I would have wanted to go all the way."

His face turned serious, his eyes showing so much love in them I thought my heart was about to burst. "I'm asking you now… Do you want to go all the way?"

There was so much more to that question than just sex. I answered immediately, my leg swinging over his hips, pinning him to the bed. I moved gently against him and felt him respond. "Does this answer your question?"

He pulled my face to his and kissed me deeply, a primal moan escaping his lips. "I have something for you." Somehow managing to keep us in the same position, he reached down into his bag. "Here…"

I was expecting maybe a picture or couples rings, but what he pulled out was a wooden spoon. It was gorgeous. The stem was made up of two different designs of chains and a Celtic knot that twisted elegantly and intricately together. The bowl of the spoon was deep, and when I ran my fingers into it, I felt the smooth ridges of a keyhole. "What is it?" I asked.

"It's a love spoon. It's usually given to someone you consider most dear… someone you can imagine spending your whole life with…"

It was better than a ring or anything else he could have given me, and with it came his everlasting love. I ingrained every curve of the spoon into my mind, not wanting to let it out of my sight, but with a mischievous smile, I placed it onto the bedside table, my legs tightening around his hips.

Pulling open his shirt, I ran my hands up his chest, feeling every muscle, but I abruptly stopped. I hadn't noticed before, but… All over his body I could feel the rise and dips of scars.

Some were white with age while others were tightly stretched pink. I found the one on his abdomen where Îbris had stabbed him…

How did he get all of these? How many wars, battles, and duels has he fought for them to leave their mark?

I purged the thought from my mind as I pulled off my own shirt, Bowen kissing my neck, his arms around me like a vice as I simultaneously moved against him. Breaking free, I rolled him over and scraped my nails up his back. There were more scars there as well, but what really caught my eye were the five rows of inked tally marks on his shoulder blade.

"What are they for?" I asked, tracing each one with my finger.

"They're for the most important friends that died in my lifetime."

My hand froze, my fingers feeling like they were stroking gravestones instead of tattoos.

"There aren't as many as I expected." It was a stupid thing to say. It would have been impossible for him to document the thousands of brothers-in-arms he had lost or friends that had died of old age. "What about this one?" I traced the first tally mark, inked in deep green.

"That one?" He turned over, his body languid as he took me into his arms. "That one was you."

"But I didn't die." I giggled. "I'm right here."

"But you changed my life forever. A far greater significance than the rest put together."

I moved in closer to him and heard his intake of breath as my hands ventured lower to stroke the V of his hips, his body arching at my touch, hot and ready. I pulled off the rest of my clothes, the last barrier between us, and Bowen did the same, throwing them forcefully across the room.

I straddled him between my legs, my spot already wet and waiting for him, until finally he was inside me. My body moved tight against him, our moans low enough that only we could hear them. I was right on the cusp when Bowen grabbed me and slammed me into the mattress, his strong arms propped either side of my head. He moved deeper in me, my cries muffled by his hungry lips.

My eyes opened to see Bowen's beautiful form positioned above me, but that's not what kept my attention. It was the small wisps of magic that floated off both our bodies. I wasn't surprised by the green of my own, but Bowen's... his was plum—as if the fruit itself deemed him worthy of carrying the pigment.

With a final thrust, he buried his hips deeper into mine and I could feel the rush of energy surge through him, pulling me closer, the movement making me tighten around him. Bowen moaned deeply into my chest, biting at my breasts.

"*Dwy galon, un dyhead, dwy dafod ond un iaith, dwy raff yn cydio'n ddolen, dau enaid ond un taith,*" he whispered, his breath heavy.

"'Two hearts, one wish, two tongues but one language, two ropes that join connected, two souls but one journey.'" I repeated back to him.

XI
Finch

Finch sat with Gwenllian in the living room, the other two having already retired for the night. If he had told his past self he would be a guest in Gwenllian's home, let alone sitting this close to her, he would have balked at the idea. He had set everything up perfectly twenty-one years ago when he had followed Bowen out here, enabling him to perform the one spell he had perfected during the Dark Ages: to steal another person's magic. It wasn't a complicated spell and didn't call for the person to possess much themselves, but it was taboo. Now all he had to do was keep playing his cards close to his chest and make sure everyone else was holding the wrong hand.

"Is there something you want to ask me?" Gwenllian had her laptop propped onto her lap, the sound of the mouse clicking away as she navigated the screen. She picked up her glass of neat Penderyn whisky and took a sip, replacing it afterward. He had seen the label when pouring a glass with ice for himself, the limited edition bottle costing twelve hundred pounds sterling.

There were so many questions floating around inside his

head that he didn't know where to start. Since 1890 he'd thrown himself into finding the Tree, finding answers about himself, but now he stayed quiet, not wanting to risk slipping up.

"Your silence says a lot," she said, her eyes never moving from the screen.

"I have questions, Your Majesty, but I imagine they're a bit prying." He pulled out his best diplomatic voice—confident, smooth. Already he could sense the wheels behind her eyes whirring to figure out his part in all of this.

"Gwenllian," she corrected. "No one cares for titles anymore."

That wasn't true. When he was in the Order, titles meant everything.

"Ah… right." He took a sip from his own glass, the cubes of ice slowly melting into the smooth whisky. It tasted a bit off, but that could have been due in part to it being a one-hundred-and-ten-year-old bottle. He chanced it. "What do you know of the Tree of Life?"

Gwenllian's hands stopped, her gaze now glued to him. With a quick stroke, she closed her laptop and set it next to her. "I know about your past, Finch." She practically spat out the words. "And I know everything you have done to my daughter."

A pang of fear crept into him and he tried to hide it away. This was exactly where he didn't want the conversation to go. He knew her powers was almost gone, but that didn't mean she couldn't call on *Y Ddraig Goch* if the situation came to it.

"Let me tell you a little story." The leer that crept to her face was nothing short of terrifying. "Once upon a time, there was a mother who loved her daughter very much. But one day, a group of men found her and knew exactly who she was and what they thought she could do."

Finch's heart raced. He knew this story... had read the reports of the incident from the Order...

"She told them she had no idea where the Tree of Life was hidden, and that awakening a sleeping dragon was never a good idea." She crossed her legs, bringing her glass to her lips again. "The men had a different idea. They believed that with her magic, and the magic of her child, they'd be able to covet the Tree and control everything that happened in this world."

He tried to act cool but couldn't hide the small bead of sweat that ran down to his chin. A tingling started at the back of his throat and he coughed in an attempt to dislodge it, doing little to relieve the feeling.

"In their blindness, they overlooked the fact they were standing in front of a mother dragon and her baby, and made threats against her and her child... to use her for their own personal gain. That didn't sit too well with the mother." She stood, towering over Finch, his cough now racking throughout his body. "Graciously, with the help of her friend *Y Ddraig Goch*, she kept one alive so he could tell everyone else to never darken that woman's doorstep again. That she was a *fear* to be reckoned with."

His glass fell from his fingers onto the shaggy white carpet, the strength in him nonexistent.

Panic now consumed his mind, no longer able to put up a front. He looked to her own glass, noting that not a drop of ice was placed in it.

"And do you know whose name popped up in all of this...?"

Finch grew paler.

"Yours."

She wrenched him up off the couch by his tie, restricting

his airway even further, and pushed him so hard he collided with an expensive highboy, its body strong enough that Finch didn't put a scratch on it.

Blood ran down his lip where it had split, a lump forming at the back of his head. "You don't understand," he said, choking. "I had no affiliation with the Order when they met with you. I had made mention of you in the past—centuries ago!—before I even knew you would travel to the twenty-first century, and the Order used this information against me."

"But you created it. You started the search for the Tree and planted the idea in their minds," she shot back.

"They were—*are*—way off the reservation. My views no longer align with theirs. That's why I left." It wasn't exactly true. He had been excommunicated, an excuse he knew Gwenllian had no patience to listen to. "On paper, yes, I'm still the First Knight, but outside of the society, I'm nothing but a stranger."

He stayed on the floor, bleeding, dizzy, and out of breath.

She sat back on her heels, slightly out of breath herself, and Finch could see how sick Gwenllian really was. Her lips were cracked, the insides smeared with a layer of blood. She hid it well, but he could feel her hands shake as she brought his face close to hers, the grip on his chin forced with feigned power. "Why should I believe you? Do you know how long I've had to run from those bastards? What giving Jade up did to me?"

"Please…" he said as innocently as possible, "Gwenllian… I didn't know…"

She held on for just a second longer, then finally released him. "I doubt that." Standing, she left him there, the click of her heels deafening as she sauntered away, leaving him to clean himself up.

XII

The next weeks were filled with exhaustive training. I was getting hit on both fronts—Bowen taking the physical and Gwenllian the magical—but it was better this way. I was too busy to think of anything else, and now that Bowen was back with me, I could take my dreams head on. The weather was surprisingly good moving into June, with sun and blue skies. My magic... not so much.

"Flick your wrist!" Gwenllian yelled for the eighth time, as the spell fizzled from my fingertips instead of exploding as she hoped for.

We stood outside the front of the house, Bowen and Finch watching from within.

"You make it sound easy," I countered, already feeling the onset of carpal tunnel settling in.

"You're just not concentrating enough."

She was right. I couldn't concentrate. There were so many things running around in my head—adapting to my new surroundings, meeting her, training, the Order... My focus was clouded.

I felt the slap of Gwenllian's hand across my cheek, its

sting catching me off guard as I stumbled to the ground. "Pay attention!"

Bowen was next to me in an instant, pulling me up from the dirt, my palms raw where I had landed on fallen pine cones and needles.

"Enough," he barked.

"No, I'm fine," I reassured them both. Though her training was Spartan-like, it was needed. I had to adapt again to my new surroundings. Having magic in the twenty-first century was extremely different to the fourteenth, where ingredients and the Tree made calling upon my power easier. "You're right, Gwenllian, I'll try harder."

I centered myself again, meditating as my body connected with the earth beneath my feet. The wind chime clinked slightly in the breeze, helping me to focus on the music to block out everything else. My breath came evenly, the minutes that ticked by as I concentrated feeling like eons, until I could feel the small tendrils of magic slither beneath my skin. Sweat beaded down my neck as I opened my eyes and flicked my wrist to see green sparks dance around like mini fireworks.

"Good, that's step one complete." Gwenllian wore a genuine smile, her white teeth flashing behind blood-red lipstick, the color too bright for me to look at. "Think of it as a flash grenade. Once you're able to control it for longer, the light will brighten, blinding your enemies."

A handy trick I could have used when the Brotherhood stormed Saint David's Cathedral—a moment I tried not to dwell on too much.

My breath caught for a second as Finch came out to the entrance.

"Drinks!" he announced.

I shook the thoughts from my head, for once the forest shadows nowhere in sight.

Bowen took my hand and led me into the kitchen, where an array of drinks were already laid out on the table. I grabbed a glass of orange juice and snuck a bagel as well, smothering it with Philadelphia cheese and strawberry jam. If there was one thing I absolutely missed when in the Dark Ages, it was bagels.

"I'm sorry about that..." Gwenllian sipped at her black coffee, the strong smell of it wafting throughout the kitchen.

"It's okay, really. I know you're just trying to help... Mind you, Master Lewis was a hell of a lot stricter." I winced as his name left my mouth, a bitter taste replacing that of sweet jam.

"How are you faring?" she asked, the boys on the other side of the kitchen getting their own drinks, unsuccessfully trying not to eavesdrop. "I mean... being back. It was hard for me at first, acclimatizing to a new time period, and with everything you've been through..."

"I'm okay," I lied. How could I tell her I woke up every morning in a cold sweat, or that every shadow made my instincts jump or that red reminded me of the broken bodies and deaths I had witnessed, their blood pouring out...

"If you need anything I—" Right then her phone pinged, and when she looked at it, her face fell. Her chair scraped loudly against the tiled flooring as she pushed back from the breakfast bar and sped out of the room.

The three of us looked at each other in concern and raced after her, making it to her office door just in time to hear Gwenllian's booming voice.

"*What do you mean you've found nothing?*"

I wasn't sure I wanted to go down there. For almost a week I had barely heard her raised voice, let alone how it was now.

"If you don't get your shit together, Quinten, then I have no need to abide by our deal!"

We only heard a second's pause before she jumped down his throat again.

"No! I told you that if you didn't deliver then I wouldn't pay. That's how buying and selling works. Now either get me the information I need or find me someone else that can," she finished with.

I cocked my head toward Bowen. She had always been so… calm. There would only be one thing that would make her snap like this: her contact in Scotland hadn't found anything.

"You three get down here!" Gwenllian yelled from inside.

I didn't want to be the one who went first, and luckily Finch took the lead, then Bowen, leaving me the last to enter the dragon's den.

Gwenllian was sitting in her desk chair, the back of it swiveled away from the screens, waiting for us. "Please, sit." She gestured to the couch on the other side of the room, where we all squashed together, her cheeks flushed from the earlier argument.

"Did your contact not have anything?" I asked.

"No." Her jaw jutted out in annoyance.

Finch stood up and stared at the screens in front of him, trying to decipher their meaning. "Is this how you're guarding against the Order's hackers?" he asked, reading the code that was on display.

"Yes. I've been able to keep them out, but they've also been able to keep me out. I can't get anywhere close to their systems. That's what I was having my contact look into, a way to breach their security."

"And what did they say?"

Gwenllian's eyes crinkled in weariness. "*That they didn't find anything,*" she stressed, her temper getting short. Yet another trait we had in common.

Finch switched gears, his eyes glued to another screen. "Have you tried setting up an alert system? By data-mining, you could sift through everything and find only what you need."

That seemed to strike a chord.

"Don't you think I've already tried that?" she reprimanded curtly. With a swift movement, she swung her chair around, her fingers typing rapidly on the keyboard in front of her. "There's been chatter over the web about the Tree of Life. Nothing too prominent, usually folklore and the like…" She opened a screen on the wall of monitors for us to see as Bowen and I stood to get a better look.

"What are we looking at?" I asked, squinting, trying to make sense of the jumbled mess of words and numbers on the monitor.

"It's code," Bowen chimed in.

"Well, I got that," I said a bit too harshly. "What does it mean?"

"It means that there's nothing. *Nada.*" The vexation in her voice wasn't lost on us.

"You need to sequence it properly and get rid of that bit of rubbish," Finch said, pointing to a section in the middle.

"I think I would know computers better than a fossil like

you." Gwenllian said it so smoothly I almost didn't hear her, her fingers moving a mile a minute. "There's one other person I can try... He's the only one I can think that would be willing to help us, but we'll need another friend's help to get in contact with him."

In an instant, her phone rang, and I was ready for a second volley of verbal assault, but instead, it looked like she was about to melt with glee as she took the call.

"Simone! I was just talking about you."

We couldn't hear what was happening on the other side of the line, but as Gwenllian twirled her hair between her fingers, her body seemed to relax more into the chair. They only talked for a minute or so, but it was long enough for her to invite Simone over here.

She hung up. "I'm having a friend over tonight. She'll help us get in contact with her friend up in Scotland. He's a genuine genius when it comes to computers." Gwenllian stood up from her chair and made her way up the stairs and back into the kitchen, her face filled with joy, her earlier anger forgotten.

We tripped over ourselves trying to follow her. Considering she seemed to be such a recluse, she sure did have a lot of contacts, but I guessed that connections were good to have in a crisis.

"What do you mean she'll help us? Who is she?" Bowen asked, his lips turned down in disapproval.

"As I said, she's an old friend." Gwenllian refreshed her coffee and went to cut a croissant.

"That doesn't tell us much, Gwenllian. How do you know her?" he continued.

"That is none of your business. Simone will be here tonight

and you will meet her then. Do not"—she held up her knife threateningly—"for any reason, think she is against us. I trust her with my life."

Finch went over to his brother, trying for once to be the voice of reason. "Bowen, I think at this point the more help we can get the better. I trust Gwenllian, and if she trusts Simone, then I trust her too."

"I second that motion," I said, raising my hand as if we were in court.

Bowen didn't look happy. I could only imagine the many scenarios that were playing in his head at the new, unknown equation, but he put his worries on hold long enough to agree. "Alright. I guess there's not much we can do then. And *you*," he said, pointing to Gwenllian, her mouth stuffed with a bite of pastry, "put that away. I'm going to start dinner soon."

I had begun to notice how much I seemed to have in common with Gwenllian; like her, I was still starving.

XIII
Gwenllian

Gwenllian went and sat in the living room, leaving Jade and the others in the kitchen to get dinner ready. Going to the stack of music on her shelf, she picked a record that reminded her of her late husband, its smooth jazz soon letting her drift for a couple of minutes. She hadn't even realized she'd fallen asleep when she noticed a weight on her lap.

Jumping to her feet, she heard the soft *thump* of padded paws hitting the ground. She attempted to cough, blood and mucus spewing onto the tissue she quickly grabbed for, her face flushed and sweaty. Once finally calm, she was able to speak. "Simone... Do you really need to do that every time?"

Were this years earlier, Gwenllian would have heard the laughter of the cat hissing, but now that she was getting sicker, Simone's face showed only concern.

The cat jumped back onto her lap and purred, Gwenllian running her fingers through her black fur, noting the hints of brown in it. What always drew her to Simone was her eyes, their deep hazel flecked with strands of blue, a telltale sign of a Shifter.

In the moment it took Gwenllian to blink, the short hair of the cat turned into shoulder-length human hair, her light brown skin perfectly smooth against the cream cardigan that was two sizes too large for her.

"Gwen, are you okay?" she said in her thick South London accent as she hugged Gwenllian to her. Simone was one of the few outsiders who knew everything about her—where she had come from, what she was—it was why she always came in cat form, to throw people off her trail. *Transformation* was a dead practice, Simone being the only one who could still use the spell. "It's getting worse, isn't it?" She came and cuddled closer to her, their hands entwined together.

"I passed out about a week ago after getting into it with Finch. The others don't know that…" She paused, not wanting to say the words herself.

"You're dying?" Simone finished for her.

Gwenllian nodded. "I've only just got Jade back in my life. I don't want to add to her worries. I still don't know what's going through her mind. Does she like me? Should I be hovering over her more, or giving her more space? I don't want to seem like I'm one of them," she said, pointing to the kitchen, "but I can't help it. We've been apart for so long…"

"And the boys are getting in the way of your quality mother–daughter time?" Her upward inflection hinted at the answer.

"There is that." Gwenllian nudged her shoulder. Simone always seemed to have the knack of knowing everything that was going on in her mind, even when she didn't.

"Then send them away. They can give you at least another day together."

"A day would never be enough." Gwenllian could hear laughter and there was a mouth-watering aroma coming from the kitchen, her stomach growling in response.

"It's a start though."

They sat listening to the jazz record, its needle finally coming to the end of the disk.

"Dinner!" Bowen shouted from the dining room.

Simone slapped her thigh and hopped off the couch. "That's our cue."

Gwenllian got up slowly and put on a brave face. She hid the stained tissue in her pocket, making sure no evidence of her sickness was left for someone to see. Joining the others at the table, she saw that Bowen had outdone himself. There was a huge spread set out: roasted chickpea burgers, potatoes, vegetables, Yorkshire puddings, onion gravy… It all looked delicious.

"Are you Simone?" Jade walked in carrying a handful of wine glasses and set them down while Finch started to pour their drinks. "I didn't hear you come in. Where's the cat?"

Simone stared at her with the most quizzical of looks and answered like she should have already guessed. "I *am* the cat."

"You're joking!" Finch exclaimed in amazement, the wine sloshing. "You're actually able to perform the *Transformation* spell?"

"Yes," she replied, a jauntiness in her step as she sat down in the chair next to the head of the table. "Everybody, sit before the food gets cold." Simone left it at that, keeping the details about her body hidden, though Finch looked like he wanted to prod further.

Jade sat across from Simone, Bowen to her left and Finch

taking the seat next to him. As always, Gwenllian presided over the meal at the head and, flicking her serviette out, placed it on her lap.

"Well, Bowen, this looks absolutely amazing." It wasn't until Gwenllian scooped a ladle of peas onto her plate that everyone else dug in. After that, the atmosphere seemed more relaxed. Simone filled the meal time with stories about her life, her work as a sales representative for a cosmetics company and how many of the high-powered men and women that came into her work loved to gossip about the market.

"So, Jade"—Simone speared a carrot with her fork—"how were the Dark Ages?"

Gwenllian's face went pale at her question, everyone around the room silent awaiting Jade's answer. Simone hadn't heard the screams Jade believed no one but Bowen could hear when they woke in the mornings, or how her mind would drift, Jade's every action needing more energy than she was able to give. Being reminded of the past was hurting her more than she would ever admit.

"It was… good. Eye-opening. Obviously, the history books got it wrong." She took a gulp of her wine, seemingly content to talk about the topic, but Gwenllian could see a vein in her neck pulsing.

"Well, who can really trust history books? They're only one of many perspectives an author can take," Simone added, feeling the strain of tension at the table, trying to smooth over her blunder.

"I suppose that's true." Jade looked to Bowen and Finch, an unvoiced conversation passing between the three.

"So," Bowen said to Simone, "how did you meet Gwenllian?"

"Bowen," Jade snapped back at him, warning him against prying too much.

"What? I'm curious." It was an innocent enough question, but it seemed Jade had already caught on to their relationship.

"Do you really want to know?" Simone leaned in closer to him. "I met her in a pub..."—she stood and came to her side—"and did this." She grabbed Gwenllian's face, planting a huge, wet kiss onto her lips.

Simone cackled at the looks on the boys' faces, Gwenllian pushing her away and wiping at her mouth in an attempt to remove Simone's lipstick. Though she loved a good joke, this wasn't one of them. They had what few could achieve in life.

"Prudes," Simone mumbled, as she took her seat again. She gave Jade a wink, and she smiled back, a womanly bond forming between them.

Gwenllian composed herself and started up a different conversation. "Simone, why did you call me earlier? You wouldn't have known we needed to get in contact..." She got up to fill her glass, taking a minute at the cabinet to steady herself from the dizziness that had overtaken her. They had already finished two bottles of wine, and fishing through the cabinet nearby she found an eight-year-old Sauvignon Blanc. "You said we needed to talk in person."

Simone set down her glass, her full attention on Jade, the mood turning somber. "They know you've returned."

Bowen's hands stayed flat against the table, but even from where she stood, Gwenllian could see as he tried to reign in the rage beneath, while Jade looked shell-shocked.

"The Order?" Jade asked in a panic. "I've only been back for less than a month. I haven't talked to anyone."

Gwenllian could guess who had leaked this information, her eyes squinting at the culprit, but Finch maintained a look of innocence.

Simone looked to Gwenllian, waiting for her to sit with her refilled glass and continue. "They're still hell-bent on the Tree of Life."

Gwenllian stayed quiet. This wasn't news to her. It wasn't news to anyone—except Jade.

"What! Why are they looking for the Tree?" She glanced at Bowen, her voice flat. "Did you know?"

For once he was lost for words, his hand running through his beard, but his brother answered instead.

"Yes, that's what we were trying to tell you before you got taken away by *Y Ddraig Goch*."

Power radiated from Jade as she stood, her food forgotten, and paced the dining room, her hands shaking either in fury or in terror, Gwenllian had no idea. If she looked hard enough, she could see the faint pulse of her magic eager to break from her skin, the light translucent against the dark mahogany cabinet.

"Why are they after the Tree?"

It was such a simple question, but the answer was anything but…

"We don't know. It could be any number of reasons"— Gwenllian made a point not to look at Finch, knowing full well he wouldn't talk—"but it's not the reason *why*, but *when*."

If Finch had been looking for the Tree, that meant it had been centuries since they'd first started, and thank God they hadn't found it yet.

"I've found some documents that could have some answers,

but they're up in Scotland," Finch said, a little too easily. "I have some work to do up there. I wouldn't mind checking them out while I'm there. Malcolm has been looking for leads since he started working for me," he continued.

"Your PA?" Bowen asked.

Finch nodded. "He said there may be some pages that make reference to the Tree. It could be nothing…"

"Or it could be everything," Jade countered.

Gwenllian trusted the man even less than she trusted the Order. She wasn't going to let him out of her sight. If he was going to Scotland, then so was she. "What a coincidence, the contact I told you about lives in Scotland. Simone, you're still friends with Ian and Iz, right?"

"Of course! Iz and I meet up every now and again when she needs to get out of the high country. Do you think Ian knows something?"

"We can only ask."

Forgetting the rest of the meal, Gwenllian and Simone went down into the basement, the rest clomping down the stairs after them. Gwenllian took up her position in front of her monitors, and reaching over her, Simone brought up a secured chat screen, a ringing tone resounding throughout the room.

Ian was another name we hadn't heard before, but when a man popped onto the screen in front of us, I cried out in surprise. He was the spitting image of Tristan, but older. His golden hair and blue eyes were as soft as I remembered them, but they were now crowded with crow's-feet, his temple creased with age. Instead of his long hair, the man in front of us had his cut short and prominently spiked at the front. When I glanced to Bowen for support, his face mirrored my own, eyes hardening at the memory and loss of his best friend.

All of that was pushed aside when we heard his voice.

"Simone, you alright?" His Scottish accent sounded odd coming out of that mouth. I had been expecting an English one, just as the original Tristan had spoken with. "You're only supposed to use this line in case of an emergency. Oh, Gwen, it's nice to finally meet you. Simone talks about you nonstop!"

"Enough with the pleasantries, this *is* an emergency," Gwenllian growled. "The Order is looking for the Tree of Life and we believe there are documents that could help to find it up your way."

The screen jerked as Ian wrestled with his phone, a slur of curses in the background. "Goddammit, Simone! I told you! I warned you something was happening!"

"You can blame me later," she said, her eyes sharp against a nasty retort she was holding back. "It seems the world is falling faster and faster into chaos and the Order is keen to get to the Tree first."

"And we have to get there before them," Finch interrupted. "Hello, Ian."

It seemed Simone's contact and Finch already knew each other, Ian giving him a look of loathing.

"So you've teamed up with this bastard?" Ian asked.

"The lesser of two evils," Gwenllian countered.

Ian grunted.

"So do you have any leads?" she asked.

"Jesus, woman, you've only just told me about it. Can you give me some time to find things out?"

"Time isn't on our side. Have you seen the news? Wildfires, earthquakes, floods… It's practically the apocalypse," Simone retorted. "We need your tech skills to help us find the Tree."

Ian shook his head. "A week at least. Then I'll have something," he replied.

"That's too long," Gwenllian snapped. There was a long pause as she thought what to do.

"We'll *all* go to Scotland then," Finch said, cutting into her train of thought. "A plane trip would be faster than just waiting here for news."

Gwenllian considered this, her mind ticking away, but it seemed it was an acceptable compromise. "Bowen, get everyone's things together."

"What do you want me to do?" I asked.

Ian positioned his phone to see me better. "Who are you?" he asked, side-tracked, his face suddenly a mask of shock as he put two and two together. "But… your…"

"My daughter," Gwenllian finished. "Yes, now, can we stay at your place?"

How does he know about me?

"Yes, of course, we have more than enough room," he answered.

"Get Iz down there as well," Simone chimed in. "We'll need all hands on deck, just in case."

It was another name I didn't recognize, but my question still stood.

"Is there anything you want me to do?" I repeated. I didn't

want to just sit on my hands. If the Order was after the Tree, we needed to find out why... and fast.

Gwenllian turned to me. "You? Nothing. Simone will take care of arranging our plane. Sadly, Myrddin will not be allowed outside the Welsh borders, otherwise we would be taking him as well."

I could feel my annoyance rise by the second, my hands tingling. Everyone in the room seemed to notice, and Bowen took my hand before I could say something I would later regret. I wasn't here to be used for my magic, or a burden on my friends and family. I could help... I *wanted* to help. But still, everyone else went to work.

I gazed at Gwenllian, and I imagined her in her medieval gown, a golden crown on her head... This was how she would have ruled if she'd had the chance, her decisions made with ease and carried out swiftly by those around her, no doubt in their minds.

Simone jumped onto Gwenllian's laptop and was booking us a private flight from Cardiff International into Edinburgh, as Bowen led me upstairs to our room, throwing our clothes into the bags he had brought with him.

I sat on the bed, looking at the deep creases in my hands. *What have I done with these hands...?* "Is this all my fault?"

Bowen stopped packing and came and sat beside me, cradling my hands into his own. "No, *cariad*, Fate is at play here and no one can escape her."

I wanted to cry. Why was everything so hard? So complicated? It felt like the world was working against me at every step. Bowen took me into his arms, his body supporting me.

"You smell like mulled spice and wood-fire," I said absentmindedly, inhaling his scent deeply, his blue cashmere sweater soft against my skin.

"Does it bother you?" he asked, moving away a bit.

I pulled him back closer. "No, I love it."

We sat there until Simone knocked on our door. "We need to leave now," she said from the other side.

"We'll be down in a minute," Bowen called, his voice vibrating against me.

"I don't want to go." My arms linked in a vice-like grip around him.

"You're going to have to face reality at some point," he chided, his hands rubbing meditative circles on my back.

"Is this our reality? Magic? Secret orders?"

He brushed his hand over my hair, kissing the top of my head, my cheeks, and finally my lips. "It is for now."

Gorau adnabod, d'adnabod dy hun.

The best knowledge is to know yourself.

XIV

The flight into Edinburgh was thankfully short and not as bumpy as my first flight into the UK, the process of getting through security even easier with Bowen and Finch's private memberships (because of course they would have them).

Ian was already waiting for us at the arrivals gate and I had to check myself to make sure I didn't run and fling my arms around him. Tristan would have had the same rough lines on his face were I able to have seen him grow this old. To his left was a woman who stood almost as tall, his mirror image, though compared to his blonde hair, hers was more a strawberry blonde.

"Ian!" Gwenllian hugged him close to her.

"Gwen. It's good to finally see you in the flesh… I thought you'd never leave that cabin of yours." His smile made my heart ache a little more. "And this must be your daughter."

"Jade," I said, my hand held out for him to take, and when he did I could feel the strong grip. I looked at the woman next to him and held out my hand. "And you are?"

"Hi, I'm Isolde, Ian's sister, but you can call me Iz." It made sense now who Simone and Gwenllian had been talking about last night and why she and Ian looked so alike. I shook her hand lightly, glad that she was friend not foe. If I hadn't been so tired I would have laughed and cracked a joke about how I'd had a friend named Tristan, and how they were almost a perfect match.

"Shall we get going?" Ian grabbed Gwenllian's suitcase and we followed him to his van, all of us fitting in.

"Is there any news?" Gwenllian asked, strapping in.

"Let's get back to the manor before any of that. You all look like the walking dead."

He was right. We had rushed so much in packing our things and getting here that none of us had even thought about sleep, all too on edge.

It was only a thirty minute drive into the heart of Edinburgh, yet I couldn't stay awake. Bowen was in the same predicament, his head propped onto the front of his chest, lightly snoozing away.

"Jade!"

I turned around and found myself enclosed by stone walls, the overpowering smell of incense burning in the air. I would never be able to forget that smell, not in my lifetime. I was back in Lampeter's hill fort, Bowen lying bloody on the ground in Tristan's arms.

"Tristan!" I went to hug him, only to find that my body passed right through his. He was lifting Bowen to his feet, shouting frantically for me. He still wore his captain's uniform, the white and red fabric torn in places, while his face looked as if he'd been fighting with a cat.

"Tristan, please, stop screaming," Bowen muttered, his strength gone. "She's right here."

"No, she's not! She disappeared right after she... brought you back."

There was such panic in his voice. I wanted to calm him, tell him it was going to be alright, but every time I tried, my voice wouldn't work, my words stuck in my throat.

"You do not think she sacrificed herself for me...?" Bowen looked up, as if the idea was too much for him to handle, that he rather he'd died.

It pained me to my very core.

Tristan looked no better. "Come..." He guided him into the hallway. "We must see to Master Lewis. He will be waiting for news."

I woke with a start from the dream, causing Bowen to do the same, my hand gripped tightly around his. He could see the fear in my eyes, the pain and loss I had taken for granted. For that brief moment, I had seen exactly what my absence had done to both of them.

"What's wrong?" he whispered, trying not to wake Finch, who rested next to him.

"I'll tell you later." I nestled deeper into him and tried to use his smell to drive away the lingering scent of incense.

Staring out the window, I watched as the the summer-chilled night flew past us. It was the first time I had ever been to Edinburgh, and the old streets that we passed were lined with closed shops and open pubs.

I wasn't sure what to expect when we pulled up the driveway to Ian's home, but it hadn't been the giant Elizabethan-style manor that greeted us. Its square foundation spanned two-stories, while corner towers with angled turrets spanned higher at four, dominating everything around it. Its smooth sandstone exterior was lit up with floodlights, allowing everyone who passed it to see the intricate detailings around the windows and entrance with a small clocktower indicating it was well past midnight. Its gray slate roof was almost invisible in the night, except for the cast-iron tops of each tower that glowed green against the lights, flags flapping in the chilled air. Had it been daytime, I imagined women in beautiful gowns taking a turn around the grounds that surrounded it, or military nurses rushing about, its size alone making for a good retreat center.

We all piled out of the van, the location seeming welcoming and protective. With our bags in hand, I stood there gawking until Iz came over to guide me inside.

"You live here?" I asked in amazement.

"Ian does, me and my husband and children live just outside of Edinburgh, but we come here every weekend to keep Ian company." She walked through the entry door with the others, letting me fall behind and marvel at the interior of the building.

In comparison to its size, it felt very homelike. The black and white checker-tiled floors looked like they hadn't been updated for decades, while the intricate crown moldings and baseboards felt even more ancient. As we moved through the foyer, the inside seemed crowded with heavy Victorian furniture and it felt more like entering a museum rather than someone's home. Just as in Bowen's house, large portraits were hung like monuments to their patrons, the colors brightening the dark walls.

Ian directed us to an elevator, our rooms in the west wing of the top floor. "Everyone get a good night's rest because tomorrow the work begins. We're going to have to find the Tree of Life before those bastards and we'll need all the help we can get." He eyed Finch while saying it, the ever-present elephant in the room.

The elevator was just big enough to squeeze us all in, Ian's voice loud in the confined space. "The east and north wings are for the School for the Deaf and the rest are private flats. We have the whole west corner to ourselves."

When the doors opened we practically fell out, Ian not skipping a beat in directing everyone to their assigned rooms.

"I'll try and wake you last, Jade," Gwenllian said, straggling behind the others as Bowen took our bags into our new quarters.

"That's fine… Have a good night, Gwenllian." I closed the door behind us. All I wanted to do was sleep, but Bowen had other ideas.

"Do you want to talk about what happened in the car?" He put our suitcases in the corner of the room, leaving them until tomorrow to be unpacked, while I sat down on the bed to consider where to begin.

"I was back in Lampeter's fort. You and Tristan were there… It was right after I saved you…"

He came and sat next to me.

"You were both frantically looking for me because…"

"Because you had vanished." The pain in his voice matched that in the dream.

"I didn't mean to leave you like that," I quickly blurted out.

"No, I imagined not, but all the same, it happened."

The room quieted as we both sat there reliving the past. It was only as the lighting of the room flickered that my senses came back to me and I finally had a look around. It was nice, not as ostentatious as some manor house rooms could be. Its dark red walls were offset by gold drapes and bedding. We had our own bath, the lion-clawed tub deep enough to fit us both in if we really tried. A small bookcase stood in one corner of the room, old Agatha Christie titles and the like lining the shelves.

Lying on the bed, I felt the cool satin of the sheets, the pillows fluffed to perfection.

Bowen got up and turned off the lights. "Sleep," he said, climbing in next to me.

I got under the covers and snuggled closer to him, his arms wrapped around me, and I could feel his chest rising and falling against my back.

For once, my night hadn't been hijacked by my horrors, and when Gwenllian knocked on our door we were already awake, lounging in bed, our arms and legs intertwined with each other. With my head resting on Bowen's chest, I played with the short strands of hair there, his hands softly stroking the side of my stomach. It wasn't until Finch unceremoniously banged on our door that we made a move.

After taking a quick shower together, we threw on some clothes (a hard chore when Bowen wouldn't stop stealing them from me), which took us another twenty minutes, before we finally made it to the dining room, where a cold breakfast was waiting for us. There were some annoyed glances at our late arrival, but Simone and Gwenllian beamed at us as if they too had had a slow morning.

The dining room matched the rest of this area of the house with its grand gold-framed paintings and ceramic floral vases sitting around the perimeter of the room. The dark mahogany table and chairs took up the rest of the space.

I went and sat down next to Simone, who gave me a little nudge and a wink.

"Seemed like you two weren't ever going to join us," she whispered, wincing as a leg kicked her under the table, Gwenllian's face flushed with embarrassment. I giggled and grabbed a piece of buttered toast and some sausages.

Ian started talking to get everyone's attention at the head of the table. "It's good of you two to join us. As I was just telling the others, the first thing we need to do is figure out what the Order knows."

"The documents I mentioned before might be of some help. They're up at the castle," Finch said, taking a sip of his black coffee, something stronger undoubtedly added to it. We all knew which castle he was talking about. Edinburgh Castle was one of the most famous in the UK. "I can get them while I'm at the office today."

"That would be very helpful," Bowen replied, content for once to let his brother take the lead.

"And why is that helpful?" I asked, a bite of toast between my teeth.

"Because I have an office *in* Edinburgh Castle," Finch said, smiling.

That sounded outrageously fancy. *How was he able to swing that?* "What is it you actually do?" With everything going on, it hadn't even crossed my mind that the people sitting around this table would have day jobs.

"I work for the Welsh government as a diplomat and we have an office there."

"Doing what?"

"This and that. Meetings mainly." He shrugged.

It was jarring to know he sat in such a position of power. "And the documents you're talking about…"

"My PA found some papers that might indicate where the Tree could be and why the Order wants it so badly."

"I'll come with you," Gwenllian offered, her smile borderline sardonic, as if she was making sure one of us was always with him, to watch him.

"No need. I'll be stuck in meetings for a lot of the day. You'd be bored senseless."

"I'll bring a book," she countered.

Iz put her hand up as if she were in school, trying to gain their attention. "I think it's best if I go along. I… I am a skilled linguist, and we won't know what language the documents might be written in. They may even predate your knowledge, Finch."

He looked as if he doubted that, but nodded in agreement. I hadn't even thought that we wouldn't be able to read the documents. With Master Lewis's language spell still affecting me, my mind could decipher spoken languages easily, it was the written word that still stumped me, but if she could dictate everything to me, it would make her job much easier. "Then I'll go too."

"No." It was a resolute word that escaped the lips of everyone in the room, Gwenllian offering up a more detailed reply.

"The Order is after you. You can't go around willy-nilly."

"It would be faster than spending hours trying to figure out what's in the documents," I countered. It wasn't that I didn't have faith in Iz's abilities, it was just that, in this case, magic beat brains.

"It will be hard to get them out of the castle. The director specified they weren't to leave the grounds." Finch took another sip of his coffee, seemingly unconcerned with whatever we decided.

"I'm going." If there was a chance in finding the Tree of Life and ending this shit-show once and for all, which was putting my life in danger—again—it would be worth it.

"You're not," Bowen growled.

"And the rest of us?" Ian cut in, looking annoyed. "You're telling us just to sit by and do nothing?"

Bowen speared a piece of tomato with his fork. "For the time being, yes."

"Well, that's bullshit," Ian chimed in. "This is my home and I will not be frightened onto the sidelines." The creases between his eyes had grown deeper. Being told by a man who looked thirty years his junior what to do didn't seem to sit well with him.

"I never said you couldn't leave… Just that Jade can't."

I whipped around to him, venom coating my words. "Seriously? You're going to treat me like a prisoner?"

Bowen's body tensed as he could feel the shift in my energy. Everyone else seemed to as well, as the temperature in the room seemed much warmer now than it had been seconds ago.

"Jade," Gwenllian said in a cautious tone, "your magic is seeping. Keep it in check."

It was a curt reprimand and it managed to quell my magic in an instant, but not my temper.

"Not a prisoner," Bowen corrected me. "But we need to lie low and you have your training to work on."

It was a poor excuse that I wasn't buying at all.

"Then it's settled." Finch pushed back from the table, his plate clean and his mug empty. "Iz, I'll let you know a good day to come and check out the documents. I still have my day job and the meetings won't stop, even for humanity's sake." He nodded toward us and quickly took his leave.

I grabbed that opportunity to take my own dishes, still laden with sausages and half-eaten toast, to the kitchen, any excuse get out of the room. Ian followed behind, his face now calmer than a second ago.

"He means well," he said, the words sounding forced. I turned on the faucet, the only sound in the room the water hitting my dirty plate.

"You know, you look exactly like my old friend."

Ian leaned against the counter next to me. "You mean my great, great, and so on, great-grandfather Tristan?"

I did a double take. I knew that they looked exactly alike, but I thought it was more a case of him being a doppelgänger rather than ancestry-related. My hands rested in soapy water, the basin almost full with it when Ian turned off the faucet. On instinct I moved closer to him, his broad shoulders towering over me. I finally gave in and went in for a hug.

"I miss him so much."

"I can't imagine." Ian crossed his arms and rested them around my shoulders briefly before letting me go.

"Do you know what happened to him?" I hadn't asked

Bowen; I didn't want to dredge up whatever memory he had of Tristan dying, but the thought now got the better of me.

"He lived a peaceful life. Married his wife, Elian, and they had five sons. From there you can see how we've branched out. Elian was homesick so they moved back up to Scotland."

"Wait, Elian? As in red-haired, freckled face, *my lady's maid*, Elian?" I couldn't believe Tristan and Elian had married! I was sure he was going to end up with Anwen, the Gruffydd's youngest daughter and my somewhat step-sister. Elian was so young, and Tristan... Tristan was a captain of the Royal Guard!

"I think that's the one. It was only decades later that they grew old together and died."

My heart ached for him—not out of sadness, but pure joy that he was able to live a full and happy life. I longed for that, for going quietly with the person I loved and married. Now I didn't know if the world would be around long enough for me to see my twenty-second birthday.

Bowen walked into the kitchen looking apologetic, but I wasn't concerned with what had happened in the dining room. If it really came down to it, he wasn't going to stop me from leaving the house. Instead, I was now enraged at the fact that he hadn't told me that those two had ended up together.

"How come you never told me Tristan and Elian got married?" I hit his arm, bringing my anger front and center.

He glanced away, guilt in his face. "Because I didn't know how you'd react. She was your lady's maid."

"They were *both* my friends and I'm happy for them." Frustrated tears sprang to my eyes. I wanted them back. I wanted *everyone* back: Master Lewis, Tristan, Haf, Elian,

Anwen. The room shook with my longing, the plates and glassware clinking together in their cupboards.

"Jade…" Bowen's voice cautioned my emotions, but I couldn't help it. Everything was moving too fast. I didn't want to be in a world where my friends were dead, an all too real future that still loomed over me if the Order succeeded in whatever they had planned.

My feelings poured out of me, red and green tendrils of pure emotion slithering all about my body. I tried to suck in a breath only to feel my throat clamp shut. I couldn't breathe, stars dancing around my vision as I tried to steady myself. Bowen stood in front of me, his hands on my shoulders trying to get me to calm down, but I couldn't. Sounds receded and it felt as if a knife had been plunged into the middle of my back. I broke away from him. I needed to go somewhere, *anywhere*, that wasn't near them.

Before anyone else could follow, I ran out of the kitchen, letting my feet lead me deeper into the house.

XV
Finch

Finch quietly made his escape and found Ian's other car keys by the elevator door, hung up on a hook with a flashy Fiat symbol dangling on the chain. The weather had been good to them this morning, letting the sun shine through the fluffy white clouds that spotted a serene blue sky. Once outside, he put on his sunglasses.

He had taken the elevator ride down to roll himself a cigarette, the smooth tobacco tight within the confines of its paper. Taking a small match he lit it against the side of the house and held it up to the cigarette between his lips. He liked the routine of rolling, each step bringing him closer to the perfect cigarette.

He sucked in the much-needed nicotine, the chemical running through to his brain and then the rest of his body, each muscle slowly relaxing with each intake.

Walking down to the car, he hit the *unlock* button, got in, and fiddled with the seat and mirrors until they were to his liking. His cigarette hung out the window as he pulled down and out of the driveway. If the manor had been what it was sixty years ago there would have been a security guard at the small gatehouse, patrolling who came in and out, but that had died out when the O'Conner's had let the city council take charge of the place, leaving Ian a too-big-of-a-house to manage.

Following the side roads, Finch made his way to the Royal Mile, and finding a big enough parking space, he paralleled into it. The street was the same as always, stores and restaurants lining all the way up to where you could see Edinburgh Castle at its peak.

As he got out of the car, a group of pedestrians stared at him, his tailored navy suit and sunglasses making him look more important than Jade would ever think possible. But he liked the attention, beautiful women ogling him up and down. He started his ascent to the castle, the stone streets flooded with tourists and shoppers looking for a perfect souvenir.

At the castle gates it was more crowded today than he had ever seen, masses of school field trips commencing that day. For him, getting in was easy enough, just a flash of his badge and they let him through, the waiting tourists looking impressed at his all-access pass.

With an air of importance, he zigzagged his way up the path, people taking pictures of the view and toward St Mary's Cathedral. Finch thought of those poor bastards pushing and shoving their way through the Royal Palace, the Scottish Crown Jewels on display for sucker tourists who didn't know the originals were locked up in his private vault, safe from the grubby, smudged hands of little children pressing them against the glass to get a better look.

He headed for the Governor's House, which sat right at the top of the Southern Outlook, the smell of fresh coffee and biscuits wafting from the little cafe just next to it. He could have parked underneath the castle and taken the stairs straight into the house, but where was the fun in that? He wanted to see all these people, people who had no idea just what was really happening to the world, who lived in guarded peace protected by him and Jade.

Finch opened the door to find Malcolm already there, a stack of papers ready in his hands.

His short ginger hair was parted at the side, his face clean-shaven. The three-piece suit he wore was a poor attempt at mimicking his own, a topic Finch complained about ad nauseam. "Here are last week's reports. There have been multiple terror threats within our borders since last month—not that they have gone public—and we have to decide what we want to do now that the UK will no longer remain within the EU. It doesn't look good."

"Does it ever?" Finch took the manila envelopes and, as they walked into his office, sifted through them to get a better idea about what was happening.

Malcolm went to the small bar behind Finch's desk where a new bottle of Glenfiddich sat, already a quarter of the way drained. He poured a glass for his boss and forewent the alcohol for himself, replacing it with a cup of tea.

"This is just a shit-show"—Finch took his glass graciously—"if the Tories win this time I will personally go up and slap the prime minister. All our resources will be cut, and I'm not just talking about the country—my connections will dry up too."

Malcolm gazed at his cup, swishing its contents. He took his place in front of Finch's desk, its dark oak and studded green leather top something straight out of the gentleman's club that used to dwell on the corner of the Royal Mile and had been replaced by the Bank of Scotland. "Are you going to tell them now what you'll really do with the Tree of Life?"

Finch stopped mid-drink and placed his whisky back onto the desk. "Not yet. I need to bide my time. The Order still thinks it's playing a game of cards, trying to collect better assets to strengthen its hand, when actually we're playing chess, strategically finding a way for our queen to gain all her power." It was at times like these that Finch could feel his age. The past was thought of as simplistic, but it was anything but that, more like cut-throat and messy. "We need her to train harder. I can only do so much with what little magic I've collected from Gwenllian, and making Jade's nightmares more vivid isn't going to suffice for much longer. She has a connection with the Tree that Gwenllian can't call on anymore. I believe she's the only one who can find it."

Malcolm still didn't know the whole picture of what was happening. Finch had made sure of it. In any situation, a contingency was always needed, and as much as he depended on his PA, he knew he would never go along with what he really wanted to do with the Tree. In a sense, Malcolm was the person he was closest to; first as a patron to a poor boy, then as a father figure, and now a boss.

Malcolm was just about to argue the point when a hard knock rapped at the door. Finch looked up as a man came in, not waiting to be invited.

"Finch," the man growled, his stride powerful as he strode into the room.

"Aaron," Finch acknowledged with an artificial smile, "I'm surprised the Secretary of the Order would take time out of his *very* busy schedule to come and interrupt my day. What brings you here?"

The man that stood in front of him had a scowl, the feature only interrupted by the deep scratch above his chin *Y Ddraig Goch* had left as a parting gift years ago. He was much older than Finch appeared to be, a shock of white hair trimmed to perfection and wearing a pristine black blazer and trousers. If Finch didn't know any better, he would have guessed Aaron was a descendant of the Black Prince himself. Behind his spectacles, his gray eyes resembled those of the dead prince, but it was the way he carried himself, the arrogance of his stature exuding confidence with his every move.

"You know *exactly* why I'm here. You have her, don't you?"

Finch couldn't look past the anger of the Order member, the insult that they expected him to tell them his every move slapping him in the face. He stood, his hands placed firmly in his pockets to keep him from backhanding the man in front of him. "As you and many others constantly remind me, I am no longer a member of the Order, and therefore I don't need to answer to you."

He could see he had him there, as Aaron seemed about to say something but then didn't, but it seemed he was taking another approach. "How long have we been looking for the Tree of Life? How much longer must we wait to find it? You can see what the world is coming to... Let us have her. Let her find the Tree for us."

Every word he uttered with venom. Finch knew that behind every question was a complicated agenda that no longer coincided with his own, but he wasn't going to let the last twenty-one years count for nothing. He would play along with the Order for as long as needed, just until Jade found the Tree of Life for him.

"What do you want us to do?" Finch asked in a huff, his tone relaxed compared to Aaron's.

"Get her to London. Force her into the archives so she can find something, *anything*, to point us toward the Tree. I have no idea why you thought it worthy of visiting our northern territories, but there is nothing here that will help you."

That was wrong. Aaron didn't know the lengths it had taken Finch to get everyone there, away from the Order. He wanted them all in Scotland so they could bide their time and finish what he had in store for Jade. If past research was correct, then one of the Tree's roots was still active in Edinburgh. He needed Jade to reconnect with the Tree. If they were to leave for London too soon, not only would everyone fervently disagree, he would lose the little trust he had gained from the group.

Finch glanced at Malcolm, his PA's brows pinched with worry. He shook his head slightly, enough for Aaron not to notice but to let Malcolm know not to do anything. "It may take us some time to get there—"

"One month," Aaron demanded. "Get her there in one month or we'll come after her."

Finch knew it wasn't an empty threat. The Order had as much control over the royal guards and security as the Queen herself. He could feel as his jaw tightened against a colorful reply, only trusting to answer with a nod.

"Good. Then I'll see you in London in a month. Oh, and make sure that brother of yours is out of the picture when we meet. We don't need a scene when we take Jade." Aaron left without further ado, neither Finch nor Malcolm making a move until he was out of the room.

"What are we going to do?" Malcolm's voice was frantic as he collected their now empty cups. "Wouldn't it be easier to just explain the situation to them? We need to get Bowen and Jade involved."

"Do you think they would believe me?" Finch knew Jade's trust in him only stretched as far as his pinky. "No," he said, huffing, "the only thing we can do is break her further." He sat back at his desk and pulled out his tobacco pouch. Instead of rolling a cigarette, he pulled out the small knife he always kept in there and went to work carving a spell into the desk.

"What are you doing?"

"The *Ysbryd* spell," he answered, deep in concentration, leaving Malcolm lost. Once the carving was complete, Finch ran the point of the knife across his hand, producing blood to smear onto it. "We need to push Jade further than before, and only one person will shake her into action."

XVI

My legs could barely support me as I found one of the many rooms to hide in, its furniture draped in dust sheets, and locked the door behind me. I heard no pursuit from Bowen or anyone else, a small reprieve from their constant prying, and slid to the floor in a corner of the room between two windows.

My mind buzzed as I tried to figure everything out, the noise growing as the secrets and lies of everyone's past piled up into the present. I wanted to know how they lived—if they were happy in their lifetime—but I knew that in gaining that knowledge I would also learn the hardships they went through and how they died. I just wasn't ready for that.

Placing my head between my knees, I breathed deeply, the atmosphere seeming thicker in the large room. The hot sun that beat in through the windows did little to alleviate my sticky movements.

Can I really take on the Order? Would it be better to help them? Am I the cause of all this?

Pain shot through my chest, and I screamed at the top of my lungs, the floor-length mirror on the other side of the room shattering into pieces, along with all the glass in the picture frames. My mind went completely blank, my arms and legs heavy. Minutes passed as I leaned against the wall, letting its musky smell and coolness rest on me.

What am I supposed to do?

My unfocused eyes drifted lazily—seeing nothing, hearing nothing—until a glint from the broken glass of the mirror caught my attention in the center of the room. I felt my heart pounding in my chest, my blood running cold as a figure stepped out into the sunlight.

Standing in front of me was the Black Prince.

He was wearing his regal clothes, the black fabric moving like smoke around him while his icy eyes held mine in his gaze. A second later he was facing me only a foot away, the overpowering scent of incense following him like bad cologne. He lifted his right hand and I flinched. I hadn't meant to, but all the same he saw it… and he liked it.

Gently, he ran the tips of his fingers across my face, feeling the ridges of my cheekbones and the softness of my lips. It felt like one of my nightmares had come to life, my body going numb and my breathing accelerating to the point of hyperventilation at the appearance of the physical phantom.

"*Hello, Jade,*" he purred.

It was enough to send chills running down my back. My body shook as I tried to form words, but all that came out was a broken cry; I was too scared to say anything.

"*I see you're looking… weak.*" He looked me up and down, assessing me. "*You've changed somewhat.*"

My heart raced as tears welled in my eyes. My stomach turned as he wiped them away. "*Do not fear… I am only here to remind you what you should be fighting for, that I am the* most frightening thing in your mind, and that the Order's power is nothing compared to yours. Don't trust them, whatever they may bribe you with."

Before I could get a word out, he took my shoulders in his hands, his bony fingers digging so deep into my skin I knew it would leave bruises. I felt his breath on my face, my mind reeling. He moved his lips close to my ear, making sure I heard what he was about to say. "*Trust Bowen and Finch, for they will help lead you to the Tree.*"

In the blink of an eye, he was gone. In a moment of adrenaline, I stood and ripped away the dust sheets from the furniture, making sure that he wasn't hiding under any of them, when a banging at the door startled me.

"Jade!" Bowen called from the other side.

There was the sound of shuffling as someone else knocked more lightly, her voice soft.

"Jade…" It was Jackie.

When did she get here? Or the better yet, *why* was she here?

I made my way hesitantly to the door, not sure if this was another trick the Black Prince was playing. My head rested against the wood, the room spinning as I unlocked the door. I was greeted with the shocked faces of my family and friends.

Bowen was the first to move as he grabbed me. *Not a dream?* I tried to wriggle away but my muscles were uncooperative, my energy levels having plummeted.

"Let her go, Bowen." Jackie stood next to and tried unsuccessfully to separate us.

"You've been missing for ages," Bowen said, more than worry conveyed in his words. My body swayed as he released me, and he and Jackie reached out to steady me.

"What? I've just been right... here..." I looked around at those gathered by the door. It wasn't just Jackie that had now joined our group, but Mom and Dad as well, their eyes red-rimmed and wet.

Mom stepped up to me hesitantly, her arms outstretched. "You look tired. Do you want to go to bed?"

"*No!*" I shouted, a little too adamantly, everyone staring at me with concern. I didn't want to go back to sleep, at least not anytime soon. "I just need some air." I moved to leave the room, only for my legs to buckle, Bowen unable to catch me before my knees hit the ground.

More bruises.

I lifted my arms just enough to feel my shoulders, their tenderness a reminder of the the prince's bony hands around them.

"*Cariad*, what happened?" There was more than concern in his hard eyes as he helped me up from the floor.

"Nothing," I lied too quickly.

He saw right through it.

I looked to Mom and Dad, who were giving me a wide berth, their faces filled with caution and worry. I straightened in Bowen's grip and held onto his forearm, my stance unconvincing. "Why are you guys here?"

I felt Bowen's voice reverberating against my back, his body supporting me as much as it could. "After you ran away, I thought it best to leave you for the time being. But when I heard you scream... it tore at me. And then, when all the glass in the house shattered... We searched and searched but couldn't find you. Did you enchant the room to hide, *cariad*?"

"No, I..." Had I? I just wanted to be alone for a while.

"You must have lifted the spell because I finally found a door on the wall I'd passed three times," Iz butted in.

"We tried everything to get in, but the door wouldn't budge," Jackie said, her mouth pinched at the corners.

"After three hours we just waited," Bowen continued, his voice strained. "And then a day... We even tried breaking the windows from the outside, but they wouldn't shatter." He peered down at me with those honey-colored eyes, the creases of his face etched deeper and deeper. "But when all the glass in the house basically exploded..." He could barely get his words out. "I'm sorry I'm keeping things from you. I'm honestly trying my best..."

"I know..." I said, his lies now the last thing on my mind. They had been replaced with paranoia and panic at the fact that I had been hallucinating during the day. And the most unnerving thing about it all was that the Black Prince was trying to help me for some reason.

I heard his words play over again in my head: *Trust Bowen and Finch, for they will help lead you to the Tree.*

Another bout of dizziness came over me and Mom ushered us to the living room, giving me time to sift through my thoughts.

The living room was large. As with everything else in the house, its crown molding and wood-paneling were dark but the French doors let in so much of the twilight that it balanced everything out. Cushioned couches and armchairs were positioned close together in a way that suggested the room was for family use and not just for entertaining guests.

My mouth went dry as I tried to muster the courage to tell them what I'd seen, but everyone understood enough to realize what had happened, nodding in sympathy and their eyes filled with pity.

"What can we do for you right now?" Simone asked.

"I think finding the Tree should be the priority. It will take my mind off everything and give me something to focus on."

Everyone shifted uncomfortably, as if the last thing I should be doing was obsessing over the Order and finding the Tree of Life. Gwenllian had been silent throughout, Simone shooting worried glances in her direction.

"Where's Finch?" I asked, realizing he was the only person not in the room.

"He's at work…" Bowen replied.

"Has he discovered anything about the documents?"

"He hasn't found anything yet," Iz admitted. "It seems they were nothing more than accounts of oral folklore that told 'fake tales of the past', as Finch put it."

My mind moved on from the conversation on that note, too numb and tired to process anything. Mom finally convinced me that if I didn't at least have a nap that I would fall over from exhaustion.

Reluctantly, I went with Bowen to our room and he tucked me in, lying down next to me to make sure nothing else would happen.

XVII
Bowen

Bowen silently crept out of bed, making sure not to wake Jade. She had finally fallen into a deep sleep, her breathing easy as he made his way out of the room. He had never seen her like this. He knew her coming back after everything she had been through would be hard, but that's why he was there now to help her.

"How's she doing?" Ian asked.

Bowen grabbed an apple off the breakfast table. Everyone was sitting in their pajamas, waiting to interrogate him. "As good as can be…" He ran his hand through his beard, frustration and anguish consuming his mind. "There's not much else I can do."

He didn't know what the next hours would bring, whether she would wake to find him gone and feel a crushing loneliness… Helpless—that's what he was—a feeling he thought he'd rid himself of that day weeks ago when she had finally come back to him.

"I was going to wait to bring this up, but I think it's best we start now." Everyone looked to Finch. He had returned to the manor earlier that morning, Simone unfairly reprimanding him at his absence. "I think Jade is the only one who can actually find the Tree of Life, and I've figured out where we need to go."

That got everyone's undivided attention.

"Where?" Simone asked.

"London."

Tension grew once the word hung in the air. Finch and Bowen knew of the city's past, untold histories the others would never be able to understand, especially when it came to the Order. Bowen hadn't been there in years, and for good reason. London had changed drastically once it had become the hub of the Order in 1590. He didn't want to go back there if he could help it.

"Explain," Bowen demanded.

"*I've* been looking for the Tree since 1890." Finch poured himself a glass of Scotch. "It was during a time when our country was plagued with political and economic strife. There were riots every year, sometimes every month for those of you in the Americas."

"I remember," Bowen commented. "I was an advocate caught in the Bloody Sunday in eighty-seven, among others."

"Exactly"—Finch downed his drink—"and can you see how the world is now? The States' politicians are fucking trolls, Brexit isn't anything to smile at, wars are breaking out in the Middle East, climate change is kicking our asses, and the growing tension between races… don't get me started on that fucking—"

"Get to the point," Gwenllian snapped, a cough racking through her. "What does all of that have to do with Jade?"

"The world is going to shit, and taking the long way 'round. For those of you who don't know, the Tree is what holds the world together. Jade damaged that infrastructure when she sucked the magic out of the world, but now… She is the *only* person on this planet who can find it and bring life back to it."

"How is Jade supposed to do that?" Dave was sitting at the edge of the couch, concentration etched into his features.

"I'm not sure, but she is somehow connected to the Tree of Life and it to her. That's why you need to train her harder." He directed this at both Gwenllian and Bowen. "We don't know what we'll come up against in finding the Tree and she needs to be prepared. Especially when the Order shows up."

"*If* the Order shows up," Simone interjected. "They've been absent all this time…"

Bowen shook his head. "The Order has its eyes everywhere. It's why I would prefer that Jade didn't venture beyond these walls."

"But that's unfair," Jackie began. "She's always wanted to see Scotland and I promised we'd at least visit the castle. You can't just lock her up and expect her to play dead. Give me one night. Just one night where we don't need to have a care in the world."

Jackie was right. As much as it pained him, he knew Jade wouldn't stay put for long. "Fine, one night," he agreed, against his better judgment.

Bowen could see the mischievous smile spread across her face, Jackie already plotting her next course of action.

"If earlier was any indication as to her magical abilities," Finch said, fingering one of the many broken picture frames now scattered throughout the house, "then I'm sure she will have no problem learning quickly." He glared at Gwenllian. "She just needs to train harder. She *needs* to learn the higher magic."

"I'm teaching her as best I can…" Gwenllian whispered.

Bowen could see the sweat that soaked her brow, the small tremors that vibrated up her arms. She was sick, and he knew that things were only going to go downhill for her.

"It's not good enough," Finch berated her. "She needs to learn more, and faster."

"I can't. I—" Her lungs heaved with a heavy cough, Simone reaching for her.

"You *need* to!"

"Enough!" Simone replied sharply. "Gwenllian, you don't owe him an explanation."

"I think she does if we're to know why she can't help Jade," he said.

"I'm dying," she tersely gave up. "Soon after I arrived in the twenty-first century I found that I wasn't able to use my magic. I lost it quickly and my body can't keep up."

"Why didn't you mention this before?" Janet asked, looking shocked and worried. "Does Jade know?"

"She knows I can't use magic anymore… but not that I'm dying. I hid it very well, up until now. Only Simone has ever seen me at my worst, and during the days I've spent with all of you I've known when I have to have time to myself," she stated.

"Medicine? Isn't there anything you can take?" Janet asked.

Gwenllian shook her head. "It's like having stage four cancer. You know something's wrong, but you don't know what will happen or when your time is up. It could be in a month or it could be tomorrow."

"All the more reason to speed up Jade's training and find the Tree as soon as possible." Finch set down his glass. "Malcolm's combed through every piece of intel and book we can get our hands on up here, but we haven't found much. He's even better with computers than I am."

"Everyone's better with computers than you are," Gwenllian wheezed.

"Is that why you want us to go to London?" Bowen asked. Soon day would break, and with it more challenges lay ahead. Everyone knew that each day now counted; they couldn't afford to waste any time.

"I think London is our best bet. There are more and bigger libraries there that could have something. I've looked there in the past, but who knows how much their content has grown over the last few decades."

"And you suggest we leave now? With Jade like this?" Dave asked incredulously.

"Not yet," Gwenllian replied. "It wouldn't be smart to move so soon. We'll take the time to train her, get her ready for whatever trials lay ahead. London is too crowded. Someone will notice us—the Order especially if we're caught using magic."

Finch and Bowen nodded in agreement.

"Let us know then when it's the best time to leave." Bowen stood. "Sooner rather than later would be ideal."

"No." Everyone in the room turned toward Janet, the lines of her face etched deeper than ever before. "I don't want Jade to be like this anymore."

"Janet—" Bowen began.

She held up her hand, her voice soft. "I don't know what

everyone else sees in that room, but *my daughter* looks as if she'll be blown away with the next rain." Tears sprang to her eyes and then began running down her cheeks.

Gwenllian went and sat next to her, placing her hand lightly on Janet's. "Janet... You have been the best mother Jade could ever ask for. You've raised her *so* well." Each word was packed with emphasis. "But she's a grown woman now. I know to a mother that doesn't matter... Even though I never played a part in her upbringing, I'm still happy to have met her as an adult. One who sees me as a person and not the makeshift god so many children make their parents out to be. She will get through this. We all will. And we'll do it together." She squeezed her hand tightly. "No one is alone in this world."

Janet looked at everyone in the room, each of whom had brought support in one form or another. She lingered on Bowen, pleading for once, instead of the schooled hardness she had adopted toward him before. "I'm trusting you to keep her alive."

"I wouldn't live without her."

XVIII
Finch

Finch's plans had worked more perfectly than he had expected. It was cruel what he was putting Jade through, but he needed to push her, needed to push *everyone* in the right direction, and this was the only way he knew how. He had taken a gamble in forcing Jade to reconnect with the Black Prince, but he didn't realize it would work so well, the magic he used conjuring up a physical phantom to haunt her. Finch needed her to understand the seriousness of the situation and knew full well that anything he would say would be met with contempt and mistrust. The Black Prince on the other hand… They would take his appearance seriously, Jade's trauma enough of a reason to have them picking at the puzzle in finding the Tree of Life.

After leaving the others to talk training and how to prepare Jade for any potential fights, Finch made his way back to his room.

"*Sêl,*" he chanted as he closed the door behind him, sealing it tight so nothing would be able to penetrate it.

By siphoning off Gwenllian's powers, his strength had grown over the past twenty years. He still couldn't use it frivolously, making sure to save up as much as he could for when they finally found the Tree of Life, but he still made sure to practice with it so he wouldn't lose touch. His attack spells were harder to produce and took up too much power, making him feel as if he had gone from being an Olympic-level athlete to a junior varsity player in the blink of an eye.

Going over to his dresser, he opened the bottom drawer and, reaching right into the back, pulled out his Browning that sat in its holster. He remembered when he had first bought it in the mid-sixties, before the Firearms Act of 1968 was put in place. It felt comfortable in his hand, the gun almost welcoming. Since then he hadn't had a need for it, especially when he became a Welsh official, his position helping him to stay under the radar. If the government ever found him trying to buy anything newer he would have been kicked out. But he made sure to keep it clean, especially during the past year, the process methodic.

He reached back in and found the bullets for it, their cases clinking against each other. He felt the outside of one of the bullets, the rune symbols engraved into its casing allowing him to meld old magic with new. His research had pointed him toward one of the remaining roots of the Tree of Life, one of the last that remained deep beneath the earth. Gentrification had turned the once lush Edinburgh into a metropolis, buildings and roads clearing the area of the old magic, but Finch still remembered the older layout. Not two hundred yards away from the O'Connell estate was where the root should dorm, the line of copse he could spy from his window indicating its resting place. This was the real reason they were there.

It wasn't just the Tree he had researched, but the remaining documents and grimoires that still possessed spells—old links to a forgotten history. Most of them were gibberish, the thoughts of people from Salem or Transylvania who believed they were the descendants of witches and sorcerers and could still use their ancestors' magic. He knew better, and thanks to Zanna's harsh lessons, he knew just how to mold the spells to actually work. The spell he had cut into the bullets was simple in its execution, its purpose to void the use of any magic. The hard part was trying to figure out a way to enact the spell while also making sure he didn't drain all of his energy. He couldn't die—not yet—but that didn't mean he wanted to become incapacitated when the moment counted. He had figured out that a conduit would work just as well, hence the gun. It would enable him to use it at both close and long range depending on the situation. There was no way to tell what would happen when they found the Tree of Life, but he was going to be prepared for anything that came at him.

Now that he had met up with Gwenllian, the pull of his magic had become stronger, letting him enchant the bullets in preparation, the magic stored within their casings.

I hope I never have to use you on anyone.

He had resolved his heart long ago. No one was going to take away the chance of him getting to the Tree. Not Bowen… not even Jade.

XIX

Days had passed since the incident in the room, my body on high alert for another unannounced visit from the Black Prince. There wasn't the time for sleep or food, my body somehow running purely on adrenaline.

I spent most of my time in my room, hidden away from my family and friends so they wouldn't have to look at the complete mess I had become. I saw how they glanced at me now, so full of concern that it made me cringe.

When I looked into the bathroom mirror I could see the new, sharper angles of my face. Deep bruises hung under my eyes, as if I had been punched twice over. I didn't want *anyone* to see me like this. I made Bowen sleep on the couch in the living room, adamant that all I needed was time, but I knew at some point they were going to get sick of me…

I crawled back into bed, my body heavy as I lay there contemplating everything. My mind was just about to drift off further when Jackie burst into my room, my heart almost giving out at the noise. She was wearing a tight white dress that accented her curves way better than it would on me. Her long, puffy curls were now braided and pulled up into a high ponytail, gold cuffs strategically placed here and there, and her makeup was on point, complete with a burgundy lipstick.

"Get up," she commanded, as she threw a matching black dress at me.

"I don't want to go anywhere right now, Jackie." I pulled the covers over my head, emphasizing the fact.

She took no pity as she tore the covers from me. "I don't care what *you* want. *I* want to go out and drink and party and make out with someone, and by dammit I will have you come with me." She left the room as she went to get my shoes and I was thankful as she handed me ballet flats instead of the high heels she was wearing. "We're in Scotland, for fuck's sake!" It seemed that was a good enough reason for her. "And since we're here, you will not be walking around like a freaking zombie if I can help it. Here." She pulled me off the bed, told me to take my clothes off, and pushed me toward the shower. "Scrub," she commanded.

Once I was showered and dressed, she sat me in front of the bathroom mirror where all her makeup was set up, ready to attack me. At this point, I was too tired to resist.

An hour and several Q-tips later, I was fabulous. Compared to Jackie, my makeup skills were child's play. A pang of sadness hit me at the memory of Elian and Haf, how they used to fuss over me as well.

"There…" She pushed my handbag at me. "Let's go."

As we made our way down the stairs, I saw that Bowen and Finch were already at the entrance waiting for us.

"Took your bloody time," Finch mumbled, while Bowen stood there looking awestruck. Usually men only looked at you like that as you came down the wedding aisle, but here

I was, descending the stairs to find that look on his face. I wobbled a bit on the last step and he casually came over to take my hand. What was more surprising was the fact he was actually allowing me out in this state.

"You look—"

"Hot," Jackie finished for him, pushing us all out the door.

"Exactly." Bowen gave me a peck me on the cheek, looking like a god-incarnate himself. He wore a dark tailored suit with a white shirt, the buttons at the top undone. Gold cufflinks glinted as he looped his arm around me. Though he looked like he was ready to walk the red carpet, his hair was more relaxed than usual, its soft waves bouncing as he moved.

Finch wore something similar, the cut of his suit just a tad tighter than his brother's, which accentuated the lines of his body. As we walked out into the fresh June night, he lit a cigarette, the smoke billowing behind us in the soft breeze.

It seemed we weren't taking a car tonight, pubs and clubs easily accessible to us, so we didn't have to go far. Jackie had a full itinerary lined up.

We started off at an old bar that served cocktails that knocked you on your ass, the room full of people beginning their night just like us, then headed into Old Town to hit some of the places with live music. Of course—Bowen being the perfect man he is—he joined in on the piano while Finch fiddled his way into getting almost every girl's number in the place (not that he did anything with them).

Jackie and I were less conspicuous and settled for throwing back vodka martinis. I had lost count several bars ago how many places we had visited, but it seemed Jackie was still determined in making one more stop.

"*It's here!*" she slurred, pointing at the two-story building in front of us.

"You want to go here?" Finch asked skeptically.

I looked at the entrance of Cotton Nightclub, which didn't look all that bad. Though it was situated down an ankle-breaking cobbled alley, it was close to home and that was all we needed. A line of people were waiting outside the door, music and lights escaping through the doorway.

"What's wrong with here?" I was slurring just as bad as Jackie, making the sentence sound like one elongated word.

"Well, for one, their staff are absolute shite," Finch said, crossing his arms.

It didn't matter at that point. Jackie had already cut the line and gone straight to the bouncers at the front, the rest of us following quickly behind. I wanted to pull at her and tell her she had to wait like everyone else, but what actually came out was "*WOOOOOO!*" The bouncers at the door miraculously let us in, though I'm sure I saw Finch pass them a crisp hundred.

The entrance funneled people into the back, where bars were situated on opposite sides of the room. The floor was already littered with forgotten drinks, my shoes sticking in some places as the waft of stale beer and sharp spirits hit my nose. Mirrors lined the back wall, creating a mirage of people and disco lights. Moving up to the next level, we found a relatively quiet section where the boys could sit as Jackie grabbed my hand and led me onto the dance floor. We merged with the throng of people, swaying to the music's beat. I hadn't felt this good in weeks, perhaps even months, the imminent future always looming over me. But now… now was a chance to let loose and seize the night.

When we made our way back to Finch and Bowen, martinis were already waiting for us. I quickly downed mine and Bowen handed me a bottle of water.

"Drink," he commanded.

I pushed it away, only wanting one thing. I stumbled up to the bar to get a rum and coke, disregarding the cardinal rule about mixing drinks. The night was going perfectly until I turned around and saw a group of women sit down next to Bowen, jealousy spreading through me in an instant. When those women reached for their drinks, instead of liquor touching their lips, mice quickly scurried away from their glasses, screams erupting from the women as they threw them to the ground.

Bowen fixed his gaze on me, not impressed. He excused himself and joined me at the bar.

"That wasn't very nice, they were just taking a break!" he yelled over the music.

I shrugged. "There were literally so many chairs they could've taken, but they sat next to you!" I yelled back.

He let it lie, and I coaxed Jackie back into the horde of dancers and over to the other side of the club where the other bar was situated. Behind the counter was a guy, no older than me, dressed in a black vest and jeans. His left eye had been painted over with the clubs dragonfly logo, while his hands spun each bottle with a dexterity I could only wish for.

We made eye contact and he came straight over. Or maybe it was the twenty-pound note in my hand?

"Four shots of Chartreuse!" Jackie yelled into his ear, leaning in close so he could hear her over the pumping music.

He nodded and produced four shot glasses, filling them

with the clear green liquid. Downing my other drink, I switched it out for a shot glass, only to have Bowen's hand shoot out of nowhere, grabbing them.

"Heeeeyyy!" I said, too slow to stop him as he gulped them both. "Those were mine!" I whined, pouting.

"I think you've had enough!" He banged the glasses onto the counter and took my arm, pulling me in the direction of the door, but I wasn't ready to leave. This was the first night in a *long* time when I could let go and not care about anything else other than drinking and dancing, and he wasn't about to ruin that for me.

"Bowen," Jackie said, "you promised me one night."

"I agreed to it for her sake," he shot back. "She needed to do *something* before she lost all sense of the world. She needs healing… but this isn't it."

I didn't like what I was hearing, and before he had the chance to take me any further, I took a bit of magic and boosted my own strength to flip him to the ground, innocent bystanders also getting hit.

When I turned around, Finch was right behind me.

"You gonna try and stop me too?" I said, pointing with a finger.

He knew better than to get in my way, hesitant as he threw his hands up in surrender.

"I wanna play a game!" I shouted at him, my mood bouncing back and forth. Jackie came up behind, her eyes twinkling with devilment.

In an instant, my hand waved across the top of the DJ's booth, producing a number of shot glasses, my body following after them. Grabbing the microphone, I flipped a switch on the deck, lowering the volume of the music as the sea of people booed in unison until I spoke.

"Guys! Guys! SHUT UP!" Feedback from the mic did the trick, the pitched sound causing our ears to ring. "Now, we're gonna play a little game," I slurred. "Up here we have twenty shot glasses. If you can find the shot glass you'll get an endless amount of drinks for the night!"

The whole crowd cheered rowdily.

"Let's begin!"

I tapped the first glass with two fingers, filling it with Fireball. The sweat-filled energy in the room buzzed, and I did the same for the remainder, alternating between strong spirits.

I had no idea how I was doing it, but at that moment it didn't matter. When I was finally done, I waved my hand and all the drinks disappeared.

The room went into chaos.

That's not right… It's a game of hide-and-seek. You're not supposed to stampede in hide-and-seek! My mind slowed as it tried to process everything through my alcohol-induced haze, wondering how the night had come to this.

Bowen pulled me from the DJ's booth, his hands grabbing tightly around my shoulders, the action reminding me of the Black Prince's, and my body began to tremble.

"You need to stop this!" Bowen ordered, shaking me.

What does he want me to do? Freeze the whole room?

"Fine!" I brought my foot down hard onto the ground, cold ice spreading from me to cover every inch of the room. The music cut out as party-goers slipped and slid so much they couldn't stand, let alone search for the shots. "That better?"

Bowen's eyes went black with fury. The only other time I had ever seen him like that was when Finch had been performing the rite of passage on me.

"Finch!" he yelled across the way.

He and Jackie were holding onto bar stools, trying not to fall themselves. "Yes?"

"You and Jackie meet us outside. *Now!*"

Finch maneuvered Jackie as best he could, her arms reaching out at anything and everything to keep steady. I, on the other hand, had no problem walking on my own ice, and it seemed neither did Bowen.

"You were out of line, Jade," he growled as we left the club. People were still trying to get in even at the early morning hour, everyone watching our argument. "You know you're not supposed to do that in public."

By the time I gave a shit we were already standing in front of Edinburgh Castle. It was gorgeous, all lit up. I would have to come in the daytime and actually have a roam about. Better yet, Finch could take me on a private tour and I could see all those secret places tourists weren't allowed in.

"I get it!" I yelled, exasperated.

"I don't think you do," Bowen said, still hot on my heels.

"It's not like the High Elders can come and banish me from the world! They're dead! AND I KILLED THEM!"

That stopped him.

Drunken tears streamed from my eyes, ruining Jackie's hard work on my makeup.

"You think I don't know what I've done? I've killed millions—billions—of people," I stammered. "I'm probably one of the most lethal killers in history and nobody's heard of me!" I stood there, screaming at the three of them. "The Order probably only wants me so I can revive that stupid Tree and probably kill even more people!"

"Is that what you think?" Bowen took a step toward me but stopped when I held my hand up in protest.

I was tired, not only from the drinking and dancing, but tired of everything.

I stepped backward and found myself in our room.

Bowen forced his way into the room, the door giving way as its hinges bent with the force. Though he was worried about Jade, it was sheer anger that drove him to her. Anger not only at himself for letting her perform magic like that, but also at Jade for thinking that every event, every death after she depleted the Tree of Life, was her fault.

"Jade!" he called from the doorway, Finch and Jackie following close behind, their minds clear in the mayhem of it all.

He saw what was happening to her, the fear, the paranoia, the dreams... It was an experience he knew about only too well, his own memories of war ever-present.

"Leave me alone!" she shouted from inside the bathroom, and a second later there was the sound of shattering glass.

Bowen threw himself at the bathroom door, and all the commotion had now woken the other occupants of the house.

"What's happening?" Janet asked. She was in a pink robe, her hair up in curlers.

"What else? Your daughter is overdramatizing everything and won't come out of her room," Finch replied.

"Watch it!" Dave and Bowen said together.

Bowen continued to push, until finally, the door of the bathroom gave way under his strength, and he found Jade sitting in the middle of the tiled floor. He spied the broken mirror, and then saw her knuckles, all cut up from the glass.

Janet and Gwenllian tried to rush in, only for Dave to hold them back. "I think it's best if we leave them alone."

Bowen looked to those around him and they nodded in agreement. If he hadn't just broken the door down, would he have found a different scene playing out in front of him? A chill ran up his back at the prospect.

"Jade…" He inched into the room and sat next to her on the floor. "Jade, please talk to me," he pleaded.

She looked like hell. He hadn't seen her like this since the Dark Ages. Maybe not even then. Back then she still had a semblance of hope, but now it was nowhere to be seen.

Jade finally looked at him. "There's nothing to talk about really," she answered numbly. "It's like I said, I'm a murderer."

He brought her closer to him, taking her body into his arms.

No longer does she wear a smile on her lips that used to ignite my faithful and foolish love. Now its appearance comes and goes, carried by a breeze that has left me pierced by its sadness. It was an old adage, one that fit the situation too perfectly.

"*Cariad*, you are the farthest thing from a murderer," he said, brushing the hair from her face. He had met real murderers, seen them in action on the bloody streets of Cardiff at one point.

"But I've killed people. They could have lived for longer if magic had been around."

"The one thing we know about life is that it will end, no matter what, and magic may halt the progression for a time, but in the end Death always comes for us. It's not your fault nature took its course."

"But if I hadn't drained the Tree of Life…"

"That fault lies with another, who has paid over and over for his sins." He pulled her in closer, wanting to protect her as much as he could. "I know it will take some time for you to understand and accept this." He could feel the soft tears fall onto his jacket and made to wipe them away, only for his thumb to come away covered in black eyeliner.

She chuckled. It wasn't much, but it was enough to let Bowen know that the worst was over.

"Sorry," she said, as she tried to remove the makeup from his finger. "Waterproof doesn't always mean cry-proof."

"That's alright, *cariad*." Even under all that makeup, he could see the bruises under her eyes. "Come on, you need to sleep." He could see the fear those words instilled in her. "I'll be here when you need me."

He picked her up and carried her to their bed, the duvet already pulled back. He settled into the pillows beside her, Jade's eyes fighting to stay open as he held her against him until she fell soundly to sleep. He checked first that she was completely out before he snuck from the room, everyone else waiting for him.

"It's worse than before," said Janet in a panicky high-pitched voice.

"I know," Bowen growled. He had no idea what to do. His

own dealings with his emotions after war had been nothing compared to how Jade was handling hers. He'd had centuries to sort everything out, but Jade… He cursed her mortality.

"Train her," Finch stated resolutely. "She needs to feel like she's in control of *something* if she wants to get past this. Even if you only find out exactly how much magic she has, it will be enough of a starting point for her recovery."

All of them looked to Gwenllian.

"Alright, we'll start in a couple of days. In the meantime, try and get her to build up her strength again. I can't help her if she's not willing to help herself."

Bowen nodded. If Jade wouldn't be able to get past this, then he would be there to support her in any way possible.

XX

I woke in my room to find dim light streaming through the open curtains. Bowen wasn't lying next to me anymore, but that didn't matter. I'd slept. Really slept. I don't think I'd had such a good night's sleep since coming back from 1351. And I didn't dream, a thankful reprieve. Last night's drunken revel had somehow snapped me back—rested my mind to the point where my shoulders no longer felt stiff and my back didn't feel as if a knife had been stuck in there. I had been holding onto so much inside that finally telling the truth made me see myself for what I had become... A damsel in distress. A broken woman. A murderer.

    I pulled myself from bed and readied a steaming hot bath. Had Elian been here, she would have scented it with lavender and mint to help speed the process of healing. How much I took her company for granted... and the rest of them. I didn't even know how they had lived, how they had died, too scared to pick up a history book and read the lies about their pasts, the truth forgotten to the modern world. I looked into the bathroom and saw that the mirror was cracked where I had punched it, the rough ridges of my knuckles that were speckled with dry blood only confirming the reality of it all. Someone had already been in to clean up, the shards of glass nowhere to be seen.

What am I doing?

I had never been this person, never struggled with life in such a way. I'd always had my anxieties, but compared to this they seemed like a child's problems. It felt now as if I had been thrust into a CEO's chair, handed the keys, and told to run a company without any experience.

I slipped into the tub, the hot water relaxing my tense muscles.

I have no idea what I'm doing...

But did anyone really? I thought back to when I first met Bowen, the rage inside him, the anguish. He probably went through a similar process when he found me gone, our battle suddenly over.

But look how far he's come.

I couldn't fathom the other horrors he had faced in the past, but he'd had centuries to figure out how to deal with his issues. I, on the other hand, had a time limit, one that was quickly running out...

From the tub I could see my distorted reflection in what was left of the mirror.

Push it down. Don't feel it... Don't think about it. Don't think about them. Concentrate on what you need to do.

As much as it went against my nature—as much as my body screamed for me not to—my mind was made up. If I was to find the Tree of Life, I had to stay in the present and think about the future, not carry on mourning for the past. Everything else—my feelings—could wait. The world couldn't.

I got out of the tub and grabbed for a towel, its texture soft against my skin as I dried off and pulled on my clothes. The warm weather had lasted a couple of days (a British summer they had called it) and was once again back to a cool dreariness.

Taking a shawl with me, I looked around for everyone, surprised no one had come to find me yet. My stomach had started its symphony and I ventured to the kitchen, its fridge full to the brim, but where were the others…? Either everyone was out doing something or they were all avoiding me.

I found the ingredients for a sandwich, too hungry to put any real effort into a full meal.

Taking my chicken and mustard sandwich with me, I went to sit in the living room. I was going to watch something on the television, but that too was broken, the screen looking as if someone had taken a crowbar to it. It didn't matter though, Gwenllian walked in a minute later, seeming hesitant as she looked to me for confirmation that it was okay for her to join me on the couch.

"You alright?" she asked, her eyes glued to the broken screen, as if she could will it to come alive again. It was clear she was a bit out of her depth, and I couldn't blame her.

"For now," I replied. Though I had decided what I was going to do, who knew when my next ordeal would hit, incapacitating me again.

Mom walked in, a bit taken aback that Gwenllian was already with me, and came to sit on the other side of me, placing a hand on my leg. "You can talk to us any time."

Seemed like they were doubling up on me. I half expected Simone and Dad to walk in, have the whole parental support thing, but they didn't, thank God.

"I know," I answered sheepishly, "but I think I got everything out of my system last night."

Mom raised an eyebrow, as if to say "Yes, you did", while Gwenllian just sat there quietly.

Never would I have thought that I would be sitting in a room with my two mothers as they looked on in understanding at the foolish actions of their child, but here we were... and I could hardly believe it.

"Okay, well, I'm going to find Bowen"—I got up, ending the mothers-daughter moment—"see if he wants to spar."

"I'll join you," Gwenllian said, quickly standing at my side. "I think you need more guidance in your magic. It seems to be a bit… disjointed." She emphasized this as she motioned to all the broken panes of glass in the photos around us.

I nodded in agreement, embarrassed that my outburst had caused more damage than I ever intended. "Great. Let's go."

We found Bowen and Finch having a duel outside in the grounds, the impending storm clouds just a mile off. Thankfully, none of the house's other tenants were out, leaving us to practice in peace.

Bowen and Finch stopped as we joined them, their shirts already drenched in sweat.

"You good?" Finch asked.

I guess it was just going to be one of those days where I had to repeat myself. "For now," I said.

He threw me the practice sword he had been using and I caught it easily.

"Actually, Gwenllian's going to teach me more magic." I

threw the sword back to him and took a position in the middle of them all, ready for her instruction.

"I think we need to take off the training wheels and go full force at this point." She unbuttoned her light sweater and dropped it on the ground. Seemed shit was about to get real. "Hit me with your best shot."

That drew me up short. I wasn't about to unleash my powers on her with no way for her to defend herself. "How about me not killing you today?"

"Ha!" Gwenllian snorted back. "Like you could ever hit me that hard."

Probably not, as I knew I would subconsciously hold back against her, but I had a feeling that if I really tried I would get close. "Okay, but the safe word is *kiwi*." I wanted some backup at least, just in case anything got out of hand. I heard Finch make some off-handed comment about what safe word Bowen and I might have, only to hear a resounding slap behind me. I would have felt bad but he really should have known better.

"Give me everything you've got."

"Shouldn't I… you know… make us invisible or something so no one sees us practicing magic?" I thought of the tenants of the other flats and the school—I didn't want them to start questioning their own sanity.

"Good idea. Do you think you can hold a barrier and spar?"

"We'll see how long I last."

I concentrated on the space around us, the smell of the grass as the sun hit it, a congress of ravens swooping down into the trees before us, the soft lull of traffic from the road behind us. Taking my time, I held my hands out in front of me, the strain of the spell making them shake. I had never put up a barrier before except when fighting off the Brotherhood, but even then it was more for defensive purposes than camouflage. It took me five minutes to distort the air around us, and from the inside it looked like the oily remnants of a bubble.

When Gwenllian was satisfied with the size of the barrier, she began the lesson. We went over the movements time and again until they felt familiar, all the while my magic storing up for the practice. I concentrated on the target in front of me, Gwenllian standing like a pillar fifteen feet away. My breath came in heavy waves as my magic collected in the palm of my hand, its green luminescence turning white with every passing second. She readied her stance, my own wobbling at the immense power I now held. Curling my fingers inward, I made a fist and punched the air between us, unleashing my spell onto her.

My body swayed with the sudden draining of my magic, Bowen steadying me. "You alright?" I yelled to Gwenllian, who had been knocked back farther than I had anticipated, my body hot from the exertion.

She stuck her thumb up, giving the *all okay*. Slowly, she stood and rejoined us. "Now, again. See if you can hold it for longer, build it up more."

"Gwenllian," Bowen said, in a cautionary tone, as if a silent conversation was passing between them.

I wiped a trickle of blood away from my nose, smearing it onto my arm. "No. It's fine. I want to know—*need* to know—how much power I really have."

He crossed his arms over his chest. "Well, you're not going to use Gwenllian as a punchbag. You could seriously hurt her." He peeked over his shoulder. "Finch. How about you stand in?"

"Why me?" he asked incredulously.

"*Kiwi!*" Finch panted, his T-shirt dripping with sweat. Mine was no better.

"You're not even the one training here," I said, huffing heavily. My vision blurred for a millisecond, but it gave enough reason for Gwenllian to agree.

"I think I have the data I need."

I hadn't paid much attention to the phone in her breast pocket. Each time we had stopped she would type on it. Now she pulled it out again. "I've recorded everything so I can analyze it later."

"But she cloaked us. How will you be able to see her using magic?" Finch finally piped up. He had collapsed to the ground, his chest heaving up and down from exhaustion. It was almost awe-inspiring how durable he was. Had he still possessed his magic, he probably wouldn't have batted an eye at any of my spells.

"How do you think technology was created?" *Like that answered anything.* "Plus, it's actually easier to see magic through a phone's camera. They are remarkably innovative devices."

"I'll have to take a look at it for myself as well then." He got himself up from the ground and headed back into the manor with Gwenllian, both glued to the screen of her phone, leaving me and Bowen to continue my physical training.

"Ah, Jade," Gwenllian said, calling back to me, "don't blame me if you hate me by the end of all this! I *will* have you prepared for whatever happens when we get to London, Order or no."

XXI

It was already on the cusp of August, the physical toll exhausting as I trained harder and harder with Gwenllian and Bowen every day. I had pushed away the annoying thoughts of the Black Prince and my actions during our night out. There was no time to have such things swimming around in my head.

"Come on! Use that powerful body of yours! How are you going to listen to the enemy?" she yelled from across the field. We had moved on to more subtle magic, training in heightening my senses.

"What enemy?" The Order was more of an inconvenience than an enemy at this point as we *still* didn't know *why* they wanted to get to the Tree, or me for that matter.

"The enemy that could be listening to us right this second!" she shouted like a drill sergeant, but I rolled with it. In the short weeks that had followed our initial training, I was already getting used to how my magic reacted in this century, and if this was going to boost my magical powers enough to find the Tree of Life, then it was well worth it.

I whispered a short spell that increased my hearing to the

point of painfulness, and I was able to detect a deer eating from a bush three hundred yards away.

"Good!" she yelled.

I covered my ears at the backlash. "Jesus. Gwenllian, not while my ears are bat-like. You want to deafen me?"

"I don't know, sign language can come in pretty handy. Perhaps you should join the school here and learn a new trade?"

"If I live long enough…" I mumbled under my breath.

"You *will* live as long and happy as Fate sees fit," she scowled, reprimanding me tersely. She had been acting weird lately. Since meeting her and having made the decision to go to London, it was like she was trying too hard to steer me in the right direction. "Alright, we're finished for the day."

I knew I needed to prepare for my encounter with the Order, as well as be ready for whatever magic was needed to find the Tree, but this all felt too detached. I had no idea what threat they posed to me or the world. With the Black Plague Brotherhood, I at least knew where they stood in the grand scheme of things.

I went back into our bedroom and found Bowen on the bed staring out the window at the garden. The grass was still as vibrant and green as in spring. After my recent breakdown, Bowen was now more open about his life, our relationship no longer based on half-truths and secrets. I had told him it was a secondary problem compared to my unnerving meeting with the Black Prince, but he assured me he wanted there to no longer be any walls between us.

"I feel like we're getting nowhere," I complained as I plopped down next to him. "Do you really think I can do this?"

Finch and the others had told me what they wanted to do.

London felt like a far-off place, separate from my world. My training needed to hurry up so we could get there and start a more effective search for the Tree. Jackie had taken to the Internet to help Gwenllian and Ian find more information, but everything was steeped in lore from one corner of the world or another. We still needed more definitive answers.

Bowen wrapped his arms around my waist and rolled me over to stare at me, his eyes hard against the dimming sun, yet his voice was soft as he answered. "Of course, *cariad*. You are not alone in this fight, remember that."

He flung me onto his lap, his arms around my body, and I ran a hand through his thick hair, the wave in it enticing, as a smile spread across my face. "I love you."

We were still for a moment. It was the first time I had said it out loud. These past couple of months we had been able to progress our relationship substantially, and it seemed as if those words were implied in every action we made toward each other, but to hear them ring so clear…

He pulled my lips to his in a rush to devour them. His strong hands felt hot as they ran down my back, my breath catching as they crept under my shirt. His hands were ice-cold, my body on fire at the contrast.

"Don't singe me now, witch," he quipped playfully. I could see the magic starting to rise again from our bodies. This was the first time he had touched me like this in weeks, convinced abstinence somehow healed the pain I was going through. But all I wanted was him.

I pushed him down onto the plump covers of the bed, our bodies in sync as my hips moved against him. Our movements slowed as we moved under the covers, our clothes strewn onto the floor. If it were possible, I never wanted us to part. His lips traced my neck, his hands venturing down to the crease of my thigh and then further. My breath caught as he found exactly where I was most sensitive, and then he rolled me over into a better position. His mouth found its way to my breasts, nipping at them playfully as I ran my hands up his back, until, finally, I could feel him hard against me. He entered slowly, the ecstasy of the moment prolonged. I brought his mouth to mine, my moans captured against his lips as he moved. His tongue traced me until it reached my ear.

"I love you too," he whispered softly, thrusting harder with the words.

I didn't think I was going to make it, but by the time we finished together, I was still in one piece—well, maybe two, as Bowen completed the other half.

Night had fallen, the house deathly quiet as Bowen and I slept in each other's arms, the sheets half-strewn across our bodies. The cool breeze from the open window caressed against my skin and my hand reached toward Bowen's sweatshirt that was permanently draped on the edge of the headboard behind us, only to find the space empty. Squinting around the room, I saw it perched on the chair across from us, and stepping onto the cold wooden floor, I lazily made my way toward it.

"Jade."

My feet stuck to the wood as a soft whisper of a voice sent the Devil's fingers to run up my neck. My breath caught in my throat as I looked out the window, the soft glow of something on the lawn capturing my full attention. I could see sullen eyes, their stare boring into my soul as the phantom's billowing black cloak melded with the night.

"*Jade*," he whispered again.

"Bowen," I croaked through tight lips. "Bowen!"

Nothing.

"Jade!" He was still out there. I glanced down again and saw him beckon me with a finger. "*Come here.*"

"No..." I didn't want to be anywhere near him.

"*Now!*"

In an instant my body seemed to become weightless as it passed soundlessly through the panes of glass and I found myself standing in front of the Black Prince. I was only wearing Bowen's sweatshirt, the hem falling just past my hips, the summer breeze against my bare skin sending goosebumps all the way down my legs.

"*Care for a stroll?*" He held out his arm, and without question I responded, hooking my own around his. I had felt this way before, my will meaning nothing in his hands, and panic quickly rose in my chest.

Wake up, wake up, wake up, wake up. I tried my hardest to suppress my emotions and keep a poker face so he wouldn't see how freaked out I was, but I wasn't convincing enough; the prince glanced at me as a chuckle escaped from him.

"*How has the training been going?*" The Black Prince led us away from the house and across the garden. There was a copse at its perimeter, and the moon shone brightly, illuminating our path toward the trees.

I said nothing as I walked beside the prince, the grass flattening beneath my feet while an iridescent trail was left by his own. Distant sounds of wildlife echoed from the sparse backdrop, insects whizzing past my ear as they hurried along toward a waiting supper.

"*Come now, Jade*"—he came in closer, his lips by my ear, the all-knowing grin on his face reading my every move—"*you're the one who keeps seeing me.*"

Revulsion ran through my body—my hair standing on end. He was right. This was some sort of sick joke my mind couldn't stop playing on me.

"*Have you made any progress in finding the Tree of Life?*" One look at my face and his lips turned down in disapproval.

We had made it across the lawn and entered the line of the copse, tree trunks and branches looking haunting against the shadows of the night.

I looked in every direction, convinced that if the Black Prince was here then other Brotherhood soldiers wouldn't be far away, hiding among the trees.

"*This conversation is getting to be pretty one-sided… I know everything you are doing. Everything you are feeling. How you're struggling to advance your magic… How your mind is completely fractured… I even know where Bowen last touched you…*" He emphasized the latter fact by grazing his fingers across my cheek.

"I need to go back," I stated, numbly, the blood in my veins running cold as he gripped me tighter.

"*There's no rush. Everything is quiet in the house and you will not be missed.*"

You will not be missed. The words rang in my head. *I would be missed*, I tried to convince myself. But it was the middle of the night… no one would notice.

"*This way. There is something we need to do.*"

My body betrayed me and I followed him deeper into the woods, the light of the manor barely visible from this distance.

"What are we going to do?" I asked hesitantly. I was reminded of every horror movie I had ever seen that was set in the woods, and the end result was never good.

He stopped us in a small clearing and all signs of life disappeared. "*Do you know the premise of Yin and Yang? Good and evil? Dark and light?*"

I stood there with my arms by my side, their weight heavy, my mind blank as I answered automatically. "Everyone does. There are two sides to every coin… The balance of the world."

"*Correct.*" He circled around me and I never let him out of my sight. "*And what do you think happens when one holds greater precedence over the other?*"

"The balance shifts to one side and things are thrown off." I didn't like where this was going.

"*Exactly.*" His icy eyes sparkled. "*Now, what is needed to equalize these two sides?*"

My mind tried to keep up, to decipher what he was throwing at me. "A counterbalance." Fog seemed to blanket my brain with each question asked, the prince's steps not faltering as he continued to circle me.

"*You see, the world as it is today is off-balance because the Tree is almost dead. You are that counterbalance. You are the only one that can find the Tree and bring order back to the world. Magic is too far gone to be saved, but this world… There is still time.*"

"Why does this concern you?" I mumbled through numb lips, the air around us growing colder and colder by the second. The Black Prince was vindictive, tyrannical, basically psychotic, but here he was pleading for the world's salvation? Something didn't add up.

The prince continued circling, his iridescent footprints fading with every step he took over the spongy moss. There was a moment when he stopped and placed a small stone at my bare feet, a symbol I didn't recognize scratched into the surface, then he continued. The moment the stone touched the ground I could feel every pulse of the world—everything that was living and dying all at once.

"*It concerns all of us,*" was his simple reply. "*Now, concentrate. Feel the strands of magic around you.*" He finally stopped in front of me and placed his hands on the tops of my shoulders—grounding me. "*You and the Tree of Life share a bond stronger than magic—stronger than time—and you need to reconnect that bond.*"

Reconnect? How am I to reconnect with something I can't find?

"*By concentrating,*" he said, answering my inner thoughts. "*You still lack power, but if you can at least recall one of the roots, then perhaps it will help you in your search.*"

The fog became thicker in my mind and my eyelids started to close, the prince's face going blurry as my magic wandered beyond my reach and into the soft earth.

Then I felt it, like a searing hot poker being plunged into the arches of my feet.

I woke to the smell of morning dew and mud, moss and leaves squashed underneath my body. I thought I had been dreaming the whole thing up as I had done when I'd been locked in one of the rooms of the manor, but I was wrong. Lying next to me was the stone the prince had used in whatever ritual had happened earlier, and the searing pain that encapsulated my feet all the way up to my ankles was too painful to be unreal.

I stared down at them, a soundless cry escaping me.

Thick black veins wound their way up from my arches, twisting and overlapping, reaching to the tops of my ankles, where they disappeared deeper into my skin.

No… Not veins, but roots.

My hands instinctively went to wipe them away, but instead they collided with raw skin, as if I had just spent all night in a tattoo parlor, the black roots bleeding and scabbed.

Painfully, I made my way barefoot out of the trees and back to the manor, dawn just breaking past the horizon. When I got to the French doors at the rear of the house, I could see the carnage of last night in the reflection in the window. My hair had clumps of mud stuck in it, while Bowen's sweater was soaked and dirty. My lips were light blue, the cold air causing a spasm to pass through my body.

I wiggled the handle of the door, but it was locked. I had no energy, no will to smash a pane of glass, nor to call up to Bowen, my throat feeling as dry as sandpaper.

Placing my back against the wall, I slid to the ground, my head resting on my knees. There was total silence, and it allowed my thoughts to wander back to last night.

How was I going to explain this to the others? Would this help me to find the Tree of Life? I looked down again at my feet, the redness slowly fading, somehow answering my question.

XXII
Bowen

Bowen felt the cool, empty space beside him in bed and squinted against the early morning sun to the bathroom, hoping to see Jade there, but instead he found the place completely empty. In seconds he was out of bed, throwing on his shirt and shoes, running into the hall.

"Jade!"

Scenarios ran through his mind. He was hoping for the more positive one where he found her in the kitchen having an early breakfast. The less positive thought… He didn't even want to contemplate what it could be. Perhaps they had been too naive, too lax in their thinking that the Order couldn't find them.

He ran to the kitchen in the hope that he was right, and opening the door, he found everyone else instead.

"Why are you up?" Finch licked at his finger as he caught a bead of whisky falling from the bottle's neck.

"Why are all of you up?" he asked, out of breath.

"We thought we'd brainstorm a way to get to the Tree and let you and Jade sleep in." Simone capped the pen she had been using to write down their list of ideas, and Jackie was already typing them up on her computer.

"Jade." Bowen got back to the situation at hand. "She's not in our room."

That got all their attention.

"Well, she's not here," Jackie commented.

"Has anyone seen her?"

Ian stood up to get another cup of coffee. "Hasn't she come back from her walk?"

Every head turned in his direction.

"A walk at this hour? Do you know the woman?" Jackie asked incredulously. "I could understand if she were drunk, but she hasn't touched alcohol since... well, the last time," she finished awkwardly.

Bowen didn't stay for the coming discussion. He ran out of the kitchen and took the stairs down and out through the back door, where he found her sitting.

His heart pounded from the extra adrenaline, his breath heaving as he tried to calm down. "Jesus, woman..." he sighed, but when he finally took in the state she was in, it made his heart weep for her. Mud was caked all over her, and she smelled of fresh earth. There were small cuts on the soles of... her feet... and ankles... Bowen took in the patterns that snaked up them.

"Jade, what happened?" He approached her cautiously and placed his hand onto her shoulder, but she squirmed away. She was like ice.

"Black..." Her teeth chattered. "He..."

The sound barely escaped her lips, but Bowen caught it, the blood in his veins running cold. Bowen cursed that name.

After he had woken to find Jade gone in 1351, so too had he found the Black Prince and his shadow no longer there. He had heard rumors that he was in Oxfordshire, then France, but back then he was more caught up in trying to find Jade. It was only years later, in 1376, that Bowen had the satisfaction of learning that the prince had died of dysentery. It was a painful way to go at that time and Bowen reveled in the fact.

"What did you say?"

"I tried to wake you…" She sounded weak.

What has he done to her?

"*Cariad*, you didn't. I would never have left you alone if you had."

She looked confused, and sat up, only to sway back down. She brought her hand to her temple, her brow furrowed in pain.

He lifted her into his arms and took her back into the house as Simone came toward them. Bowen motioned toward her, and in a second, her feline paws scampered back up the stairs.

He maneuvered himself into the elevator, making sure to keep Jade's head close to his chest, and by the time the doors opened again, everyone was already waiting for him.

"What happened?" Janet said, inspecting the state her daughter was in, sounding horrified. "What's that on her feet?"

"Let's move to the living room and find out." It was becoming a common occurrence for their meetings to take place there, their personal headquarters in their time of war.

"Ian, can you get her some water?" Bowen placed her on the love seat near the bay window to let her get as much sunlight as possible. "And a first-aid kit!"

"I'm fine, really," she replied unconvincingly through

chattering teeth, pulling the nearby blanket around her shoulders.

Ian handed her a glass of water anyway and gave Bowen a small green bag with a white cross on it. He pulled out antiseptic cream as Janet tried to lightly dab away the dirt and leaves that had caked onto her soles. The small red cuts had to be cleaned and treated before they got infected.

"Start from the beginning," Gwenllian demanded eagerly.

The color in Jade's face returned slightly as she retold her tale, Bowen trying not to strangle the bandages as he applied them to Jade's feet.

"So you were sleepwalking?" Jackie asked her when she was finished.

"I don't know," she replied.

"But you said the Black Prince was trying to help you?" Gwenllian seemed agitated at the news. They all were.

"Maybe help isn't the right word," she said, looking down at her feet.

He had done this to her?

"What are they?" Simone asked, lowering her voice.

"Roots," Jade replied. She looked at Bowen, the corners of her mouth only just pulling up. "Now we both have ink."

He managed a sad smile at the forced humor in her comment.

"I think it's time to go to London," Finch interrupted. "We need to find the Tree *now*." He paced alongside the fireplace, its ash stone cold.

"And what will you have us do?" Gwenllian retorted. "Snap our fingers and find the correct spell that will lead us to the Tree?"

Finch's eyes squinted at her tone. "Better than doing nothing."

"And the Order? We still don't know why they want the Tree. Wouldn't its death be just as bad for them as it is for us?" Jade pointed out, her voice soft.

Everyone's attention turned to Finch, hanging on his every word.

"I don't know," he growled in frustration. "I was excommunicated from the group a hundred years ago. I've no idea what they want to do."

"Why were you excommunicated?" Jackie asked, her eyebrow raised.

Bowen silenced Finch before he could answer. "For once, I agree with Finch. We should go to London."

"Right into the lion's den?" Simone asked incredulously.

"They'll never suspect we're right under their noses." Finch poured a glass of Scotch for both himself and Jade. She looked like she needed one and Bowen didn't stop him as he handed it to her. "The documents we originally came here for have led us nowhere. I think we need to make a stop at the British Library."

Jade's eyes seemed to widen at the prospect. Bowen knew she had never been to London, never had the chance. He would have liked to take her under better circumstances, and perhaps once this whole ordeal was over they could travel to the ends of the world together.

Finch continued. "I've pored over the records in the British Museum and library for centuries and have come up empty, though I haven't been in some time. They get lots of new material every day. I'm hoping you'll be able to see something I don't."

"Gwenllian?" Bowen asked. She was being unusually quiet about the situation.

She hesitated, her eyes filled with dread. "It's just that they're so pretentious—the British Library. I tried to get in once and they said I had to be a member to access that part of the library. If I had known the pup over here could get in I would have used him," she said in exasperation. She didn't want to have to depend on Finch, but then again, neither did anyone else it seemed.

"Well, I'm all you lot got, so..."—he stood, a bit of a bounce in his step—"who wants to go to London?"

A fynno glod, bid farw.

The best way to gather praise or recognition is to die.

XXIII

Despite peaceful nights after my tattoo session in the woods, Bowen had stayed vigilant, making sure he was nearby at all times. My feet had fully healed in a day, the soreness no longer prominent compared to the rest of my pale skin. The dreams and sleepwalking had ceased as well, leaving me to battle against the demons that haunted my conscious mind.

We were all sitting around the breakfast table, everyone silent as they nibbled their way through the morning meal, the only interruption when Ian made a purposeful cough.

"I won't be coming with you to London," he announced as he raised his cup of coffee to his lips.

"Why not?" Gwenllian asked, spreading a glob of apricot jam onto her toast. Though her appetite seemed to be growing, she looked like she was getting thinner by the day. Simone sat perched on her lap, her soft purring bringing comfort to all of us. "Don't you want to see what happens when we find the Tree?"

"Truthfully, yes"—Gwenllian grunted in approval—"but I feel I'm no longer needed."

I looked into his blue eyes, their pure color seeming

to reflect his pure nature. If he were Tristan he would have followed me to the end of the world, but he wasn't, and I couldn't ask that of him.

"Though I don't agree you're no longer needed, you're entitled to stay if you wish."

"Thank you, Jade, but I do believe my involvement ends here."

"We'll be sad to leave without you," Bowen said, sipping at his orange juice. Everyone had become fast friends, the impending events of the future bringing us all closer together.

"Well"—Finch clapped his hands together, making us all jump—"the plane is booked. Will we be staying at the townhouse in Fitzrovia or the Barbican?"

Both those names meant nothing to me.

"Fitzrovia," Bowen answered resolutely. "The Museum Mile may be clogged with students and tourists at this time of year, but at least its closer to the library."

"You have more than one house in London?" Jackie asked, mouth agape.

"Jade owns one of them, the one in Fitzrovia actually."

"You wanna pass on that wealth, Jade?" Jackie slyly pushed her eggs around, as if all she was asking was for me to pass the salt.

I couldn't wrap my head around the fact that I actually *owned* a house, and more than one, according to Bowen. I thought I would be lucky to find a house-share somewhere, never mind outright owning a place. "To tell you the truth, take it. What am I gonna do with…" I looked to Bowen for the rough number of houses I owned around the world.

"Fifty-six."

"*Fifty-six* places!" *What the actual fuck?* That was just excessive.

"Fifty-nine if you're counting land," Bowen answered with a flashing smile. "But only eleven are for living in. The rest are either rented out or used as storage units."

"We need to sell some of them off," I protested.

"Jade," Dad said in a cautionary tone, "maybe we leave that alone for a year or so… Just until your mother and I visit every last place."

Now there was an idea.

Our luggage took up most of the sidewalk outside of Edinburgh's airport. We left Ian and Iz at theirs, taking taxis. *How did we accumulate so much stuff?* If I had visited Scotland a year ago I would have had to squish next to someone on a nine-hour coach ride, never mind bringing enough stuff to last a month.

We hauled everything to the private check-in desk, the line nonexistent compared to the others that were bursting with waiting travelers. It only took one look from the attendant behind the desk, his face stretching into a smile as Finch handed him all our documents. The whole process went smoothly, Finch's status getting us exceptional care.

It wasn't long until our flight was called, the private jet already waiting for us—something I had never experienced before. The inside felt decadent, with cream leather couches and luxurious recliner chairs. A hostess was already on board to greet us, a tray of champagne flutes filled for our leisure. It was better than flying first class.

I glanced down at my feet, my socks and jeans covering my new markings, but I could still feel them all the same.

"I'm sorry you have to go through this," Gwenllian said, her eyes full of pity.

"It's not your fault. I created this mess. It's only right I now have to clean it up."

"*You* didn't do anything," Jackie shot back, squinted eyes fixed on the real culprit.

I knew I should have felt angrier toward Finch at the situation, but one, I just didn't have the energy, and two, at least he was trying to help us find the Tree of Life. We needed all the help we could get, and without his connections, who knew where we would have ended up.

Our time in the air was short, an hour and a half at the most. In America it would have taken me over two hours to fly from California to Washington state. My whole body tensed as we started our descent; I still couldn't get used to touching down in planes, my hands instinctively gripping the armrests and my nails digging deep.

Bowen put his hand beneath mine, risking it being crushed, but we landed way before I had time to do any permanent damage.

Getting settled into the limousine was a breeze. This was the first time I had visited, the city already bustling as we pulled out into the morning traffic. We drove into the heart of London, past the River Thames, Little Venice, and Madame Tussauds. Commuters had their heads down as they rushed to get where they needed to go while tourists milled around trying to snap pictures.

"We're here," Bowen announced.

Damn... I silently cursed. That was the first time in a long while I had actually enjoyed a car ride. It had reminded me of the times Dad used to take us around the neighborhood during Christmas to see everyone's lights—a Morrison family tradition—but this felt better than Christmas.

We gathered our things and got out of the car, the house just at the back of a small close off Riding House Street. The lane didn't look like much as white stucco was falling off in the corners of other houses, their windows draped so no one could peek inside their homes and businesses.

Bowen pointed to the one that sat in the far right corner, the converted mews house proudly positioned so no one from the street could see it. From the outside, it was more robust than the others around it, with brick running up the facade. A small balcony jutted over the entryway, creating a sanctuary if one were caught in heavy rain; while lush green ivy snaked its way all around, the mid-August wisteria bringing a vibrancy to the place. It had a split barn door as the entrance, a remnant from its past occupants that was painted a cool sage green.

Bowen dangled the keys in my face, a coy smile playing on his lips. "Would you like to do the honors?"

I took them and put them in the lock, the key turning smoothly.

"I usually rent this place out, though, as stated in any contracts, I have the right to kick them out when I need it." Bowen pushed open the door that led into a long hallway.

I didn't want to know how much he charged for people to live here. Wooden floors ran from the entrance to the back kitchen, where it smoothly transitioned into Italian tiles. The walls were painted a soft beige and worked well with its tenants' pictures and nicknacks. Off to the right was a small living and dining room—plush couches and rustic barnyard furniture giving it an Italian-villa feel.

"Our room is in the attic," Bowen informed me as we ascended the stairs to the left of us. It didn't look it from the outside, but the house was big enough to comfortably fit our party of eight.

The others were directed to their own rooms as we made our way up until it was just Bowen and me who were left on the second flight of stairs. The large loft turned out to be the master bedroom, which used the whole width and length of the house, an en suite and lush king-size bed taking up most of the space. Its flooring was different from the one that greeted us, the gray wood contrasting well against the white and green accents of the room. Exposed beams in the ceiling let us see the original structure of the house, the thick, dark wood entwined with fairy lights and fake leaves. Compared to Bowen's mansion, this place was quite cozy in its close-quartered living.

"I had debated giving this room to your parents, but then I couldn't choose which parents to actually give it to," he said, chuckling, setting our stuff onto the floor in front of the bed.

It was a hard choice…

"Well, I'm glad you kept us neutral." I flopped onto the bed's pristine sheets, hints of lemon and thyme dancing to greet us.

"What do you want to do first? Eat? Unpack…?" He was just about to unzip his suitcase when Finch stepped through the door.

"Actually, I thought we'd start with a trip to the British Library…" He had already changed into new clothes and looked more ready to attend a gala dinner than enter a library. "There's someone I want you to meet."

Finch, Bowen, Jackie and I made our way to the British Library. The red-brick entrance stood proudly on the corner of Ossulston Street and Euston Road; its entrance gate was a sculpture with the words "British Library" repeatedly cut out of a sheet of steel.

"When the sun makes an appearance, the letters throw shadows onto the wall and floor," Bowen whispered in my ear.

I couldn't picture it. There was no sun today. Summer rain had replaced London's suffocating air, the throngs of people doing little to alleviate its smothering feel.

A statue of *Newton* by Eduardo Paolozzi gazed down on us as we passed from the courtyard and into the library. I was struck at the sheer size of the place. Buttermilk marble checkered the floors, its shine deceiving those visiting into thinking it was wet. To our right was an information station, library volunteers and workers directing people to where they wanted to go. Though it was packed with tourists and local readers waiting to view the many exhibitions on display, there was barely any noise, the tranquil atmosphere of a library kept in place.

We took the stairs up to the first floor, Finch leading us confidently. The inner sanctum of the library was a gigantic glass wall with books behind it. I thought we would make our way past the structure and go deeper into the bowels of the place, but we stopped by the door to the right of us, the words STAFF ONLY clearly displayed and a chain blocking our path.

Without skipping a beat, Finch unhooked the chain latch and knocked thrice on the door, then paused, then thrice again.

I gazed around us, aware of the eyes of interested students and jealous visitors wondering what we were doing.

A minute later, the door opened, a woman scowling at our intrusion.

"Sahar!" Finch barged in, giving her a hug and kisses on her cheek.

"Finch Evans." Her previous look of annoyance turned to joy, and she broke out into a smile. "What brings you to this side of town?"

We entered the room, the door closing silently behind.

Her black hair was longer than my own, and it lay straight against her back. She wore black slacks and a blouse—a uniform I presumed was dictated throughout the library—and stood as tall as Finch, their eyes level as she stared him down. The spices of red chili and turmeric scented the air around her, mixed with whatever fruity shampoo she had used this morning.

"I was just in the neighborhood and thought I'd pop by," he said innocently.

"Last time I saw you, security was escorting you out." She tapped her finger against her lip. "Somethin' about destruction of private property?"

Bowen's eyebrows pulled together in concern, his mouth turned down in disapproval.

"There was no destruction," Finch countered lightheartedly. "They wouldn't let me see a manuscript I wanted."

"So resorting to stealin' it was the next best option?" She smiled widely again, enjoying the interrogation. "How'd you even get through the front door?"

"Well, that *was* about a decade ago. I imagine there have been quite a few changes to the staff since then. I'm glad they didn't get rid of everyone," he said, winking at her.

He winked. I had never really seen Finch with any woman. For all I knew he could be a celibate monk, though I was highly doubtful after seeing the way Sahar was devouring him with her eyes.

"And still lookin' as good as ever." She lingered on him a moment longer, Jackie purposefully coughing to break the sexual tension.

"Ah, Sahar, meet my brother, Bowen; his girlfriend, Jade; and their friend, Jackie. Everyone, this is Sahar. You've been the Order's archivist for what now… twenty years?"

"Eleven," she corrected, slapping at his arm. "I'm only twenty-nine!"

"A mere child to my standards," he joked.

The three of us stood shell-shocked at the introduction. She was one of *them*. Part of the Order. And Finch had just led us in here like it was nothing.

Bowen's voice cracked against the glass walls, the insulated silence making it more pronounced. "Finch. What's the meaning of this?" His temper rose and I stood closer to him, a cautioning hand against his chest. If anyone was going to kill him, it was going to be me.

"Don't worry about it, love," Sahar said, placing her hand against her hip. "I ain't gonna tattle on you to the Order. This is neutral ground."

"I made sure of it," Finch began, "back in 1753 when the British Museum was first founded, stipulating that any and all information housed by the Order was open to the public. Not that anyone really cares about it except us. Everyone else thinks it's just a pile of ledgers about who's the Queen's favorite."

"Being a founder of the Order has its perks," Jackie said.

"It did…" Finch countered.

"Enough about that," Sahar thankfully cut in. "You'll be wanting to get into the stacks, yeah?"

"If you'd be so kind," Finch agreed.

She picked up a set of keys. "Sign in and I'll lead you down. As always, I must tell you the disclaimer for insurance purposes, no taking of anything from the stacks"—eyeing Finch intentionally—"don't do any damage to anything that is here, and no food or drink." She ended on a smile.

Finch scrawled his name into the ledger, but instead of Finch Evans as I had expected, the name Henry Eam stared back at me—a slap to anyone in the Order if they were to see it.

"Follow me." Sahar unlocked an inner door that revealed a landing and a set of spiral stairs. Though there was no natural light, crystal chandeliers provided enough brightness to let us see every nook and cranny.

When we got to the bottom of the stairs, we found that row upon row of metal shelves had been crammed together, a lever on each end to move them when needed. It reminded me of The Forest, but I knew this library would never house the extensive collection the former had.

"Look at anything you like. Cranks work clockwise to open, counterclockwise to close. Try not to get squashed between them… It happens more often than you'd think. There's another level below—the stairs just at the back," she said, pointing.

"Thanks, Sahar," Finch said enthusiastically.

She flashed him a flirtatious smile. "I'll leave you all to it then," she said, and made her way back upstairs.

We split up, each of us taking a century's worth of information, starting with my encounter with the Tree of Life in 1351. We spent hours skimming page after page, trying to find any information about the Tree. There were a couple of tidbits here and there but they were more or less things Jackie and I had already learned about on the Internet.

"The library is closing in ten minutes!" Sahar called from the top of the steps.

"We haven't even scratched the surface yet," I complained to Bowen.

"We'll come back tomorrow," he replied, rubbing at his eyes.

It had been a long day, and in the rush to try and comb through as much as we could, we hadn't taken any breaks.

XXIV
Finch
February, 1917

Finch could hear the sounds of guns firing off in the distance. Mud caked his boots as the three of them stealthily made their way through enemy lines just outside Belgium, the winter's cold freezing sweat and dirt to their faces. He reached around his backpack, unclipping a belt.

"Did you ever think we would live this long, brother?" He handed Bowen the last mine they were to place behind German lines.

"I plan on living much longer after this," he countered, carefully hiding it in some shrubs. "Just never thought we would get to this point."

"It is a bitch of a time at the moment." Finch activated the weapon, his hands steady as he set the clip.

"I would have pegged you to be a strategist rather than a frontman." Bowen took a swig from his canteen, his chest heaving as he tried to catch his breath.

"And miss out on all this action? Never."

Explosions were set off as the first of their traps was tripped, the German defenses cracking.

"That's our cue," Finch sang. "Get Richard out of here. We'll meet up with the rest of the Second Army on the northern flank."

Bowen left and helped their third brother-in-arms to his feet, his leg bleeding from a stray bullet that had passed their way, while Finch covered them. He wished for his powers at times like these, their loss a constant reminder of what he was fighting for.

When they met up with the rest of the Fourteenth, everyone was convened in HQ's tent.

"Finch," Fitz called to him, "good to see you're not dead."

Finch knew it was a sly joke. The Earl of Norfolk was his oldest friend and an ally of the Order. Not that Bowen knew this. Finch was still able to keep *some* of his secrets, knowing his brother would disapprove.

"Not yet," he jested, a look of seriousness passing between the two. This whole war Finch had been reckless—insane. He took on positions at the front line on purpose, curious to see if this day would really be his last.

"Well, the port seems to be well in hand and we should be in charge of it by nightfall. Come." He replaced his cane with a glass and goaded Finch over with sherry, the good stuff that only an earl would have been able to smuggle in behind the front lines. "Did you find out anything?"

Finch knew exactly what he was talking about. The Great War had started in part due to the assassination of Archduke Franz Ferdinand by the Black Hand. Or so the world believed.

In truth, it was on the Order's call, the archduke getting too close and knowing too much about their dealings with the Tree of Life, claiming he had information about its location.

"Nothing," Finch replied, venom in his words. "If the Order had just waited until I got there to interrogate the archduke, then perhaps we wouldn't be in this huge mess."

"Twenty-seven years we have been searching," Fitz reprimanded. "We weren't going to let the German's have it first."

"And centuries before that I've been looking," Finch growled in frustration. "Do not for a *second* think we'll find it that easily. I doubt the archduke really found anything—a mention of it perhaps, but not the real thing."

Fitz stroked at his white beard. Time had not been kind to him, the lines on his face growing deeper with age. "Then this was all for naught. No matter," he said, waving off the subject as if it were a bad smell. "I hear you and your brother are to be sent back home. Tired of the fight already?"

"We have drawn a bit of attention from our dealings in this war. Time to lie low and let others win it." He finished off his glass, his dirty hands smudging the crystal as he set it down. "I can't believe you came all this way, and at your age!"

"I've still got some fight left in me, old boy. But I think it right to accompany you home on your journey. There have been… whispers."

That wiped the smile from his face. "What kind?"

"That the King has personally stocked our treasury—put a backing onto our horse, as they say."

"It would prove useful, no doubt." Finch poured himself another glass, the sweet contents going down smoothly.

"The viscount wants to see you when you get to London. Something about information pertaining to an all-powerful witch, if you can believe it."

Finch's heart dropped. Of course, the Order knew about what happened in the Dark Ages, but he had never been specific, leaving out names and dates so nothing was ever marked down on paper. It would be too permanent. But if Grey had found something…

He glanced at Bowen, enthralled with the other officers about their plans once back home. "We need to go. *Now.*"

Finch and Fitz left Bowen at the boat and stepped into the car that was waiting for them, forgoing a ride home and one straight to Westminster. The snow-covered cobbled lane they drove up was quiet, a silence Finch hadn't heard since entering the war.

He adjusted his lieutenant's cap in his arm. "They can't seriously think a witch is in this time…" he probed. "They died out centuries ago. Even my own magic doesn't exist."

"I can't say, old boy. All I know is that there are rumors flying about… Just here please," he called to the driver.

They got out of the car, Fitz needing help to get from his seat and onto the street. Clouds rumbled overhead, their impending presence just moments away from a shower.

They entered through the side door of the house, its bricks almost black from the constant smog and soot from the chimneys of London. A section just to the left of them had crumbled away, the bombings leaving lots of places in rubble while sandbags lined the rest of the street.

"Everyone here?" Finch asked, handing his gloves and cap to the butler at hand.

"They should be. I sent word that we were to meet today." Fitz did the same, adding his cane to the mix.

They went through to the meeting room. Since Finch had joined the London branch all those years ago, it had become their regular spot to congregate—the Round Table, they had dubbed it. He always thought it was a funny name, as the faces he saw around it were no comparison to the legendary knights of the Arthurian tales. Yet each year new faces appeared, the others dying off one way or another. Fitz didn't look like he was too far behind and went to settle himself in his usual chair.

Their newest member, the fifth Marquess of Bath, Thomas Thynne, had a pretentious smirk, his eyes sparkling with whatever news he was waiting to tell. Unlike the others in the room, he had changed from his military uniform into more relaxed tails.

"Is this all who came?" Finch asked. With him and Fitz added to the room, they only totaled six.

"Not enough for you?" the marquess scoffed.

"Know your place, Thynne. As the newest member, you have little say in what is going on here." Finch missed the old days, when he was revered as somewhat of a god among men. Now he was being treated just like Fitz: as if he had one foot out the door.

"Can we hurry this up," the Earl of Beaucham, William Lygon, groaned, his Australian accent punching the words out. "I'm supposed to meet Robert in an hour."

The men shifted uncomfortably at the statement. It was known in most high society circles about his proclivities toward men—not that it ever hindered his political career. For a time he was known as Lady Lygon, his beauty captivating not only the men that trailed after him but the women as well, all fawning over the man who not only had the confidence but the bravery in a time when there was little when it came to such gossip.

"Quite," Viscount Edward Grey commented. He was a traditional man when it came to his appearance, the parting in his hair nearly as straight as his nose. The gray hair around his temples was cropped short, his captain's uniform tailored. "Sit, Finch, and we'll get a move on."

Finch took his seat, the rest taking theirs, leaving their other brothers' chairs empty. "Thank you, Grey. Fitz tells me you've found a witch who can locate the Tree?"

"It's not a powerful witch we've found," started Thynne.

"It's a powerful *book*!" Grey finished.

"I can't believe we're talking about this," Hardinge, Baron of Penshurst, sneered in a curmudgeonly fashion, his mustache turning up. The thinning of it was as pronounced as the hair on his head. He adjusted one of the medals on his uniform, the war creating heroes of those who never ought to be.

"Your right-wing politics standing in the way of change, Baron?" Grey goaded, tipping him a salute with his glass. "If you want to look outside the window and see where the world is at the moment, then be my guest. It will only go downhill from here… If we manage to live through this war that is."

"It's that sort of liberalism that's getting us to follow fairy tales and fantasies," Hardinge reprimanded.

"Are you saying my existence is a fantasy?" Finch interjected, his voice biting at the insult.

"Can you blame me?" Hardinge puffed. He leaned forward, his hands clenched on the smooth surface of the table. "All we have is your word, a thing too many these days can mold to their liking."

Everyone started as they heard Fitz's hand slap against the table, his face red. "If it wasn't for Finch, then the Order would not be what it is today," he snapped. "Mind your tongue, Charles, for I can just as easily tell the King about your wife and the lineage of your family."

Finch had never seen Hardinge silenced so quickly, the others hanging on their elder's words, curious to know what the secret could be.

"Tell us more," Lygon inquired, for once his personal life not being the topic of conversation.

"Enough," Finch commanded, his hand raised in a gesture of submission. "You are entitled to your opinion, Charles, and if you would rather not be a part of this meeting, then, by all means, you may step out." He emphasized the last words, implying that severe repercussions would ensue were he to leave.

The room was still, waiting for the baron to make his choice.

"No?" Finch asked when he made no move to leave. "Then shut up." He quickly turned his attention to the viscount. "Grey, you were saying something about a book?"

"Yes…" Sweat beaded down the side of his face. "Our researchers have found a book that could potentially give us information about the location of the Tree of Life."

Finch's breath caught. How many years now had he been waiting to hear those words, to finally be on track?

"It was hidden in a manuscript on loan to us. As you know, the museum has made it their top priority to be a safe haven for knowledge in this war, and we just happened to luck out, as the Americans would say."

"Do you have it with you?" Finch asked, eager to make sense of what was needed to be done.

"It's under heavy protection. Every time one of our researchers touched it, they came away unable to remember what they saw. Its owner mustn't even know its true purpose! Thank the heavens we finally had them working in two-man groups and not by themselves, otherwise we would have overlooked it again," Grey explained.

"Where are you keeping it now?" Finch stood up, his brow furrowed in concentrated frustration.

"With the Order's stacks at the British Museum."

Fitz rejoiced. "Good, good! We'll make a trip there after this and have a look for ourselves, eh, Finch?"

Finch was stuck in his own thoughts, and a somber look passed across his features. "Gentlemen," he started, "we are at a turning point. If we can find the Tree, then this could stop the war, and every war in the future."

Every head in the room nodded, except for Fitz's, whose stone-faced reaction left Finch feeling guilty.

Finch was led from the building, Grey accompanying him and Fitz to the museum. The others were left behind, the meeting over for the day. Though the Museum Mile had been packed to the brim with sandbags and makeshift medical tents, it was still the fastest way to get to the museum, the outside roads blocked with checkpoints and fallen buildings that slowed down traffic.

Finch looked around the Mile. So much war he had seen… but never on this scale.

"It's horrible," Grey commented as they ascended the stairs into the museum.

"Not something one should get used to," Finch agreed, his own past actions creeping into mind.

They made their way to an abandoned section of the museum; a hallway that only the Order used was marked DO NOT ENTER for everyone else. Finch had been here countless times, either to donate more books or to try and research for himself where the Tree could be located. It was only once he gained the trust and backing of the other Order members that a research team was put in place, giving him a reprieve from the endless task.

"Which manuscript did you find it in? Is it a grimoire? Did you leave it where it was?" Finch had so many questions, he could barely contain his excitement.

"We didn't remove the pages if that's what you mean. It was quite the story the research team presented to us when they found it, the book practically hiding in plain sight." Grey opened the door to the stacks, the room filled with tables piled high with books, people's noses stuck far into them searching for more clues. "Letty should have more information."

They zigzagged their way around the people and books, typewriters clicking away as they wrote up their reports.

"Letty!" Grey called from the other side of a bookshelf, the shelves dusty in some areas where they hadn't yet removed the books.

The woman that turned toward them was a gorgeous creature. Her brown hair was curled in the fashion, her red lips parting ever so slightly as she recognized who had called for her. She wore trousers (of all things) with calf-high strap-up boots. Her burgundy coat clung to her waist with the help of a belt, the velvety folds of it falling to her knees.

Finch couldn't take his eyes off her.

"Edward Grey," she said with a smile. "And Finch Evans… My, my, the big dogs have come for some answers. How are you doing, soldier?" Her Irish accent practically sang with the words as she shook Finch's hand.

He hadn't been down there in years, the war taking up most of his time, so Letty had taken charge of the search. It was the first time he had met her in person, her personality shining into the deep cracks of his heart. "As best as I can," he replied. It was a roundabout answer that most soldiers gave to civilians. They didn't need to know the horrors he had seen.

Letty nodded, knowing this was the best he could give. "Well, no need to beat around the bush, gentlemen. I'll take you to the book." She shut the tome she was reading, its weight looking hefty in her delicate hands, and led them deeper into the stacks. "We did our best to keep it contained, unsure whether other books or objects might react around it."

"Smart," Finch commented. He liked the way she thought. He had met too many people in the past who flippantly abandoned caution when it came to the preternatural. To find someone who still had a head on her shoulders made a nice change.

They came upon a guarded room, the sentry armed with an Enfield strapped over his shoulder. Finch thought it overkill.

No one was going to be coming for this book as they were the only ones who knew about its existence… so far.

Letty pulled out a ring of keys and, flipping to the third one on the chain, unlocked the door.

Inside, the room was dark. A dim light swung slightly overhead to save what electricity they could, and it cast long shadows into the corners of the room. In the middle was a steel table, its legs worn and surface scratched, the edges looking almost as sharp as a blade. The only thing on it was a hefty-looking bookstand, but it paled in comparison to the volume that sat upon it.

Finch stood horrified. He knew that book, had seen it countless times on Bowen's shelves.

"Here it is, gentleman," Letty pronounced triumphantly.

"What's wrong, Finch," Grey asked.

"That's impossible…" His disbelief consumed him. When was the last time he had been to his brother's house? Four, maybe five years ago… "When did you get this?" It had been staring him in the face all along, taunting him.

"The owner is off in the war and lent it to the museum for safekeeping," Letty explained. "I begged him for us to be allowed to look at it but he had said no, perhaps knowing the secret it kept." She sighed dishearteningly. "But my curiosity won out in the end. And a good thing it did."

No one knew Finch had a brother, or vice versa. It was something they rarely told outsiders, their privacy kept as much to themselves as it was to strangers. But Finch knew his brother had no idea what this book really held. For Bowen, it was a reminder of Jade, how she'd saved him, but for him… For him, it was a reminder of his immortality, of the countless cursed lives he had lived.

TO THOSE WHO SURVIVE

The Monksblood Bible.

"We have examined its contents," she continued, unencumbered by Finch's reticence, and pulled on a pair of thick gloves, "and the most interesting pages we have come up with are those splattered with blood at the back. We have sent them for analysis, but I'm not going to hold my breath." She picked it up carefully, flipping through the pages. "All in all, it looks like a regular Bible, yet bring it close to a light"—she lit a candle and placed it so close to the page Finch wished it would burn it right then and there—"you can see there is a slight glint from the parchment."

"Fascinating." Grey moved closer to her, looking from every angle. "And the gloves let you handle the document without forgetting what you saw once you release it?"

"Correct," she said, placing the candle and book back in their respective places. "We haven't been able to get much farther than this, I'm afraid, but we can only assume a huge amount of magic would be able to do this."

Finch was the expert in this area and they all looked to him for confirmation. All he gave was a curt nod. He needed to get that book back to Bowen.

This was more dangerous than he had expected.

XXV
Finch
February, 1917

Finch climbed silently over the gates into the museum's delivery entrance, the unmanned position perfect for his infiltration. He found a window that was close to where the book was being stored, and with a knife, he unhooked the latch that held it shut. It was well past midnight and the researchers hadn't been there for hours, Finch waiting until every last one had clocked out before making his move.

He had to get that book back to Bowen.

What was he thinking, parting with it so easily?

He crouched through the window and dropped onto one of the tables that lined the side of the room. Papers shifted under his foot as he moved onto the floor, having to replace them as best he could. He hadn't stolen anything in centuries, the last being a highway job in 1738 that ended with him in jail for three years—the only sentence that could be carried out—while the others hanged.

Using what little moonlight crept through the windows, he

found his way back to the room where the Monksblood Bible was being kept. There was an absence of sound except for the light touch of his feet against the ground. There was no guard keeping watch at night, the Order arrogant enough to think no one would be stupid enough to try and steal it from them.

Taking out a piece of thick piano wire, Finch curled it until it matched the key hole. It went in smoothly, and with a *click*, the door swung open, when he heard a voice behind him.

"Looking for something, old boy?"

His heart raced as he whirled around, sure he had waited until everyone was gone. So what was Fitz still doing there?

"Fitz," he exclaimed, bent over, his hand reaching for his heart. "You nearly gave me a heart attack. What brings you here?"

"I could ask you the same question, but it seems you have already found what you're looking for." He gestured toward the book behind him and took out his handkerchief, wiping his mouth. "You think the Order will let you get away with stealing that when they have come so close?"

Finch stood straight, his eyes piercing. "You know what I have gone through to find the Tree."

"I know." He bobbed his head in understanding, a cough afflicting him. Fitz didn't look good, the pale sweat on his forehead glistened even in the darkness. "You want to find the Tree and see if plunging one of its branches into your heart will finally kill you."

Finch stood silently, the weight of his friend's words hanging heavily in the room.

"I have lived too long already, Fitz." Finch's eyes pleaded for understanding, if not for Fitz's sake then for his own. But his friend didn't react. Finch backed his way further into the room and picked up the book with his gloved hand. "This can solve everything."

Fitz's cane struck the ground as he came closer to him, the handkerchief placed over his mouth and nose in an attempt to subdue another cough. "I fear you have barely lived at all, old boy. What have you done in your life except be eaten by your guilt and obsess over something that could already be dead and gone? My own days are numbered, I know that, but I have my wife, my children, my grandchildren. Stop this vendetta you have toward yourself and go *live*. Fall in love. Teach history to future generations, but stop living as if you already have one foot in the grave." He took the book from Finch, making sure his handkerchief was placed around it.

Finch faced his best friend, the white handkerchief speckled with blood.

"Fitz..." he started, but was swatted away.

"I know, I know. My time is almost here. That is why, old boy, what I am about to do is out of love, not malice."

He shoved the leather binding of the book into Finch's face, connecting it with his skin. Finch stumbled back, grabbing Fitz on his way down, both falling to the floor.

Finch felt woozy as he came to his senses, the metallic tang of magic in his mouth a dryness he hadn't felt in eons. He pushed up onto his elbow to steady himself as he tried to stand, his body heavy. He couldn't get his mind straight, the stars dancing around his eyes taking precious seconds to clear.

But he wished they hadn't.

Lying on the floor in front of him was his best friend, a pool of blood around him.

Finch moved unsteadily as he made his way over to him, his fingers hesitant as he felt his neck for a pulse. There was none.

"Fitz." He shook the man by the shoulder. There was a deep gash across his forehead. Finch examined the room, trying to find the culprit, but he only found a trail of blood at the edge of the corner of the table. "Fitz!"

There was no rotary dial in the room to call for help, no other signs of life anywhere in the vicinity, and he wouldn't leave his friend's body in such a public state. He looked down once more, trying to find some sign of what had happened and found Fitz's arm outstretched, his handkerchief in his hand, but it wasn't the only thing he was holding. Finch's jaw went tight at the sight of it.

What is he doing with my brother's book?

He put two and two together as he picked it up. The museum wasn't meant to have this book, no one was. It was a stain on his past, but a treasured remembrance for Bowen. Finch glanced back down at his friend.

What happened?

The only plausible conclusion was that he had killed his best friend while trying to recover the tome.

Finch stood, hands shaking as he placed it into his satchel and ran from the room.

There would be no going back to the Order now.

XXVI

A headache was already working its way into my mind as I closed the twentieth book I had read through. So far we hadn't found anything that would even point us in the right direction.

"Useless," I said, as I shoved the thing away, my nerves already fried.

"Do you want to take a break?" Bowen reached over and tucked a strand of my hair behind my ear, his touch warm.

"Yes. No. I don't know," I confessed, my head in my hands. "Why can't we find anything?"

"We're looking for a magical tree in a world with no magic," he retorted softly. He moved closer, his mouth hovering over my own, and parted my lips with his tongue, kissing me deeply, as if by doing so he could solve all our problems.

"Bowen…" I pulled away, his eyes gleaming in the fluorescent lighting. "Sadly, that's not really helping us."

"No, it's not." Jackie stepped out from the end of the aisle, a sour look on her face. She continued down to us, a small volume in hand. "I might have found a mention of something. I think it's about the Tree of Life, but I'm also seeing references to the *magna pythonissam*." She sounded out each syllable. "I'd finished reading all the English texts, and though my Latin is a bit rusty..."

Bowen and I stood, our kiss forgotten.

"The Great Witch," I said in awe.

Bowen held out his hand for the book, Jackie readily giving it up. "*The Great Witch*—as we can assume, the Exalted Witch—" he translated, "*is a creature of immense power. No one knows who he is, or what the nature of his power holds, but I have been told that their appearances have been few, the last to be found in the Middle Ages.*" He cocked an eyebrow in surprise. "This is about you." He continued on. "*It is said that the creature had reign over the elements and was strong enough to tame seas or set alight a great fire. If such a creature were to exist then we can all but hope they are the key to finding the TOL.*"

We stood there stunned, my hands thrumming with magic as I could feel its tingling move all the way down to my feet.

He closed the book and handed it to me, letting me inspect its cover, which had worn gold filigree letters that spelled out the word JOURNAL. I flipped to the title page, where in elegant script was written: *The Thoughts of Henry Fitzalan-Howard, 15th Duke of Norfolk.*

"I know that name..." Bowen took the book back, running his fingers along the text, his eyebrows pinched together in concentration. He flipped back to the page we had been reading before. "*The First Knight, who has been a friend since my acceptance into the Order, has been searching for centuries for the TOL. I fear that his obsession with his internal questions has consumed him and may lead to his death. If this continues, the Order may have no use for him, and vice versa.*"

"First Knight?" I asked.

"Henry Eam," Finch interrupted, popping up out of nowhere. "Me." His stride was languid as he came over and took the book from his brother, his hand hesitant as he reached for it. Finch cradled it with the tips of his fingers, the diary almost floating upon them. "I didn't even know he kept a journal." His face was heavy with regret, and he seemed to try and hide the tears in his eyes.

I had never seen Finch so emotional. He had begged me for forgiveness, but even then he'd had a sort of pride to uphold, but now…

"He was my best friend," he said, breathing out, a past pain consuming his emotions.

We stood there unsure of what to do—what to say.

"The reason I was excommunicated from the Order was because I killed him. I'd killed a fellow member. I didn't fight the ruling, knowing what I'd done." He looked to his brother, trying to find understanding in his eyes. "You remember 1917? When you loaned the British Museum the Monksblood Bible?"

Bowen nodded, his face straight. "I was convinced that the bombing might reach all the way to *Y Goedwig*. The museum was a fortress and they had better facilities at the time," he explained.

"I didn't know that. All I saw was that he had the book. I can't even remember how it happened, but I must have snapped at seeing him with it." He stroked the cover of the journal, feeling the rough leather.

"You can't blame yourself, Finch," Bowen said.

"I never met another man like him," he mused, and

dismissed the memories, returning to the present. "This is dated the year he died. We should split up and look for other journals. Other Order members may have kept some as well."

Bowen nodded sympathetically.

We found an old registry of the people who had once been members, dating back to 1348, and divided the names among us. Searching at the end of the room I found another member's journal, this one looking in better condition than the last.

I reached for it, only for another hand to bump into mine. "Oh, sorry, if you need that then go ahead."

"No, Miss Morrison, it's all yours."

I peered to my right to find an older gentleman looking down at me. He was tall, with a shock of trimmed white hair. Thin wire-framed glasses were perched on his nose, giving him an older scholarly look, but he couldn't have been more than fifty-five. He stood with an arrogance I could see up close, the gray of his eyes like storm clouds ready to strike. His black suit was immaculate, a shield of gold with a black cross stitched onto his breast pocket a bright contrast.

He reached for the book and held it out to me, our fingers brushing briefly at the exchange. They were cold, and I saw the glint of a pinky ring with an emblem forged into the metal.

"There you are," he said triumphantly, as if he had finally found a lost item.

"Excuse me?" I asked, concerned.

"Bouncing around from Wales to America to Wales again, then up to Scotland and now England. Very smart. It took us some time to pinpoint your exact location, and by then you had already left for the Dark Ages. But when you came back… It was as if you were goading us to take you." His eyes glinted.

My magic prickled under my skin, the threat prominent in his words.

"Where are my manners?" he said, shaking his head at his blunder. "Aaron Mannheim, Secretary to the Order of the Garter."

My mind went blank at the introduction. Since arriving at the library barely anyone but us had been down there. We had gone a week being overly cautious and vigilant about the Order finding us, but since we hadn't heard a peep from them, we'd fallen into a false sense of security. And it was now costing us.

He held out his hand, waiting, but I wasn't about to grab it. He quickly lowered it to his side. "We wanted to find you in the hope that you would come and work for us."

"Work for you?" I asked, taken aback.

"Well, yes. You see, we have been searching for the Tree of Life since before you were born, and when we got in contact with Gwenllian about her help, she refused. Naturally, we thought you could be of some service to us."

"You want me to help you find the Tree of Life, so you can—what?—rule over the world."

He chuckled, the whites of his teeth flashing. "Is that the lie your mother has been feeding you? No, no, no. We are trying to make the world *better*." If *I* didn't know better, it sounded like he was the one about to spout lies. "Imagine powering a whole city with something the size of a battery, or pacemakers—electrical equipment that could save peoples' lives—that would never run out of energy."

My eyebrows were raised at the prospect. In all honesty, I had never thought of that application. The Tree was a source of natural energy, powerful energy, that had ruled over the world for millennia. Why not harness its force for more? But I knew that with every utopian outlook, there was a dystopian catch. As Dad always said: *If someone's offering you something too good to be true, it usually is.*

I planted my feet firmly, pinpointing exactly where the trick lay. "And countries would line up out the door for the chance to have it… for a price?" I countered.

He towered over me as he came in closer, his voice but a whisper. "Well… the UK would have a patent claim on any findings and building materials, and people would have to pay for it. This is a capitalist world, as you know."

"And the fact that you'd basically be taking over the world twenty-first-century style doesn't play at all into your plans?"

Panic was ascending into my chest, the intensity of my magic threatening to break free against the man in front of me. *Where's Bowen? Jackie?*

The smile he gave me sent chills up my spine, the storm in his eyes finally striking. "Not at all."

"Aaron." Finch came up behind him, slapping his hand onto the man's shoulder hard enough that he actually winced. "What brings you down to this part of the stacks?"

"Just going through some old files," Aaron said, pushing him off, "and I just happened to run into Miss Morrison here." It seemed his hair wasn't the only thing that was silver; his tongue seemed to be coated in the stuff.

Finch moved between us, his body acting as a shield. "I highly doubt that," he replied.

Aaron peeked around him and extended his business card to me. "Let me know what you think, Miss Morrison." He looked back at Finch, who snatched it from his hand. "Mr. Evans," he sneered, and walked off.

My mind felt like it was about to explode as the room spun around me. Before I could even get to my first set of questions, Finch was on me, his eyes showing genuine worry in them.

"Are you alright? What did he say? Did he hurt you?"

The prickling in my fingers magnified as I felt my magic pool into them, sweat running down my back.

Shitshitshit.

I dropped the book and stumbled down the hall, the walls seeming to close in as I burst into a private meeting room. My palms slammed against rough concrete, its coolness useless against the heat of my hands, which were now engulfed in bright red flames. It took every aching muscle in my body to force the magic back inside me.

I turned as Finch came toward me with outstretched arms, seeming to be looking to help me. "Don't come near me right now!" My stomach heaved on the last word and I emptied it onto the floor next to me. Sweat dampened the back of the neck, my legs wobbling as I tried my best to hold myself up. "I'm okay."

Finch wasn't convinced and he took my arm, leading me gingerly out of the private room and back to the stacks. He found a chair for me to sit on. "You need sugar. You look like you're going into shock."

"Bowen… I need… Bowen…" My teeth chattered, making the words staccato.

He searched in his pockets and pulled out a caramel.

"What are you? Eighty?" The attempt at a joke was unsuccessful, my jaw clamping shut, making Finch worry even more.

"Finch." Bowen spotted us down the aisle, his eyes hard as he saw the state I was in and he reached for his brother's collar. "What happened?"

"She's in shock. The Order found her. We need to get out of here," he replied.

Then everything moved quickly. We were out of the stacks within minutes and back at the entrance of the library. I don't remember how we got back to our place, a vague memory of a taxi carting us back home playing around my mind.

My body vibrated as my magic begged to be released.

Gwenllian was there, taking my face in her hands, trying to give me directions on what to do, but I could barely hear her, the world sounding as if it was underwater.

I must have blacked out at some point because when I woke up I was on the couch, Bowen sitting on the floor in front of me, his head leaning against a cushion. He looked so peaceful when sleeping, the prominent furrow of his brow smooth.

What the hell am I doing?

I thought about what Aaron had proposed. Would it be worth working with them to find the Tree of Life? There was some truth in what they wanted to do. The Tree could sustain enough energy to power the world for millions of years, but it was dying, and there would be no point in powering a world that was already on its way to destruction.

No, fixing the Tree was what was needed, and I wasn't about to let anyone else mess with the balance of things.

XXVII

When I woke, I found the sun streaming through the window, the space next to me empty. Slowly getting up, I made my way to the bathroom, the large mirror showing the horror of my encounter with the Order yesterday. I turned away and started the process of running a bath and adding salt to the water in the hope its crystals would calm the tight muscles throughout my body.

As I stepped into the tub, I could feel the warm water wash over me, my mind calming as I sank deeper. My head rested on the small pillow that dangled at the edge, wisps of my hair floating in the soapy water.

Trust Bowen and Finch, for they will help lead you to the Tree.

The Black Prince's instruction resounded once again in my head. *Trust.* I had trust in Bowen, trust in everyone that had helped me so far, but Finch... Just as the prince said, *I* needed to be the one to find the Tree—I was its counterbalance.

Much later, and with my skin prune-like, I stepped out of the now ice-cold tub and wrapped myself in a soft towel, the scents of vanilla and hibiscus wafting around me. I took my time as I dried my hair, trying to gain some semblance of normalcy for once. The black roots on my feet now felt as if they had always been there, their twisting branches beautiful. I imagined what Haf would have said at the sight of them, her aghast intake of breath bringing a smile to my lips. How things had changed since then... How even more crazy the world had become...

My mind wandered as I picked out my clothes from the dresser, the day calling for lighter clothing than usual as the sun shone brightly through the open window onto the bed, when I spotted something big and brown upon it. I thought it was Simone, her feline tendency to find the most comfortable spot for a nap astounding, but when I had a closer look, it wasn't her soft form that I found on the cushiony duvet, but the Monksblood Bible.

What are you doing here?

Gingerly, I picked it up, the binding still cracked in places, and opened it to feel the taut parchment underneath my fingers. Its roughness was meditative as I felt my way across its pages, admiring the handiwork that went into the scriptures, when a glint on the wall caught my eye. I thought nothing of it, the sun catching the window at just the right angle perhaps, but when I turned to another page in the book, the pattern on the wall changed as well.

I held a tentative hand up between the book and sun, interrupting the path of light. I regarded the book as I held it up, the pages shimmering as I turned them this way and that. It had never done this before, the question as to why it was doing it now not the only one running around my head.

What are you?

"*The answer.*"

I threw the book back onto the bed, its pages flipping erratically back and forth as the sun glinted from it.

"*It is finally time,*" it sighed in relief.

"Time? Time for what?"

The pages stopped flapping, opening onto the spread stained with Bowen's blood.

I approached it once again, hesitant of what it might do next, and before my eyes, I watched as the script drifted away.

No longer did the pages hold rhythmic calligraphy as it had before; now what replaced it was a depiction of the Tree of Life.

Its leaves were coated in filigree as bright as crystal, the thick trunk like molten gold as its branches waxed and waned on a passing breeze. Its roots extended to the bottom of the page... No, not just to the bottom, but crept past the edges of the book and down the bed to connect with those at my feet.

In that instant I felt its omnipotence consume my mind. Everything the Tree had ever witnessed, felt, and lived through poured into me in a wave until my knees buckled and I found myself in a pool of water.

I wasn't sure where I ended up, someplace between the past and present, death and life... a sort of dark limbo that seemed like a dreamer's paradise. There was water all around me reflecting my image back in its pristine, dark surface. When I looked deeper, I could see the Tree, its leaves dipping into the water, upside down.

The Tree!

"Beautiful, isn't it?" A woman's voice carried to me, the sound as smooth as honey, seductive.

I looked in the direction of the voice and was awestruck seeing the person in front of me, my excitement forgotten.

She looked heavenly, her hair as white as fresh snow on a winter's morning against an onyx backdrop. Her eyes held a soft fierceness to them, though it was more a feeling than recognition since they were clouded over, her irises barely visible. The red dress she was wearing seemed to float about her form, its shape constantly changing. She was seated haughtily on a golden cloud, a galaxy of stars behind her. There was an hourglass next to her elbow, the white sand slithering between each bulb without her needing to turn it. She held out a delicate hand, as if reaching for some unknown trinket, her fingers pulling at an invisible thread beside her.

"Yes," I replied, too awestruck to find a better answer.

"That's not the real one, by the way, just its mirror image." My heart sank. "It is a shame that it's dying…" Her eyes sharpened at the remark and I shrank away from their piercing gaze.

"Yes…" I looked back down into the water, and no longer was the Tree vibrant colors, but it had withered and sickened, all the life having been sucked out of it. I looked again to her. "Who are you?"

She sat up and stood onto the water. I would have expected ripples to form as a result, but the surface remained calm.

"I've had many names in the past: Manāt, Ananke, Kāla, Ori, Etu… But you may know me better as Fate."

The stars behind her seemed to glow brighter, the water moving out of her path. My heart beat loudly as she approached, each of her steps silent until she was right in front of me.

"So, what are you going to do about it?" She gestured toward the Tree.

"We've been looking for months now and we still haven't found anything." I could feel the prickles of fear up my spine, my temptation to flee growing with her every step. It wasn't just her physical prowess, but the way she moved, the way she held herself—the confidence, arrogance, and danger all a threat that had me trembling.

She placed a light hand on my cheek, her eyes squinting. "Stop whining. Don't think. What do you want to do?" As quiet as her voice was, she might as well have screamed the words with the amount of venom in them.

"S-s-save the Tree."

"And?"

"R-r-restore the balance of the world."

"No matter the price?"

"Yes," I answered instinctively. I would do *anything* to bring back the balance, anything to put right what I had made wrong.

"Even if that means death?"

"Yes."

I didn't hesitate with my answer. If it was a choice between my death or the thousands—millions—of lives that would be otherwise lost, then I would do it.

I won't let the past repeat itself.

She seemed to calm at my answer, the skin around her nose wrinkling with amusement. She touched my temple with two fingers, and in an instant I could feel the pull of the Tree. Images flashed before my eyes: the city of London, an old pub, a broken clock, a medallion of the Tree of Life, and my bare feet against ash. I tried to memorize the images, making sure I knew them by heart before making any sort of movement.

"Now you know where to look." She removed her fingers from my temple and turned away, seeming content to leave me with the jumble of information.

"What about the Order?" I croaked, as she made her way back to her cloud. She touched the hourglass beside her, leaving the sand suspended between the two bulbs, stopping time.

"What about them?"

"They want the Tree for themselves… to covet its power."

"They will *never* find the Tree of Life, for it has never been their fate to find it. But you…" She leaned on an elbow, her eyes shining. "You have always had a connection to the Tree, and it to you. When you first came into this world I knew you were special—more so than anyone else. And connecting you with the Tree… it's my best work yet." She sat back, her form once more languid upon the golden cloud, seeming content, and she lifted her hand as if to say I was free to leave.

A second later I was back in our bedroom. Night had somehow fallen, and with it, the room had become cooler. I was shivering, still in my towel, my hair damp and plastered against my chilled skin. I glanced down at my feet, the roots still in place. If anything, they looked as if they had risen above my ankles.

A God… I just met a God. Goddess, to be more precise, her form both beautiful and terrifying.

The Monksblood Bible was still open on the bed, the depiction of the Tree of Life staring back at me. I looked down at it and placed my fingers ever so gently to touch the artwork.

"Found you," I murmured triumphantly.

The door to the room creaked open, Bowen's head popping in through the gap. "Is it okay to come in?"

"Yes," I said, smiling at him. I hadn't even noticed there were tears streaming down my face until he rushed over to wipe them away.

He can't know the price...

"What's the matter, *cariad*?" Despite yesterday's ordeal, he looked more relaxed than I had seen him in months. His usual business suit was replaced with loose-fitting jeans that hugged him at the waist, a T-shirt with an eighties band's logo on the front, and despite the chilly weather, he was barefoot.

"I found it." I practically sang the words.

But there's a cost...

"What? What did you find?" His voice was soft with concern.

I stared down at the book in front of us.

"The Monksblood Bible… What's it doing here?" He picked it up, analyzing the picture. "This wasn't in there before."

"The Tree of Life."

"Yes, I know what it is, but there were never illustrations in this book before…"

"No," I said insistently. "I found the Tree of Life. I know what I need to do."

Shock didn't quite fully convey the emotions that played on his face. There was awe, fear, and curiosity also rolled into one. I could see the questions on his lips, yet his voice, for once, failed him.

I let him mull things over as I got dressed, the air too cold to stay wrapped only in a towel. Taking a page out of Bowen's book, I threw on jeans and a T-shirt, adding socks and shoes and feeling much more comfortable. I didn't know why I was so calm, as if nothing else in the world mattered at that moment—as if all my anxiety, all the stress and other baggage I had been carrying around with me since coming back to the twenty-first century, suddenly *didn't matter*. I had to leave now, before anyone could stop me.

"How?" he said finally.

"Fate guided me," I answered. Still in the closet, I pulled out a small duffle bag and filled it with what I thought I would need when looking for the Tree.

"Doesn't she for everyone..." he said philosophically.

"No. Fate... the actual deity, the goddess." He didn't see as I left the bag by the door, too busy with the Bible. "She was haunting and gorgeous and terrifying all at once. She sat on a golden cloud and there was a pool of water and—"

He looked at me as if I was mad, his face concerned.

"I've not gone crazy," I said quickly—defensively—switching my tone. *I'm sorry to do this to you...*

"I never said you had."

"You didn't have to, your face says everything."

He set down the Bible and guided me to sit on the bed. "I'm just... I'm worried we're putting too much pressure on you."

I stood and paced around the room, my rage racing through my veins. *I have to make it look real.* "News flash! What do you think the events of the past year have been about?"

"Jade," he said, "don't you think I wanted everything to turn out differently?"

"I don't know. You seemed pretty content with how everything's turned out."

"I'm not," he growled, standing. "I wanted you to *not* have to go through everything that you did. If I could do it all over again I'd—"

"What?" I shouted. "What would you have done?"

"I would have left you with Gwenllian! I would have made sure you never stepped foot in Lampeter! I would have protected you better!"

"This isn't about you!" I snapped back. "This is about the world. The stupid, fucking world that is going to shit because of something *I* did."

"It is *not* your fault." His hands shook with the fury in his words and he grabbed my arm. "Stop acting like a damsel in distress. You are a warrior, and warriors don't fight alone."

"You want a warrior?" I asked through gritted teeth, my body smoldering with ivy-green flames. "Fine. Then I'll give you a warrior."

XXVIII
Finch

Finch heard a great *thump* shake the whole house, the ice in his whisky clinking.

"What was that?" Gwenllian asked, holding onto her laptop for dear life.

"Sounds like it came from Jade and Bowen's room," Dave said, his work lying around him as he tried to figure out a calculation.

"I'll check on them." Finch got up from the couch. Yesterday had been exhausting, and he'd not for a second thought Aaron would show up to surprise them like that. He had left his name in the registry book so the Order could see he'd made good on his end and brought Jade to London. He had waited days for them to get in contact with him to see how they were to move forward, but Aaron had pushed him aside, no longer keeping him in the loop.

Ascending the stairs, he found their door open, both of them inside—Jade, in all her magical glory, was aflame and had Bowen pinned to the ground.

Finch rushed to them, his hands meeting with the flames as he tried to break them apart. "Ow! What the hell is going on?"

"He thinks I've gone mad!" Jade exclaimed, twisting his brother's arm further.

"She has! She thinks she's found the Tree of Life! That she met a goddess!"

"You've found the Tree?" This was what Finch had been waiting for, a breakthrough and a higher power to show them the way.

"That's not what's important," Bowen argued, squirming.

"Of course it is!" Finch left his brother to Jade. Whatever their dispute with each other, it had nothing to do with him. "Where is it, Jade? Where's the Tree?"

"It's here in London," she replied.

So close... This whole time, it was so close. "We need to go there."

"You aren't going anywhere! *I'm* going *alone*," she exclaimed.

"See, she's gone mad!" Bowen directed his next words to her. "If you think we're going to let you do this by yourself, you've got another thing coming."

"You think you'll be able to follow me? I can use magic to get there."

"Can you two stop before you break his arm, please! I know it'll be fine, but I can't help remembering the time my own was crushed under a steel pipe."

Jade finally let go of him, both retreating to opposite ends of the room. He had been witness to their sparring before, but this was way beyond that.

"Now, start again," Finch instructed. "Where in London is the Tree of Life."

"I don't quite know exactly..." she confessed. "I just have a feeling about it."

"A feeling?" Finch asked.

"A *strong* feeling."

Finch and Bowen shared a glance, like a silent conversation passing between them. "I think Bowen is right, it's not smart to go alone. And if you try to," he said before she could reply, "I'll use GPS to find you."

"I'm not an idiot. I'd get rid of my phone," she countered, smirking.

"Who said the chip was in your phone?" That seemed to wipe the smile off her face. With magic it would be easy to conceal her presence, but thankfully she hadn't mastered that technique yet.

The flames on her body softened and then sputtered out completely, the fight already won by him.

"Fine," she growled unenthusiastically as she went and threw a duffle bag back in the closet, "but I get to pick when we go."

"Deal," Bowen said before Finch had a chance to argue. "When do you want to leave?"

She thought for a second. "Give me three days."

Finch didn't stay for the rest of the conversation. He had been prepared for when Jade would finally find the Tree, but he'd not expected it this quickly. There were still threads that needed untangling.

Grabbing a sweater, he left the house, his mind buzzing about what to do next.

The Order... What will their next move be?

He made his way to The Curious Tadpole pub and sat in

his usual spot in the far corner facing the entrance. It was an old habit of his, adamant about being able to see everyone in the room and knowing where every exit was.

The pub had been there since the seventies, its original founder a bright woman with blonde hair and green eyes, one of the more outspoken women of that era, which made the watering hole an eclectic place for activists like Dora Russell and Olive Morris to meet up.

The inside was dark, the wooden features clashing with the blue wallpaper that was slightly faded in places. Framed pictures of famous old musicians and celebrities decorated the walls. For a Wednesday night, the place was full—artsy hipsters and golden oldies intermingling. Live music was playing, loud enough to hear but not deafening to anyone trying to have a conversation.

"Here's your usual, Finch." Korey placed a local ale in front of him. He had been working at the place for twenty years now, never questioning the lack of change in Finch's appearance. Finch had asked him about it once on a whim, Korey giving him a cheeky glare. "This is London. Everyone's a li'l bit different here. Plus you're never late on paying the tab."

He was right about that…

"Cheers, Korey." His phone rang. He looked at the number and rolled his eyes. "'Scuse me." He picked up the call. "I'm in the back." Then he hung up.

A minute later he saw Aaron making his way toward him, a sour look on his face. "Why do you insist on coming to this godforsaken dump?" Aaron asked as he took the chair next to him, wiping the seat clean.

"I like it here. It reminds me of a time when things were

more relaxed," Finch replied. From where he was sitting, Finch could see the chair just three tables away where he'd had his first hit of cannabis. He had liked the effects until they started experimenting with adding MDMA as well, which made his nightmares turn trippy. "You do know I'd left my real name on the sign-in sheet in the hope that you'd see that I'd played by your rules, not so you could randomly show up and threaten Jade like that? And when you slipped me your number I didn't know what to think, as I don't swing that way, but I'm glad it came in handy."

Aaron flushed at the implication, his clenched fists banging the table in front of him. "For heaven's sake, what did you call me here for?"

Finch leaned in closer, his eyes scanning the bar and the tables around them, making sure no one else was listening. "I just wanted to know what value the Tree is to you. I mean, your conversation with Jade aside, I understand why the UK would want such a terrifying resource, but you... What is it worth to *you*?"

Aaron seemed like he was assessing Finch, weighing up whether to trust him or not. In the end he took the bait. "My mortality." His eyes gleamed. "If I can get my hands on the Tree, I could end up like you and live forever."

A pang of disgust shot through Finch but he did well to hide it. He had never revealed how he had gained immortality, Aaron wrongly jumping to the conclusion that it was because of the Tree and not Jade herself. No one but her would be able to pull it off, and now that the Tree was already dying, not even she could do it.

"I see," said Finch.

"You and your brother... Imagine the things you will witness in the future, perhaps even the impact your existence will have on the world."

Finch stood abruptly, done with Aaron's nonsense. He had been considering whether to offer Aaron some information about the Tree of Life's location, but after hearing his reasoning he realized he was a petty man who knew nothing of the sacrifices and horrors he'd had to endure for so many centuries.

"Right, Mr. Mannheim, I believe I shall leave you here." He pulled on his sweater and hat, the night already cloudy with impending rain.

"That's it?" Aaron replied, his hand reaching out to grab him before Finch went any further.

Finch glared down at him. "I have no more questions," he replied.

"I thought you asked me here to make a deal! Jade's life for a chance to be part of the discovery team," he replied desperately.

A coy smile played onto Finch's mouth, his teeth flashing in the dim light. "Now, why on earth would I make a silly deal like that when our side is already hunting for the Tree as we speak?" He looked down his nose at Aaron as all color drained from the secretary's face. "If you haven't noticed, Aaron... I'm already on the winning team." He jerked his arm away, freeing himself, and walked out into the London night.

Three days...

There wouldn't be much to plan for the coming event. He had already updated his will last year when Jade had arrived in Lampeter, the main beneficiary being Bowen as he had sired

TO THOSE WHO SURVIVE

no children and had no wife. He'd left a bit for Malcolm for the years of service he had provided and some to Sahar, the only woman who had ever put up with his insane requests.

Other than them, everyone else was dead, and soon, so would he be.

XXIX

I cleaned up the room as best I could while Bowen was downstairs icing his shoulder. I had used excessive force, but it was needed. I was prepared to leave that very second, my duffle bag still sitting full in the closet, but I wouldn't… I couldn't. I had agreed to three days, and thinking back, it was a good decision. It wouldn't have been fair to my parents, not fair to Jackie, and especially not fair to Bowen if I had died without seeing them one last time. I was going to make the next three days last a lifetime.

The next morning I found Jackie in her room on the floor below us and knocked on the door to let myself in. It wasn't as grand as mine and Bowen's, but the double bed in there fit snuggly against the far wall, its light blue duvet matching the farm-y feel of the rest of the house. Clear vases of bramble lined a small shelf along one side of the room, while a group of hanging plants covered the other. A full-length mirror was fixed on the wall across from the bed, giving an impression that the room was double its size.

She was sitting on the bed, her headphones in and reading a beat-up copy of *The Odyssey*. When she saw me, she perked up.

"Hey, what's up?" she asked, taking one of her headphones out. "We off to the library again?"

"Nothing much… No… I thought we could have a normal day today. Maybe go shopping? Have lunch together?"

She jumped off of the bed. "Give me five minutes and I'll be right down," she squealed, the smile quickly fading. "Wait, what happened? Aren't we supposed to be lying low from the Order?" she asked suspiciously.

"Screw them," I answered, Fate's revelation that they would never find the Tree of Life having me throw caution out the window. "I kinda found the Tree…"

"You what? Was that what all the commotion was last night?"

"You heard that?"

"Everyone heard it. I'm pretty sure even the neighbors up the street could," Jackie said. "So which goddess was it?"

"The goddess Fate."

"I'm sorry, what? As in Ananke, that goddess?"

"Ya… How do you know that name?"

"She's one of ancient Greece's primordial deities and basically the mother of all the cosmos!" she gushed. Obviously she had encountered the name through literature, putting her English degree to use. "What was she like? Where did you see her? Did she have a spindle, like she's usually depicted?"

"Whoa, you know a lot about her."

"My minor is in classical studies, the goddesses a particular interest of mine," she confessed.

That explained it. I answered her questions in order. "She was godlike and terrifying, but also gorgeous. The Monksblood Bible somehow sucked me into this other dimension where she was. And no, there was no spindle, though there was an hourglass and a whole galaxy behind her."

Jackie's eyes seemed to brighten at the description. "Okay, give me five and I'll meet you downstairs. I'll drill you more on details when we're out."

"Haha, deal."

I left her to get ready and headed down into the living room, where the rest of the group were. It looked as if Bowen and Finch had already filled them in on all the details, the air filled with excitement.

"Well done, Jade," Gwenllian said, complimenting me as I walked into the room. "Meeting a deity… not even I have ever been given that pleasure."

I gave a little curtsy, gloating over the fact. "Thank you. It feels a bit surreal to be honest."

"I would imagine so." Simone plopped down next to Gwenllian, her mug of tea slightly sloshing onto her. "Shit…"

Jackie practically bounced into the room, ready to go out.

"You girls off somewhere?" Mom asked, as I went to grab my handbag.

"We're going to do a little shopping for the day. Treat ourselves." I was just about to head to the door when Bowen stopped me. I held up my hand. "No, we will not be taking a car, the Underground is fine. Yes, I'll be careful. No, I don't know how long we'll be gone. No, you cannot come with us—I have something planned for you and me in two days. And yes, I can pick up milk if we need it."

The unimpressed smirk on his face didn't quite reach his eyes, understanding that my preemptive strike on his questions was foreseeable. "I wasn't going to ask you any of that, though we do need milk, so that would be a huge help. I was going to give you this." He pulled out his wallet and handed me a black credit card, my name punched into the plastic.

"Holy shit," Jackie said in shock.

"It's your money, so don't feel bad about spending it. Plus, I think you deserve a little recreational use after everything you've been through."

I held the card in my hand, my stare boring a hole into it. It was another thing I hadn't thought about. All that money…

"Thanks," I replied, smoothing the worry from my face.

I grabbed Jackie's hand and we headed to the Underground and jumped on a train on the Central Line toward Marble Arch. The roads were crowded with people, school term having finished. We first made a dent at one of the largest department stores I'd ever seen, having to elbow our way into the sales sections, then continued our journey all the way up to Oxford Street, our arms already heavy with bags.

Searching for a restaurant, I found the most expensive one in Piccadilly. The place dripped with opulence as we took our seats in the booth, crystals hanging all around us.

We ended our day with a tour of Harrods and Selfridges, sales assistants more than happy to accompany us throughout our shopping spree, making sure everything was perfect. I had always imagined that living like a queen would feel somewhat like this, but the looming darkness of the coming days left me drained.

I still had so much to prepare…

We ordered a car for the ride back, the Tube no longer an option as we could barely carry all our bags.

"Good shopping day?" Dad asked as we plonked everything down in the living room, ourselves included.

"I think I've died," Jackie said, puffing in exhaustion. "Jade, pinch me… This is all real, right?"

I slapped her on the leg. "Yup, it's real."

"Let me help you guys with those." Dad picked up as many as he could. "Jesus, did you buy the whole store?"

"Almost." I laughed lightheartedly. "Tomorrow it's parents day, so be ready."

"Jade, we don't need anything," he replied cautiously.

"No, no. We're going to go sightseeing. Have the most normal family vacation day possible."

He perked up at that, realizing it suited us much better. "I think that sounds like a wonderful plan. I'll let your mother know."

"Invite Gwenllian and Simone while you're up there!" I called to him.

"Will do," he shouted down.

The five of us dominated the tourist traffic throughout central London. We started at The Tower of London and made our way to Westminster and Buckingham Palace. The London Eye allowed us to see across the whole of the city, and Mom (against her better judgment) forced herself onto the wheel to stay with everyone.

We ended the day with a couple of bottles of *Dom Pérignon* and a small night picnic on the River Thames, thankful that there was no rain to ruin the party. It was wonderful being able to spend quality time together.

Mom had asked Bowen if he wanted to join us, but I reassured her that I already had something special planned for us the next night.

"Is this alright?" Bowen asked as he finished smoothing down his jumper collar.

"Perfect." I gave him a light peck on the cheek.

"Why won't you tell me where we're going?"

"Because it's a surprise, and I spent all of this morning organizing everything."

"Ah, is that why I've been held prisoner in this room?"

"It's just one of the reasons… I wanted you to relax and have some time to yourself."

"And that explains the masseuse that showed up?" His lip curled seductively.

"That was just a little extra. Now comes our time alone." I took his hand and led him down the first flight of stairs. "Do you trust me?"

He raised an eyebrow inquisitively. "Always."

I tied one of his ties around his head, covering his eyes, so he couldn't see as I led him further down the last set of stairs.

"Is that smell… pizza?" he asked.

"Shhh. Don't ruin anything."

He chuckled under his breath, his hand tightening around mine as we reached the ground floor.

"You ready?" I asked.

"When you are."

I took the blindfold off him, waiting to see his reaction. With help from the family—who were now anywhere but here—I had moved the living room furniture to create a fort-like tent, the walls and ceiling draped in floral sheets taken from the linen closet, creating a fairylike enclosure. Cushions and pillows were strewn about the floor, Gwenllian's laptop placed in the middle, as well as bowls of chips and the pizza Bowen had rightly smelt. A bottle of Riesling was chilling on ice with the cork already popped and glasses waiting to be filled. Lit candles lined the wall creating a *cwtch*-like atmosphere.

"It's..." he paused.

"Childish, I know," I said, my face flushing, "but I thought that we'd been acting enough as adults and needed a break from it. The world is already so horrible, we might as well do something that makes us happy," I blabbered on. "And really, if you think about it, we're only in our twenties, basically just children with a license to drink, and I know you've lived longer—"

He turned to me, pure joy on his face. "It's perfect," he said. A second later I was swept off my feet and into his arms, only for him to then playfully drop me onto the cushions.

We settled ourselves in as we started watching a movie, the pizza gobbled down before any plot twists came up, but I barely paid attention. I concentrated more on Bowen as he watched, the way his lips moved when he smiled and the happiness that played in the thin creases around his eyes. How his thumb would unconsciously rub the back of my hand while his body seemed to reposition itself every time I moved, wanting to stay close to me.

I reached over to him, bringing his face toward my own.

There was hunger in my actions, the pizza not the only thing I wanted to eat that night. I threw off my shirt, revealing the new lingerie I had bought with Jackie a couple of days ago. Bowen's eyes smoldered as he took in the fine lace and straps holding everything delicately in place. He removed his own clothes, the rest of mine following close behind.

"I love you," I whispered to him. I made to move on top of him, only for him to push me against the cushions, his body strong as he hovered over me.

"You, Jade Elizabeth Morrison, are a tease."

My smile was lost as his lips parted mine, his hands running from my breasts down lower. My back arched as he felt the wetness between my legs.

My moans of ecstasy excited him as I griped his waist and brought him closer to me, my thighs rubbing against him. He responded with equal enthusiasm.

His tongue traced the outline of my mouth and I was overwhelmed with his hot breath, still infused with the scent of white wine. I could feel his groin against me, and then, finally, we fit together.

He started slowly, his movements prolonging the euphoria of the moment, but I wanted more. I wanted everything of him.

"Faster," I commanded.

It was all the permission he needed.

Bowen grabbed my waist, our faces now level. My lips parted for his; our mouths clamped together as our tongues wrestled with each other. We picked up speed, our breath in rhythm as we thrusted back and forth. His musky scent encapsulated me as my sweat mingled with it, the smell leaving me light-headed. All I could feel in that moment was him, and as he grew inside me, my own body contracted—savoring the moment as we both climaxed.

Exhausted, we both fell against the pillows, our legs still intertwined. It was a moment I never wanted to end. *How difficult will it be tomorrow?*

"What are you thinking, *cariad*?" Bowen asked as we settled back into the comfort of the make-believe fort, as if he could read my mind.

"I'm scared for tomorrow…" I confessed.

"So am I."

He didn't know… and I wasn't going to tell him.

"When do you want to go?" He grabbed some chips.

"The earlier the better, I think."

"Good idea. I'll coordinate with Finch about what we should take. We should prepare for a worst-case scenario." My heart beat faster. Had he figured it out? "I've already talked it over with him and we think that the trick will be getting back. We can deal with any traps that lay ahead as long as we have an escape route."

My mind reeled at the thought. I hadn't even thought of how to get the boys back. The planning was all so last minute…

"I'll have a look at the Bible before we go to bed and make sure there's a backup plan," I said, my eyes averting his.

"Jade, is something wrong?"

Why was it he could tell everything I was thinking… everything I was feeling?

"No," I lied too quickly, and I grabbed for his shirt, pulling it over my bare body. "Yes, actually… We've run out of pizza. I'll go make more." I jumped from the floor and ran into the kitchen.

Come on, Jade. You gotta think of something to lower his suspicions. Put on your brave face. Don't show any hesitation. He has to believe you.

My eyes watered as I shoved another pizza into the oven. It wasn't death that I feared—in some sense I relished its coming—it was what I was leaving behind. The *people* I would be leaving behind. They wouldn't understand why I had done this, the logical explanation not good enough to outweigh the emotional one, but it was something the world needed... Something I deserved.

Resolve: it was a double-edged knife.

I walked slowly back into the living room and rejoined Bowen in the comfort of the fort. From the way his shoulders were squared and the tightness in his jaw... I could feel the annoyance seething off of him, his boxers already back on.

"I'm sorry. I lied."

"You kept saying I was keeping secrets from you and then you turn around and do it to me," he mumbled, pulling me back down to him.

Resolve.

"I'm not nearly as ready as I should be and I feel like that might cost someone their life." It was a half-truth that rang with sincerity.

"Stop thinking this is all on you. Finch and I will be there to help, and we're indestructible... No one is going to die tomorrow."

I knew he was wrong, but there was a part of me—deep, deep down—that really hoped he was right. Not for my sake, but for theirs.

XXX

We all woke before dawn, wanting to leave right after daybreak. Even though the house was pretty full, everyone was quiet—solemn—as we prepared for our departure. I still hadn't told the boys where we were headed; for some reason its location was a sort of sacred place that only I wanted to know. Plus there was still Finch, a wildcard when it came to his motivations for tagging along.

"Do you have everything?" Mom asked. Each of us had a backpack full of gear for every contingency.

I finished zippering up my own, the weight of it almost as heavy as a toddler. "Yep, I think we have everything but the kitchen sink."

She laughed at the fact I had used one of her own motherly catchphrases, but her eyes were full of worry.

"Everything will be fine," I reassured her, making sure my voice didn't waver. I pulled my backpack on, Bowen and Finch already waiting at the entrance for me. From the outside, it looked like the three of us were going to backpack across Europe, not go find a mystical tree.

"It's still not fair that you're letting that asshole go and not me," Jackie chimed in as I joined the others wanting to hug and kiss me and tell me to be safe.

"I'm sorry, but they can't die, and I don't want anything to happen to you." *And I don't want you to witness my death.*

"Ya, whatever. You better come back in one piece."

I gave her a hug to hide the sadness on my face, to hide the knowledge that I might never see any of them again. "Don't worry," I reassured her, breaking away, "things will be okay."

"Be careful out there," Gwenllian commanded, her head held high as she fixed my sweater. "I've packed the potions in Finch's bag and any medical equipment in Bowen's." She fussed with my hair, making sure the strands that fell out of my ponytail were smoothed back in place.

"Thank you, Gwenllian, for everything you've done. Really, I'm so glad we found each other."

Her lip quivered at the statement, her eyes watering. She held up her hand so I wouldn't say another word.

Before she could get any more emotional I moved on to Simone, who was already in tears. "You be safe, okay?" she half blubbered.

"I will," I promised, my fingers crossed behind my back.

That just left one more person.

Dad was talking with Bowen and Finch, their conversation hushed, and they all broke away as I walked up to them.

Dad came and scooped me up into a bear hug. "I am so proud of you," he whispered as we separated from each other.

"Thanks, Dad."

Before I regretted going, I pulled both Bowen and Finch out the door, leaving the rest of my family behind.

****

It didn't take long for us to get to London Bridge station, the exit letting us out on the correct side and into the heart of Southwark. The walk from there wasn't long, just three blocks down from the bridge and left through a small alley that opened up into a courtyard beer garden.

The place was large and dead at this early hour, save for a few employees cleaning up. On the right was a Tudor-style pub that spanned the length of the concrete garden, its sign of a knight riding a white horse valiantly sticking out from above its entrance. There were balconies along the top two floors, which were made more beautiful by their carved wooden railings and pink peonies hanging from them at certain intervals. There were crooked windows along the ground floor that hung Union Jacks, their wood trimmings coated in beige paint while the rest of the outside was detailed with gray, white, and golden accents.

"The Tabard Inn?" Finch asked incredulously, looking straight ahead to another building. "This is where the Tree of Life is hiding?" He burst out laughing, some unseen serendipity playing in his head.

Bowen also had a smirk on his face, his arms crossed against his chest. "Well, I'll be damned."

"What?" I asked in all honesty. I didn't know the history of the place, especially since a name other than the Tabard Inn hung above the door.

"The actual Tabard Inn isn't here anymore. It used to reside just there," Finch said, pointing at the end of the courtyard, "in the fourteenth century, but in 1676, a fire destroyed most of Southwark. When they rebuilt, this pub expanded, taking over the place. It wasn't exactly the nicest establishment to begin with, honestly," he continued, "as it was known as one of the best brothels this side of London."

"Wow… And Fate led us here?" It couldn't be right. Such a sanctified thing wouldn't be residing below a whorehouse, would it?

"Not all its clientele were of the profession," Bowen assured me. "Many Christian pilgrims started their journey from here. People wondered if the women were that skilled, letting the men have their last saucy night before continuing on, but perhaps they knew of the Tree's link with the area and believed it was holy ground?"

"I very much doubt the latter, as Edward would have then come *here* instead of Wales," Finch said.

Just the name Edward sent my hair standing on end, the presence of the Black Prince constantly hanging over our journey.

Bowen could see my distress and moved us farther into the garden. "So, where to?"

I ducked into the main building and looked around. Fate had shown me what to look for to find the entrance; it was trying to find it in the three-story building that was the problem.

"Look for a big clock. It's somewhere in the pub." I felt a nagging sensation that came from the room next door, and in my haste, I went back out into the garden and into the Parliament Bar, leaving Bowen to argue with a tired employee who wanted to close the place. The dark mahogany panels of the walls created a cozy atmosphere despite there being no patrons, the chairs upturned on the tables for the early morning. There was little light, but the blushing dawn let me see my way around, the nagging sensation growing stronger as I made my way to the back of the room. There was nothing but an old clock missing its hands marking the entrance of a cellar door in the floor. I had seen the clock in my head, Fate's visions pinpoint accurate.

Bowen and Finch came up behind me, all of us standing over the trapdoor.

"Is this it?" Bowen asked.

I nodded, feeling the faint pump of a heartbeat from somewhere inside the cellar.

Before they could ask me what I was doing I had stripped off my boots and socks, my bare feet cold against the wood. The tattooed roots on them seemed to burn under my skin at the recognition of the place.

"Wait," Bowen said cautiously as I crouched to pull open the hatch, "I'll take the lead." He opened the trapdoor, finding a set of steep stairs leading down into the cellar.

At the bottom, boxes and kegs lined the room—other necessities for the bar crammed in as much as possible. We went deeper in, the floor slanting more and more as we made our way down.

Damp and cold penetrated my bare feet, their color turning from pink to red as the feeling in them slowly left me. We could see our breath in the air, the smell of hops and dirt mixing together, until we finally came upon a stone wall blocking our way.

"Is this right?" Finch pushed against the wall.

"I don't know. This is as far as Fate's visions showed me..."

Frustration colored Finch's voice, his slew of curses making my ears perk up. "This isn't right! There *has* to be more."

"Look for any clues," Bowen said, calmly reassuring. "Fate wouldn't have sent us on a wild goose chase. She knows this is too important."

We each took a section of the wall, looking for anything that could help us. My feet felt numb to the cold, making my movements stiff and awkward. My stance faltered and I used the wall for support, the stone crumbling beneath my hand like sand, and I could feel shapes and carvings beneath.

"Guys! Over here," I called to them.

As they made their way over I brushed away more of the stone, until, finally, a door appeared. On it was carved the likeness of the Tree, the design close to the one I had seen in The Forest, but instead of shining gems and vibrant patterns of leaves, this one was simple and had only bare branches.

"Where's the door handle," Finch asked, but before we had a chance to look for one, the tattoos on my feet spread out in front of me, latching onto the door. They crept silently up it, merging into the design. With a loud pop, the door opened, a smell of firewood entering the room.

"Guess we don't need one," Bowen answered in surprise. He pushed it open wider, pitch darkness beyond.

"Here, you'll need this." I held his hand and chanted a small spell to keep a flame going in his palm, making sure the heat would leave no damage on him.

He held the white-blue light up as he entered through the door, me following behind, while Finch took the rear.

We stepped into what was like a black aura, and once through, I saw a scene familiar to me. It was an old meadow, but the creek that ran through the middle of the field was bone dry, while dark storm clouds rolled overhead, thundering at our presence. We had prepared for booby traps, sinkholes, perhaps even a powerful barrier to keep the Tree of Life safe, but all of our preparation was for naught. It seemed that all the Tree needed to hide was a key, and I had just met that requirement.

But that wasn't what attracted my attention.

Ahead was the Tree of Life, dead and burnt as if it had been struck by lightning, its trunk torn at the top.

Throwing caution to the wind, I ran toward it, my bare feet picking up dirt and ash that swirled behind me, the boys hot on my heels. I hadn't replaced my socks and shoes, the holy place requiring my feet to be bare and needing to stay that way for my connection to stay strong.

I stopped in front of it, mumbled whispers of the Tree not making sense even at this close range. Falling onto my hands and knees, I listened closer, hoping to catch what it was trying to say.

"*You've come,*" it said, though I could barely make it out.

"Yes! Yes!"

"What's it saying?" Finch asked, his brow drenched in sweat. He looked nervous, perhaps even a bit panicked.

"It's saying we've finally arrived." I acted as the conduit between us and it. "How much time do we have left?" I asked the Tree.

"*Not long. Soon I will be gone from this world.*"

I wasn't going to allow that to happen.

Darkness passed across my face as I sat seiza-style, my knees digging into broken roots. I let my backpack fall from my shoulders, its weight finally too much for me.

Resolve, I reminded myself again and again.

TO THOSE WHO SURVIVE

My magic built quickly in my veins, the proximity to the Tree strengthening what little it had left. It felt as if molasses were flowing through my body, making it harder to extract the magic. I knew what the next step was, knew that Bowen and Finch weren't going to let me go easily.

Before they could get any closer, I raised an arm as I made to separate the Tree and me from the both of them. It was a complicated spell, one I had Gwenllian teach me during our time in Scotland. I wanted to learn it in case I ever needed to defend myself or others, not knowing what the Order had in store for us. Now I used it for a completely different purpose. With a strike of my arm, I separated us, Bowen and Finch on the other side of the thin sheet of glass extending as far as we could see. Its smooth green sheen had a slight glint to it, barely distorting both of them as I saw their shocked stares.

"Jade! Jade!" Bowen's voice was muffled as he banged urgently against the glass, falling to his knees. "What are you doing?"

I held my hand up against the wall, matching his. "I'm sorry," I said, "there was a part Fate told me that I didn't want you to know… Didn't want anyone to know."

The pain on his face… I couldn't even describe how much it broke my heart.

"What? What did she tell you?" he asked, but I already knew he had jumped to the right conclusion. "We can figure out another way," he said, his eyes frantic as he searched around him, as if he could pull the solution from thin air.

I hung my head as I shook it. There was no other way. I hadn't even tried to think of one, resigned to my fate.

I just wanted all of this to be over.

I turned away, trying desperately to block out Bowen's muted shouts from the other side of the barrier as he continued to bang his fists against the wall.

I opened my backpack and pulled out the Monksblood Bible where I had stored it safely, unwrapping the tome from its secure bindings. The Tree thrummed at its presence, the book hot in my hands as I turned to the page where the Tree's likeness was depicted. I ran my hand along it, my fingers tingling with recognition as words made themselves visible at the bottom of the page.

My final spell.

I opened my mouth to form the first word of the line, only to hear a deafening shot behind me.

XXXI
Finch

Walking into the ancient meadow where the Tree of Life had once lived vibrantly, Finch couldn't help but feel on edge. How many years had he waited, how many lifetimes? And now was the only chance he would ever get to see if his theory would really work.

The two in front of him didn't know the hoops he had gone through to get them there, the lies… the manipulation…

Finch spotted the Tree, its form broken and smoldering with its top lying a few feet away, and watched as Jade knelt at the foot of the tree, pulling out the Monksblood Bible ever so carefully.

He felt his Browning in its holster, tight against his body so Bowen wouldn't spot it. Having to carry a backpack helped as well. The magic bullets were already loaded into the cartridge, their runes etched deeply, ready for use.

He would not let this chance slip by.

Jade bent down again in front of the Tree, her head lowering each time his brother talked with her, and then in the blink of an eye she had raised a barrier even he was impressed with.

Not many could master the *Wal Gwydr* spell without having little imperfections, its foundation strong in front of them, but with Finch's trained eye, he could spot them all the same. They were like small bevels, the glass slightly warped in areas here and there, indicating where its weaknesses lay.

He readied his gun, the grip cold in his hand, as his brother continued banging onto the wall, Jade taking her position once more at the Tree's base.

It's now or never.

Aiming the barrel at one of the flaws in the glass, he cocked it and pulled the trigger, praying that his years of research, years of preparation in coveting Gwenllian's magic, years of torment, would pay off.

He hadn't imagined the sound would carry so far, thinking the meadow ended at some point, but the impact echoed thunderously throughout the place. Where the bullet pierced the barrier, a crack in the wall split, its shards tumbling like dominoes as they shattered into pieces at their feet.

Bowen stumbled back behind him and Jade had fallen in the other direction, away from the Monksblood Bible. Finch could see the shock on her features. He looked down at his brother, where disbelief turned quickly to terror, then rage.

"What did you do?" Jade asked, horrified. She probably thought he wouldn't have been able to break her spell, never imagined anyone else but her could use magic, but the world wasn't as straightforward as that.

The wall breached, Finch made his way to the Tree, his stride powerful, his head held high.

"Finch!" Bowen barked loudly. "Is this it? Is this why you were pushing so hard? You wanted the Tree for yourself!"

TO THOSE WHO SURVIVE

It was a misconception, and yet the truth.

Perhaps this was how he wanted it to end... Bowen had no idea about his past. He knew there had been troubling times, had experienced some himself, but he didn't know about the days Finch would stay awake, driving himself mad with questions about his existence. How he had painstakingly documented every attempt on his life, all fourteen-hundred and seventy-eight of them, as failures. But he only needed *one* successful one, and he wasn't going to let this opportunity pass him by. Perhaps playing the villain one last time would finally lead him to peace.

Finch sneered as he fell seamlessly back into his old persona. "Yes," he said, spitting it out.

Bowen made a move toward him, only to have the gun go off again. He knew it would do little to aim at a man who had lived half his life in battle, so the barrel was pointed just shy of his one weak spot—Jade.

"Please try not to move, brother. I wouldn't like to have to shoot her, but I will if both of you don't cooperate." He knelt by the open book, reading the inscription at the bottom of the page in his head. If he had known the Bible was the key to all of this, maybe he wouldn't have had to live so long.

"Why?" Jade asked, her eyes almost tearful. He had seen those eyes before, had felt them himself every so often when he had experimented with taking his life. From her face he could figure out what the price was for bringing order back to the world.

Because it's not your time.

"What do you think I've been doing since you got to Wales? Don't you remember the first time you met me at Folk Night, how you stared at me with intrigue and revulsion?" She perked up at that as it hit its target. "Of course I knew your fate, and that you had no idea who I was. But I knew exactly who *you* were, and from our encounter in the past, I knew *exactly* how to manipulate you and my brother."

She gritted her teeth.

"Gwenllian was the only one who caught on in the end, but she never did realize the reason she could no longer use her magic…" He let the statement hang in the air.

"This whole time?" Bowen asked in disbelief. "You haven't changed one bit!" he barked.

If only that were true, this would have been so much easier.

Jade made to move closer, only for Finch to fire his gun again, the bullet just grazing her ear.

"Stay where you are," he commanded.

Finch brought his focus back to the page in front of him and, taking a breath, started reciting the spell. He didn't know if it would work, if the Tree would accept his life in exchange for Jade's, but he knew he didn't want to live any longer, and if that meant forcing the Tree to take his life, then so be it.

He repeated the spell over and over until he felt the tendrils of the Tree's roots slither their way up his legs, restricting their blood flow. The roots dug into his skin like barbed wire, burrowing deeper and deeper, ripping tissue and muscle as they did so.

He kept his screams within, the pain a welcome sign that death had come for him. But it wasn't just that… he knew what he was putting his brother through—making him witness this brutal departure—and Jade… Well, she wouldn't hold any remorse toward him. But as he looked out of the corner of his eye he saw she had somehow made it to where Bowen was weeping, his shouts and protests going unheard. He didn't want her past to be haunted anymore, not by him... not by the screams that tried to escape from his mouth.

She was doing her best to hold Bowen back, the pity and understanding that now clouded her features a reprieve, and God-sent, that Finch didn't deserve from her. Nonetheless, she fought Bowen's advances.

I'll ask you... this one favor... Don't let him fall... as I have. Take care of him.

Finch felt it as the branches and roots finally made it to his heart, their tendrils stabbing him until he could feel his skin breaking. Glancing down, his saw his hand slowly turn gray and then to ash, the smallest movement causing more of his body to fall away. The gun fell to the ground as he crumbled and glanced one last time at Bowen and Jade.

Their faces were drenched in tears he never thought would be shed for him.

XXXII

I had thought the Tree of Life wanted my life and my life alone. I realized what Finch was trying to do, but it was too late. I don't know why his gun had worked against my magic or how he managed to execute the spell, but the Tree seemed to accept his sacrifice.

From where I stood I could see the roots that started moving up his leg, and it was the exact moment Bowen figured out his brother hadn't double-crossed us—as we had both believed. It must have been excruciating as the roots gouged their way into him, periodically ripping free, only to then start the process again.

I watched as Bowen tried to run to him, to try and reach him, but I somehow knew that if he touched his brother the roots would latch on to him as well, dragging them both down.

My body slammed against his as I pinned him down, his screams and thrashing as he tried to throw me off hurting him worse than they would ever hurt me.

My gaze went back to Finch, no sound from him as we watched the agony his body went through as it broke apart, piece by piece. It was his eyes that kept my attention... pain, fear... I had expected to see them mirrored back at me but all I could see was relief, peace that his actions had brought him exactly to where he wanted to be.

Is this what you wanted all along?

I thought back to everything he had done since I'd met him in the twenty-first century, from Folk Night to just now when a sadistic smile played on his face. Somehow he had changed—not for the worse or better, his actions falling somewhere between. On the outside he was a confident, strong, cunning, smug man, but on the inside... If we had looked deeper, perhaps we would have paid more attention to his copious drinking and smoking, and the abstinence that he radiated toward those who dared to get close.

There was still a small part of me that believed he deserved to die, that he was getting his comeuppance... Yet Bowen crumpled in my arms as we watched Finch's skin begin to burn and crack... and I couldn't help but feel remorse and loneliness for someone who had suffered so much pain and now wanted to end his long existence.

I had done this. I had cursed his life with longevity without even knowing it—and it had broken him. I always wondered what Bowen had lived through and seen in his many lives, but not once had I had the same thought about Finch. How contrasting were their experiences that they would turn out so different?

My knees buckled as I held onto Bowen; he was no longer thrashing against me, resigned to his brother's actions as we both watched Finch slowly disintegrate, his hand reaching for his heart.

He had somehow wriggled his way into my life. I hadn't

forgiven him, hadn't treated him with anything but malice since coming back from the fourteenth century, and yet he was fully prepared to take my place.

Bowen and I heard Finch's last breath, his lips parting into an innocent smile that left tears to run down my face as the roots that held him in place like some perverse scarecrow finally took all of him.

The roots retreated into the Tree, back in their original positions.

There was silence in the now stale air of the meadow, except for the sounds of breathing from both Bowen and me. I don't know how long we sat there together, hugging in each other's arms, shaking with weariness, but at some point Bowen stood and went over to the Tree, his shoulders slumped. He bent down to where his brother lay, his whole form quaking, his hands brushing through the ash as delicately as if cradling a babe.

I went over and joined him.

"The first time I saw him after the Black Plague was in 1527 during the Sack of Rome." He started to dig a small hole into the dry ground, the dirt coming away under his fingernails. "Surprisingly we were on the same side. The rebellion had thousands of soldiers, and it was only amidst battle that we bumped into each other. At first I thought him a demon, come to torture my soul even more, and I almost killed him right then and there," he mused, "but when a spear struck him deep in the leg and he pulled it out like it was nothing, I knew we were in the same boat."

I listened silently as more tears rolled down his face.

"He's my little brother…"

My heart ached at the simple sentence, so full of love. I didn't know what to say. Nothing that came into my mind would have made the situation any better. I stood by him as he completed his job, and when the time came, I helped to collect what remained of Finch and place him to rest. We found a spot next to the Tree that seemed fitting as his final resting place. If he wasn't to live forever alongside us, then at least his soul could be at peace here, where we could come and visit in private.

I didn't say anything, just to be there as Bowen wrapped his arm around my body was all he wanted.

I had only ever seen Bowen cross himself in prayer once, but now... it hit me harder than ever. I wasn't a religious person, no one in our family was, but it felt right to join him in saying goodbye. As Bowen knelt in prayer, a glint on the Tree of Life caught my eye. Curious, I went over to see what it was, the sight of it bringing a small smile to my lips.

A golden leaf, about the size of my thumbnail, poked out from one of the broken branches... enough to let us know that Finch hadn't sacrificed his life for nothing.

Bowen was in no condition to function, all his energy drained as he draped an arm over my shoulder, my body keeping him upright as I led him back through the door, up the cellar stairs and into the fresh air. Time seemed to have sped up while we were down there; it was night-time and the bar was packed with people out drinking, when a hand grasped at my shoulder.

"Miss Morrison, you have been busy... haven't you?"

I barely registered Aaron's words, his mouth smirking

sardonically. He wasn't alone, two other suited men looming behind him, the firearms holstered under their jackets intimidating the patrons around us enough for them to give us a wide berth.

"I see your little adventure has been fruitful," he said, looking at the state both Bowen and I were in. "And where's Finch? Groveling at the foot of the Tree like some zealous acolyte?"

I didn't bat an eye as my hand shot out toward him, the red flames of my magic snapping at the men behind him, rendering them unconscious within seconds. Bowen hadn't even looked up, his mind stunned, as I faced down Aaron, who now held his hands up in vain surrender.

With my hand still raised, I focused my attention onto him, his body twitching as my magic crackled closer and closer until I could see beads of sweat soaking his collar. "You better move," I snapped, "before *I* move you."

He understood the threat, his life in that moment so inconsequential to me that, either way, nothing he would do would matter. Bowen and I pushed past him, leaving his trembling form among the drinkers and party-goers as we made our way back to the main road and hailed a taxi. Our driver navigated the busy streets easily, letting both our minds wander without having to pay attention to our surroundings. Everything felt numb as I watched the city lights pass by, the shrieking from groups of hen parties and stag dos as they ran about, drunk out of their minds.

They don't even know what's happened. No one but us...

No one would ever know the long battle that had been won tonight. And no one would know of the sacrifice that was needed to make it possible. It would take time for the world to fall back into order, perhaps longer than it had taken to get this way, but we at least knew Finch would always be there, guarding it.

I took Bowen's hand in mine, acknowledging the silent tears that rolled down his cheeks. The driver looked back in his rearview mirror, and I shook my head to indicate to him to keep quiet as he maneuvered down our road and pulled to a stop in front of the house.

I paid him with what cash I had left and helped Bowen from the back seat. Being back at the house was surreal. The sage-colored front door seemed more vibrant, the ivy and wisteria that hung from the balcony lusher. It was an out of place feeling that didn't fit with the somber tone of what had happened. The world should have seemed darker—more morose—but everything appeared as normal as ever.

The lights were on in the windows, figures moving in front of the curtains and creating shadows. On our way back I hadn't even thought to text or call anyone to let them know that we were coming, or that the… two of us… were okay.

Bowen's hand hesitated on the doorknob, his face still drawn. I took his hand in mine and brought it to my lips.

"If you don't want to face anyone, I can try and make us invisible to get us upstairs," I suggested.

His lips only moved a little at the invitation, his voice strained. "Would you mind?"

"Not at all." Using the spell I had employed during our training sessions in Scotland, I created a barrier around us thick enough that if anyone looked in our direction they would see nothing.

We opened and closed the front door silently, creeping our way up to our room. Bowen was still out of it, but now being back home, I saw just how dirty we were. Our boots left sooty imprints in the white rug, and looking into the bathroom mirror, I saw that we were both covered in a layer of ash and dust.

Before I had time to think about just how much of that was Finch, I turned on the shower and let it heat up, the steam clouding up the room. Bowen hadn't moved from his position at the door, his eyes tearing up once more at the new reality.

Taking his hand, I led him into the bathroom and stripped him of his clothes, pushing them into the laundry basket to hide them from sight. I removed my own as well, and with the water now piping hot, I got us both into the shower. His eyes were red-rimmed as I grabbed for the soap, his lip quivering as another wave of sorrow hit him. Over the shower pressure I could barely hear his mumbling, and only when he pulled me closer could I make it out.

"He's my little brother... I could have done more... I *should* have done more..."

It seemed as if he were talking from a faraway place, about memories I had no idea about.

"Shhh," I soothed him.

Guilt ate away at me, but it was another thing I would shoulder. Guilt that I had tried to sacrifice myself only to have Bowen's brother be the one to die. Guilt that maybe there was something I could have done if a part of me hadn't been relieved at how things had played out. And guilt at seeing the look in Finch's eyes and knowing this was exactly what he wanted.

We stayed under the water until it ran cold, and even then it took us minutes to turn off the shower. I grabbed Bowen's pajamas from underneath his pillow and helped him dress. He made his own way into bed, his back small as he huddled under the blanket. I finished dressing, the thin cotton feeling like silk against the harshness of the day, and I turned out the light as I joined him, our bodies pressed together to make sure we could feel each other. That this wasn't all a dream.

"We'll have to tell the rest of them in the morning," he whispered, breathing heavily.

"I know…"

"And talk about why you did what you did."

I gulped. "I know."

He brought me closer to him. "Jade," he started, his chest vibrating with the sound of sobs racking through his body, his voice soft, "we did it."

Adfyd a ddwg wybodaeth, a gwybodaeth ddoethineb.

Adversity brings knowledge and knowledge wisdom.

Translations

Anesan – Older sister (yakuza)

Cariad – Sweetheart; my love

Cwtch – Snuggling and cuddling and loving and protecting and safeguarding and claiming, all rolled into one.

Dwy galon, un dyhead, dwy dafod ond un iaith, dwy raff yn cydio'n ddolen, dau enaid ond un taith. – Two hearts, one wish, two tongues but one language, two ropes that join connected, two souls but one journey.

Dyma'r rheswm yr wyf wedi bod yn aros i chi i gyd y tro hwn. – It is the reason I have been waiting for you all this time.

Et factum esset arbitrium eadem iterum, si essent interrogavit. – I would have made the same choice again if I were asked.

Magna pythonissam – The Great Witch

Oyabun – Boss (yakuza)

Persuasio – Persuasion

Sêl – Seal

Vivens lucem videret – See the light

Wal Gwydr – Glass Wall

Ysbryd – Ghost

Y Ddraig Goch – The Red Dragon

Y Goedwig – The Forest

Acknowledgments

I want to thank Beth Street for being the best friend anyone could imagine. You have saved my life more times than I can count and I can't express enough how much you mean to me. Thank you for keeping me alive to tell this story.

For those who were instrumental in the creation of this book: Rhys Thomas Lennon for any Welsh translations; Anita B. Carroll (race-point.com) for designing yet another amazing cover; Richard Sheehan (richardmsheehan.co.uk), who without your copy-editing and proofreading expertise, I would not have been brave enough to publish this book; and TJ INK (tjink.co.uk) for exceptional printing.

And as always, thank you, reader, for picking up this novel and letting me take you on an adventure.

A walking cultural experience, Isabella comes from a multicultural background: born in Australia, raised in the United States, and now resides in the United Kingdom. She has a BA in Creative Writing from the University of Wales: Trinity Saint David and an MA in International Publishing from Oxford Brookes University. After working in the publishing industry, she is now focused predominately on typesetting and writing.

By Isabella Anton

To Those Who Never Knew
To Those Who Survive

"Medieval Magic!!"
  – Amazon Reviewer

"A wonderful and fresh take on the time-travel-fantasy genre that innovatively colours a significant period of history with a touch of magic!"
  – IBellaAnton Books Reviewer

"You'll be hooked!"
  – Goodreads Reviewer